Rav

MW01134479

CRUSH Series!

"Crush is an unforgettable, stimulating romance that will have you reeling in astonishment when the unthinkable strikes in Cami's world! Which of these characters will come out of this deceitful web carefully designed by this wonderfully talented author, Lacey Weatherford! I give this book my thumbs up!" ~*Jessica Johnson, Book End 2 Book End*

"Ms. Weatherford has done what I thought impossible and given us a sequel that is just as enjoyable, if not *more* enjoyable than the first book. With *Smitten*, Lacey Weatherford has cemented her place among my favorite authors. I can't wait to see what she comes up with next!" ~*Melissa Simmons, Girls Heart Books*

"Lacey Weatherford keeps the surprises coming. Just when you think the story ended at SMITTEN, she hits us with a semi truck, POW, with another fantastic and explosive storyline. Makes you fall in #LOVE with the characters all over again!" ~*Lisa Markson, The Paranormal Bookworm*

"Dylan and Cami have done it again! They made me laugh, cry, and turned my heart into a puddle of goo! "LOVE" is the best book in this series yet, and I have enjoyed every step of the journey this series took me on*!" ~ Christina Racich, Pretty Lil Page Turners*

"You thought you had a #CRUSH. You thought you were #SMITTEN. Prepare your heart for full blown #LOVE as Dylan swoons his way to the top of your book boyfriend list!" ~*Belinda Boring, Bestselling Author of the Mystic Wolves Series*

OTHER BOOKS BY LACEY WEATHERFORD

Of Witches and Warlocks series:
The Trouble with Spells
The Demon Kiss
Blood of the White Witch
The Dark Rising
Possession of Souls
Book of Shadows series:
Fire & Ice
Chasing Nikki series:
Chasing Nikki
Finding Chase
Chased Dreams
Crush Series:
Crush
Smitten
Love
Smolder
A Fringe Novel:
Tell Me Why
A Leathers Novel:
Allure
The Story of Us
Wanderlust
Anthology:
A Midsummer Night's Fling
Faery Kissed
Novellas:
Over the River and Through the Woods

USA TODAY & #1 INTERNATIONAL BESTSELLING AUTHOR

SMOLDER

A Crush Series Companion Novel

LACEY WEATHERFORD

ACKNOWLEDGMENTS

Thank you to all my family and friends who kept encouraging me while I was writing this book. Once again, health issues have continued to plague me, and writing was difficult with all the crazy amounts of medication I was on. I've affectionately dubbed this book as my "med head" story. Haha!

I've loved this series so much, and can't believe the incredible reader support it's received. Thank you so much! You all are amazing!

Also, special thank to my editor Kim Swain for being all kinds of awesome.

I hope everyone will enjoy this!

Lacey

DEDICATION

This book is dedicated to all my readers who've loved this series and these characters so much. Thank you for all the support you've given me and for allowing me to live my dream.

PROLOGUE
Russ

My heart was racing, pounding faster than any other time I could recall in my life. I knew this was it. I was done.

It really was true—what they said about your life flashing before your eyes right before it was over. Sadly, I realized I had a lot of regrets, unfinished business, things I would've liked to try, relationships I would've liked to have had, and people I would've liked to make amends with.

But it was too late. The clock had run out for me and this was the end.

Blood dripped into my eyes, obscuring my vision and I tried furiously to blink it away, but my eyelids were too swollen. The rest of my body was just as useless, restrained and unable to move. Only my head jostled about, under the constant pressure of the gun barrel pressed to my temple.

"Make your choice or they both die right now!" Derek screamed across the room at my best friend, Dylan. His wife, Cami, lay slumped, unconscious, in the chair beside me, beaten to a pulp.

My eyes never left Dylan, who was sadly tied to his own chair. Yes, I knew I was going to die. There was only one choice he could make—and it would be me. I wanted him to pick me.

Derek shoved the gun so hard against my head, I felt like the chair was going to topple over.

"Russ!" Dylan cried out. "I choose Russ!"

Even though I knew the verdict was coming, the words still slammed into me like a bullet, marking me for death. The sound of the cocking gun reverberated in my ears and everything around me blurred to slow motion . . . frantic shouting . . . and then a shot fired.

"No!" I screamed, bolting awake so fast I fell from my bed, sheets twisted around my nearly naked form—my chest heaving as I pressed my face against the cool, newly refinished wood floors. The light scent of the wood stain filled my nostrils as I slowly became aware of my surroundings. I was in my own apartment, on the third floor of the gigantic plantation-style house I shared with Cami and Dylan.

I'm okay. I'm alive. Cami and Dylan are safe. I repeated the mantra over and over in my head until I finally started believing it again.

The nightmares were growing worse, coming more frequently, and lasting longer. Apparently my short stint in counseling hadn't helped much.

Glancing through the darkened room toward the doorway, I held my breath, anticipating the sound of footsteps running to check on me. But no one came, and I released a sigh of relief.

Dylan and Cami could never know I was suffering. They already felt guilty enough about everything that had happened with Derek. I couldn't stand seeing the pain in Dylan's eyes every time he looked at me, knowing he blamed himself for everything that happened.

No. He was not to blame—something I continually tried to tell him. He'd made the right choice when he chose to save Cami. We'd all been innocent victims of the horrible circumstances.

These nightmares were mine to carry alone. No one could know my secret.

CHAPTER ONE
Russ

"Is it safe?" I knocked on the doorframe, leaning my head around quickly to peek into the kitchen, spying Cami cooking as Dylan set the table for breakfast.

Dylan shook his head. "Has it ever not been safe?" he asked. "Name one time you've walked in here and found us going at it on the counter."

"Hmmm," I grumbled, entering the space. "There's always a first time. A guy can never be too careful in this house."

"Whatever." Cami laughed, rubbing a hand over her swollen baby belly as she continued to scramble eggs. "We aren't that bad."

"Then why am I wasting all my money soundproofing the third floor of this monstrous place?"

"Maybe it's to protect us from hearing you?" she replied, hitting much closer to the truth than she could possibly imagine. I definitely wanted to keep my nightmares hidden from them.

Rolling my eyes, I sat at the table. "Yeah, that must be it, because my love life is so over the top." That was exactly what I needed—to bring a girl over and let her wake to me screaming at the top of my lungs. Not exactly the impression I wanted to make on the ladies. "I promise you, any squeaky bedsprings you're hearing is just me rolling over in that ancient bed up there. I'm fairly certain it's original to the house."

"So, maybe you're in bed with some ghost and don't even know it?" Dylan teased.

"Well, then I hope they're hot ghosts. At least that'll give me something nice to look at, since they obviously aren't putting out."

"Poor Russ," Cami said, coming over to dish some food onto my plate. "He can't seem to find a girl he likes."

Grabbing her, I pulled her onto my lap and she squealed as I kissed her on the cheek. "That's because Dylan stole the only girl worth having. You've ruined me on all other women, Cami."

Dylan chuckled and Cami squirmed her way back to her feet.

"Whatever," she said. "I look like a barn right now . . . which is appropriate because I'm pretty sure I'm giving birth to a small calf, judging from the size of my stomach."

"And you never looked prettier," Dylan said, wrapping his arms around her and kissing her.

I was used to it by now; and I should've been immune to their constant touching and making out, but I wasn't. Seeing their love in action made me want a relationship like that of my own. But, for whatever reason, it seemed the moment I made that decision, all the women in my life just disappeared. Of course, most of the ladies I'd been entertaining myself with up to this point weren't really long-term relationship material. They were out playing just as much as I was—not that there was anything wrong with that.

The more I was around Cami and Dylan, though, the more the idea of one special someone appealed to me. Their love was unbreakable, constant, and neither of them ever questioned the depth of the other's feelings. I'd never seen two people who were better suited to each other.

Yes, I was completely and totally envious.

"So, what's the plan for today?" Cami asked, glancing between Dylan and me.

"Lots of barbecuing and lake time," Dylan replied with a grin.

"I can't wait to sink my teeth into a large juicy steak," I said, my mouth watering in agreement. "I think this is a nice tradition the department has."

"I'm looking forward to the Fireman's Annual City Barbeque, too," Cami replied. "Well, at least the food. I doubt I will get much lake-time. I couldn't find a suit I liked in whale size."

"Just wear a bikini—problem solved," I said, eyeing her as she sat down at the table, laughing as she gaped at me.

"What?" I asked, loving the horrified

expression on her face.

"You want me to just let this belly hang out there?"

"I think it sounds great," Dylan said, winking at me as he joined the discussion.

"You do?" Glancing incredulously between us, her mouth hanging open.

"Better shut that trap or you're gonna get flies," I said, picking up a plate of sausage and dishing some for myself, before passing it on to her.

Cami continued to stare at Dylan. "Are you serious or are you two teasing me, again? I never can tell."

"I'm completely serious," Dylan said, eyeing her stomach. "You look great and I don't think you've put on an ounce of weight that isn't baby related. Your body is as rockin' as ever. Your breasts are a little bigger, but that's totally normal and I kinda like it."

"I'm still here," I muttered, taking another bite of food. I loved Cami, and I agreed with Dylan's assessment just fine—the extra fullness enhanced her figure and Cami was smokin' hot, but I definitely did not need to hear the list of her assets described in detail. No siree!

Cami had the decency to glance at me apologetically. Dylan apparently didn't care, as usual.

"Your body is gorgeous and you should definitely flaunt it," he continued. "I know women who aren't pregnant who'd kill for your figure. Besides, showing that belly makes me look good, too." He winked at her and she blushed.

"Oh, yeah," I said with a groan. "Don't forget to pump his ego, Cami. You're doing all the hard work, but be sure to let everyone know Dylan's dick was involved. Maybe you should buy her a shirt that says that, dude."

Cami choked, sputtering as she reached for her orange juice, taking several giant gulps as Dylan patted her absently on the back.

"Quit trying to kill my wife, would you?" He grinned.

"Only finishing up what you started. Besides, it's pretty obvious who's been . . . abusing . . . her lately."

"Believe me, it's not abuse," Cami whispered, her face flushing a deep shade of red and I chuckled.

"I'll take your word for it." I replied, digging in for another bite.

"Trust me, Russ," Dylan said. "Someday you're gonna meet someone and all of a sudden, this," he gestured between Cami and himself, "is going to make perfect sense."

Eyeing them both, I continued to chew my food. I wasn't sure anything like that would ever happen for me . . . even though I wanted it to. The fact of the matter was that Cami had pretty much ruined me on all other girls. Secretly, I'd been a little bit in love with her since high school—like most of the male student body had been. We'd all simply viewed her as out of our league. Then Hunter, a.k.a. Dylan, the undercover cop, had swept in and claimed her for his own. He was perfect for her, and she for him, each complimenting the other so strongly.

Regardless of some of the terrible things we'd endured together, I felt privileged to have them both as my very best friends. Still, there was a tiny jealous part of me that craved what the two of them had for myself.

Swallowing, I replied to Dylan's comment. "I'll believe it when I see it."

"It'll happen," he replied, capturing Cami's hand and squeezing it lightly. "Most likely when you least expect it."

***

"How's lifeguard duty going?" Cami asked, waddling up beside me, holding onto her straw hat that was blowing lightly in the breeze. My gaze traveled over her sundress before I gazed back out at the people playing in the lake.

"So far so good. I'm glad I picked up more hours. A little extra money for my renovations never hurts," I replied, shuffling my stance. "Decided against the bikini?"

Giggling, she scrunched her nose. "No. I'm wearing it underneath this. Believe it or not, it actually kinda fits."

"So, why are you hiding it?" I teased.

She glared up at me with one eye. "You know why."

Laughing, I shook my head. "Chicken."

"Yep."

"It's just as well, I guess. I don't need Dylan rushing over here to try and peel it off of you in front of all these innocent children."

Cami snorted. "He's over at the grill, barbecuing, so I think everyone is safe."

"We're never safe when Dylan is playing with his meat."

Gasping, she lightly slapped my shoulder. "You are so bad."

I chuckled. "You know it's the truth. There should be a public alert on the two of you. 'Warning: Avert eyes or be subjected to extreme displays of affection,' or something like that."

"We aren't that bad. Besides, you're just jealous."

I wrapped an arm around her shoulders and squeezed lightly. "That I am, Cami. That I am." I was man enough to admit it.

"Don't be. You're a catch Russ. Someday, soon, you'll be the one making all of us green with envy."

"Not likely, but I love you even more for thinking so."

She slipped her arm around my waist. "I love you too, Russ. And I will always think so. You'll never make me think different. Especially after all you've done for me in the past." She was getting awfully close to touching upon that elephant in the room. Tightening her embrace, she stared at me for a moment.

"I know what you mean," I said, looking back at her, not wanting to continue the direction this subject was heading. "I'd do anything for you and Dylan."

"You've already proven that," she said softly.

A loud squeal interrupted us and I jerked my head in that direction—instantly on alert for any danger but it was just two teenagers wrestling around in the water a few feet away.

"I better go keep an eye on these guys," I said, releasing her. "I'll talk to you, later."

"I'll bring you some lunch as soon as it's ready," she called after me. "Dylan and I will come eat with you."

"Sounds good."

***

"Yep, I still got it," Dylan said, groaning as he bit into his steak.

"Props, dude. I agree. You are the grill master." Taking a bite, I savored the perfectly cooked rib-eye steak. It practically melted in my mouth.

"You didn't have to wait for me," Dylan said, cutting another piece.

I shrugged. "Someone had to keep an eye on the swimmers during lunch. Figured it might as well be me and I'd just eat when you were available." I took another bite and groaned. "It was worth the wait."

"You two sound like a porno with all that moaning and groaning going on," Cami joked.

Arching a brow I stared at her. "Been watching a lot of those lately, have you?"

Blushing a deep shade of red, she slapped me, playfully. "No! You know I wouldn't do that."

"You probably don't have time, since Dylan keeps you pretty occupied with living your own."

Dylan chuckled and stared lovingly at Cami and her skin flushed even more, her eyes wide in disbelief at the topic of conversation.

"What?" I said, gesturing to her stomach. "It's not like you can deny it. The proof is right there staring me in the face."

"I . . . it's . . . ," she stuttered. "It's not porn." Picking up her plastic cup, she glanced away and took a swallow.

"It's better than porn," Dylan whispered loudly and Cami choked, spraying Kool-aid across the table and splattering me.

Stunned, I glanced down and started laughing. "Okay. I guess I deserved that. Thank goodness I'm not wearing a shirt."

"Yeah." Dylan elbowed Cami and nodded at me. "You know he only volunteered for lifeguard duty so he'd have an excuse to go shirtless in front of all these women, today."

I rolled my eyes. "Whatever. I'm on duty and I'm the best swimmer in the department—you know that."

"Hmm," Dylan replied with a grunt, continuing to eat.

"Well, all that working out he's been doing with you has paid off in a big way." Cami smiled. "I'm sure I'm not the only woman who's noticed all those rippling abs."

"Hey now," Dylan chastised. "I'm going to get jealous if you keep talking about Russ like that."

"Don't worry. You're still my favorite." She grinned at him as he leaned over and kissed her lightly on the lips.

"Good thing."

"Can't fault the girl for noticing perfection, dude," I added, and Cami laughed.

Dylan glanced at me. "I know. That's why she's always staring at me."

I chuckled and shook my head. "Always so humble."

"Just like my best friend, huh?" He laughed and held his fist out and I bumped it. "Us ugly guys have got to stick together to be ego boosts for each other."

"Whatever," Cami said, dragging the word out. "Neither of you are even remotely close to ugly, and you know it."

Laughing, I took another bite of my steak and stared out toward the water. The sunshine glittered off the light ripples the breeze caused on the surface. Turning my gaze back toward my plate, I paused, adrenaline pumping through me as my brain registered the anomaly my eye briefly caught. Gaze darting quickly over the surface, I scanned the lake, again, seeing a hand break the water, followed briefly by a head bobbing up before sinking under.

"Hey!" I shouted, jumping from the table and briefly eyeing the beach for Jim, my replacement for lifeguard duty. I spied him further down the shoreline, out of earshot. Grabbing my floatation device, I slipped it over my shoulder. "Hey!" I shouted, pointing to the water as I ran. "Dylan! Call the ambulance!" I yelled over my shoulder as I kicked my shoes off, losing precious seconds before running into the water and diving in.

A wide ring of ripples spread out from where I'd last seen the swimmer, a woman, I thought, from the brief glance I'd gotten. Afraid to take my eyes off the spot, my arms stroked heavily through the water, propelling me as quickly as I could go—yet it seemed incredibly slow.

Again, ever so briefly, a head bobbed at the surface before disappearing.

Hang on! I'm coming! I thought to myself, unwilling to risk any energy shouting to the swimmer.

After what seemed like hours, I finally reached the spot I'd last seen her. Diving down beneath the surface, I tried to spot her, but the water was just cloudy enough that I had difficulty. Coming up, I gasped for air before plunging back into the murky liquid, swimming lower as I flailed my arms around, searching for some kind of contact.

Damn it! Where is she? I pushed lower, my hands tangling in something soft. Grasping, I realized it was hair. *Sorry*, I thought as I pulled on it, sliding lower in the water until my arm slid across her breasts and hooked under her arms. Immediately I turned and began dragging her back to the surface.

Shooting above the water, I greedily gulped in oxygen, filling my burning, straining lungs. "I need help!" I shouted toward the shore and then turned back to the victim. Keeping her head above water with my floatation device, I checked for a pulse and found a faint one, but she wasn't breathing, her lips already turning blue.

Straightaway, I initiated rescue breathing, repositioning myself and blowing heavily into her mouth as I tread water.

"Almost there," Dylan's voice filtered through the air and I glanced up from my task long enough to see him and the chief approaching in one of the canoes the department had provided for today.

Blowing into the woman's mouth, again, I felt her lungs expand. Suddenly she started coughing, water spraying from her mouth against my face. Panic filled her eyes and she struggled against me, still making choking sounds.

"It's okay," I shouted, continuing to hold her like I'd been trained. "I've got you. Help is here. Don't fight me."

Momentarily she paused, and then Dylan's strong hands were gripping her, pulling her into the boat.

"You okay, Weston?" Chief called to me and I nodded.

"I'm fine. Let's go." I tossed the end of my flotation device to him and he hooked it on the boat, dragging me alongside as he paddled back toward shore.

Relief shot through me as I heard the woman start to cry. "I . . . I got a cramp," she stuttered.

"It's okay," Dylan reassured her, sifting through the jump bag he'd pulled off the truck. "I'm going to slip this oxygen mask on your face, okay? Can you tell me your name?" he asked, beginning his assessment of her.

"Evie," she replied.

Evie, I thought to myself as I floated in the water, exhausted. *Today is your lucky day.*

SMOLDER

CHAPTER TWO
Russ

The gunshot fired and I was instantly awake, punching and clawing into the vacant air as a scream tore from my lips. Huffing loudly, I slowly came back to reality, blinking rapidly in the darkness as I shook my head.

"Holy hell," I whispered, flopping back onto my pillow and dragging a hand through my hair. It was the third time, tonight, I'd had this nightmare. It was getting to the point where I was afraid to go to sleep.

Groaning, I slipped out of bed and padded down the hall in my underwear to my spare bedroom, where I'd set up my weight center. Dylan and Cami may have been teasing me about how ripped I was getting, but the truth was that I'd been putting in massive amounts of extra weight-training time every night, trying to work out the mess going on in my head. Clearly, "exercising" my demons away wasn't working.

Maybe it was time to call in an actual exorcist to help me out.

Flipping on the light, I spied a phonebook sitting on a stack of boxes still waiting to be unpacked from my move. Ticking off the months in my head, I realized I'd lived here nearly two years. If the boxes weren't unpacked by now, I probably didn't need what was in them. Considering how long it was taking me to renovate everything on this floor, I'd probably never unpack them, anyway. Dylan had offered to pay for a construction crew to complete it, but I'd wanted to do it all myself. It made it more personal, and I enjoyed seeing the progress as the old place slowly came shining back to life, again. Too bad I couldn't work on it at night—unless it was painting or something equally as quiet. Otherwise Cami and Dylan would, for sure, realize how much I wasn't sleeping. Wandering around at night had confirmed one thing, I was fairly certain I was the only one haunting the premises.

Grabbing the phonebook, I began flipping through the pages looking for psychiatrists that specialized in Posttraumatic Stress Disorder. Cami, Dylan, and I had all seen a therapist, provided by the fire department, when we'd first moved here. Our new chief had requested the sessions for Dylan and me as a requirement of our being hired. We easily completed the mandatory eight weeks with no real issues coming up. Basically, I sat there and told the doctor what had happened, and he asked questions, now and then, about how certain things made me feel. At the time, I didn't really have any issues. Yes, I had the occasional nightmare, but it was just a dream, right? As soon as our required time was up, I quit going, as did Dylan and Cami.

I couldn't go back to the department therapist, now. I knew things were supposed to be confidential, but I didn't want Dylan or the chief finding out I was back in therapy.

Sighing in frustration, I flipped through several pages of names, before finally deciding I'd feel more comfortable talking to a woman. Last time, I felt like Dr. Milton determined my masculinity based on how I dealt with the whole event. I wanted someone not associated with the department—someone to whom I could talk freely, without feeling like every word I said was weighed as a determining factor on whether or not I was competent to work.

Searching for addresses not too far from home, my finger landed on the number for a Dr. Evelyn McKnight. Going back into my room, I grabbed my cellphone and called the number listed, not caring that it was the middle of the night. Voice mail picked up and an automated greeting gave me an after-hours number to call if this was an emergency before prompting me to leave a message.

I cleared my throat. "Um, hi. My name is Russ Weston. I'd like to schedule an appointment with Dr. McKnight. I, uh, think I'm suffering from PTSD and would like to try and get some help working through it." I left my cell number and hung up, tossing my phone down on my squeaky old bed before heading back to work-out. Hopefully I'd hear back from them on Monday.

My thoughts drifted back to the barbecue and the water rescue that had taken place. I hadn't really had a chance to interact with the victim after Dylan had taken over. The ambulance crew was waiting for us when we got to shore, whisking her off to the hospital. Dylan had insisted that I sit in one of the trucks and take some oxygen, just to be safe—which I thought was completely ludicrous, but I did it to humor him, anyway. Then the chief insisted I take the rest of the night off and not work my regularly scheduled shift. I'd been about to argue, but was interrupted when an older couple approached me, the parents of the victim.

The woman I'd rescued had been picnicking with her family on the other side of the lake from our department party. She was apparently a pretty avid swimmer from what her parents said, so no one thought twice about her going for a swim across the lake.

They both thanked me profusely before heading off to the hospital. They seemed like nice people. I sent well wishes to their daughter through them, again thinking how fortunate it was that I'd happened to glimpse her in time.

Life was so fragile. That was a lesson I learned over and over. One minute everything could be moving along normally, the next it could be drastically altered forever—a crippling car accident, a heart attack, a house fire, or the simple act of a gun barrel being placed against your head.

Life was fragile and not to be taken for granted.

***

"Well, someone has been out scoring the brownie points. Literally," Dylan said, coming in early in the morning from his night shift, carrying a pan of brownies. Pausing to kiss Cami, who was cooking breakfast, he slid the pan in front of me along with a note.

"What's this?" I asked, staring down at the chocolate squares with confusion before glancing up at him.

"Haven't you heard? You're the new local hero. Someone from the newspaper already called the station this morning wanting to interview you about the water rescue thing from yesterday. I guess a bystander at the lake caught the whole thing on video with their phone. It's already played on the early morning news."

"Wonderful," I said with a groan, not happy at all to hear this. "I was simply doing my job. I don't need any credit or recognition for it."

"Well, when you rescue a local celebrity, of sorts, word is bound to get out."

"A local celebrity?" I was completely confused. "What are you talking about? Who is she?"

"She's Dr. Evelyn McKnight, a psychiatrist. She's done a lot of local charity work to help soldiers overcome PTSD. She's considered quite the authority on the subject and is very well loved by members of the community."

"You're shittin' me." I was dumbfounded. This could not be happening. The doctor I'd called last night was the woman from the lake? "Evie. She said her name was Evie," I muttered.

"Obviously short for Evelyn," Cami said.

"Read the card," Dylan said, grinning.

Slowly, I opened the envelope and pulled out a small note card with the words "Thank You" printed in gold lettering. Opening it, I found a short handwritten message.

"Read it out loud so I can hear it, too," Cami begged, so I humored her.

Dear Mr. Weston,

My husband and I, again, wanted to thank you for saving our daughter, Evie, from drowning, yesterday. It's so nice to know our community is safer because of people like you, who train and risk your own lives for the safety of others every day.

Evie is doing well and expected to be released from the hospital later today. She sends her thanks to you, as well.

If there is ever anything we can do to be of service to you, please let us know. Our family is forever in your debt.

Sincerely,

Mr. and Mrs. Kent McKnight

Carefully, I tucked the letter back into the envelope. "Wow. That was nice of them. And she brought these brownies?"

Dylan nodded with a smile. "She must've been up at the crack of dawn to make them, too. The pan was still warm when she arrived at the department, just before I got off."

"They smell delicious," I said, peeling back the cellophane covering the disposable pan. "I'm thinking we need to have some brownies with breakfast."

Reaching into a drawer, Dylan produced a spatula and handed it to me. "I agree. The smell drove me crazy all the way home."

Cami set out three small dishes and I carefully scooped us each a large brownie as I pondered over my next move. Obviously I had to cancel my appointment with this woman. Didn't this make it some kind of weird conflict of interest or something?

Taking a bite of the brownie, I groaned. It was as good as it smelled. Staring at Dylan and Cami, I suddenly wished I could ask their advice on the matter, but there was no way I could bring up what we'd all been through together, again. We'd worked so hard to get past it. I couldn't bear to hurt them anymore. They'd been through enough. Now was the time for them to just be happy and enjoy preparing for their upcoming family addition. Their last pregnancy had ended so tragically when Cami had been shot in the stomach. I couldn't bring that all up again—not when Cami finally spent more days laughing and smiling than crying and being sad. Besides, I didn't want them to know that I was still having issues with all of it.

I decided I would call and leave a message

right after breakfast—canceling my appointment with Dr. McKnight. I'd waited this long to seek out help, it wasn't going to hurt me to wait a little longer.

The phone rang and Dylan answered it, speaking for a moment before holding it to his chest. "It's the newspaper. They'd like to do a phone interview with you."

I shook my head. No way. I wasn't going to get dragged into this media circus. "You can tell them I'm refusing all interviews. My official statement is this: 'I love my job and am grateful for the opportunity to be able to help others when needed'. That's all I'm saying on the matter."

SMOLDER

CHAPTER THREE
Russ

Wide-eyed I stared down at a picture of me in my uniform splashed across the front page of the Charleston Herald newspaper with:
Hero Firefighter is Grateful for His Job and Opportunity to Help Others written in bold letters underneath

"You have got to be kidding me," I grumbled, quickly folding it and dropping it into a nearby garbage can, hoping Dylan and Cami hadn't seen it. I was going to catch shit for this from the guys at work. Knowing we loved any excuse to razz each other, I suddenly wished I could come down with a bad case of the flu or something before my shift, tonight. Of course, if I did that, they'd probably actually think I was trying to get out of work and would come up with something even worse to torture me with. I was screwed either way.

The great smells coming from the kitchen

signaled that Cami was already awake and cooking breakfast. But, as I rounded the corner, I was surprised to find Dylan alone at the stove instead.

"Hey, man" he said, glancing at me briefly as I entered.

"Hey. Where's Cami?"

"She's not feeling well this morning, so she's sleeping in. The baby moved around a lot last night and it kept her awake. I think it made her back hurt, so I told her to take it easy today and let me wait on her."

"Not much longer, now." I smiled, going to the cupboard to get some plates. "Just a couple more weeks until her due date, isn't it?"

"Sixteen days to be exact," Dylan said with a smile. "Then we'll finally meet our little girl."

Chuckling, I shook my head. "I can't imagine you as a dad, let alone as a dad to a baby girl. But, if she's anything like Cami, she'll be a little angel. On the other hand, if she's anything like you . . . ." I let my sentence dwindle off.

"If she's anything like me, I'll need to lock her in a cage through her teenage years, for sure," he responded with a laugh. "And if she's anything like Cami . . . well, let's just say I should start practicing my 'touch my daughter and die' speech, now."

I nodded. "Sounds like a wise plan, my friend."

"It's crazy, isn't it? I mean, looking back on my life, it was all about the girls and how many I could hook up with. Now that I'm going to be a dad, my whole mentality has shifted. Just like that—in the blink of an eye—I suddenly want to strangle any guy who might look at my daughter."

Laughing, I sat down in one of the chairs at the table, crossing my booted feet out in front of me, folding my arms. "I think you just described the way Cami's dad felt about you."

Grinning widely, Dylan flipped over the pancakes he was cooking. "In my defense, he did think I was a juvenile delinquent at the time. Once he found out I was actually an undercover cop, things got a lot better."

"Somehow I doubt that would've mattered much if he'd actually known how much time you were spending making out with and groping his daughter. Cop or not, I still think he would've shot you."

Still smiling, Dylan nodded. "You're probably right about that." A wistful look passed through his eyes. "Damn, those were good days."

"Pipe down, big boy," I teased. "Your wife has had all the good days she can handle at the moment. Give the poor girl a break."

"Give the poor girl a break? You're kidding me, right? It's totally the other way around."

"Whatever."

"I'm dead serious," he replied. "Haven't you ever heard about a pregnant woman's libido? For real—I'm not kidding you. There's like all this increased blood flow down south for them and they can't get enough sex."

"You're just shittin' me, now. Come on."

"I'm dead serious," he repeated. "If you don't believe me, then look it up. Cami has been a friggin' wildcat in bed for the last several months. I probably even have the claw marks to prove it."

Staring at him for a few seconds, I narrowed my eyes. "Sometimes I really hate you, you know that?"

Dylan laughed heartily. "Not to be a prick, dude, but you *should* hate me. I've got it all."

"You do. Your life is damn near perfect—great job, big inheritance, massive house, child on the way, and a hot wife that wants to do nothing but cook and clean for you all day and ride you all night."

"You're wrong."

I grunted. "About what?"

"Cami likes to ride me during the day, too." He chuckled, winking at me.

"Way to rub it in. You're a mean son-of-a-bitch, you know that?" I shook my head, smiling at him as he lifted the pan and came toward me.

"I'm not that mean. I did make you breakfast, after all." He slapped a very large pancake on my plate and my eyes widened.

"A smiley face pancake?" I asked, glancing up at him.

"Yep. Heroes who make the front page of the newspaper get special breakfasts."

"Damn it all to hell," I breathed out. "You saw the paper."

"Bro, everyone has seen the paper. One of the neighbor ladies has already been by with cupcakes for both of us this morning. She said she just wanted to thank us brave firefighters for our selfless service to the community.

Apparently she recognized us from the video on the news."

"Great, just great," I replied.

"That's not all," he continued.

"There's more?" I asked incredulously.

"The fire department has fielded nine phone calls, since yesterday, from women needing help to rescue their cats from trees. Each of them, personally, asked for you."

I stared at him slack jawed, unable to say anything.

He patted me on the shoulder. "Better learn to deal with it, Russ. You're a bona fide hero, now. I'll take you out cape shopping after breakfast. Maybe Cami can whip you up a spandex suit– you know, something real tight to show off all those cut muscles of yours. Don't worry, I'll have her add some extra padding to your package area, so it looks adequate."

"There is no need for padding there," I retorted. "It's plenty big all by itself."

Dylan chuckled, dishing a pancake for himself before setting the pan back on the stove, grabbing the butter and syrup and then sitting down beside me.

"So, now we only have one more problem," he said, grinning.

Immediately, I was wary. "And what's that?"

"We need to come up with your super hero name."

Rubbing a hand over my face, I realized this story was going to escalate far beyond my control, and there wasn't a damn thing I could do about it.

A vibration in my pocket alerted me to my phone and I quickly dug it out, happy for any excuse to escape this conversation. Glancing at the number, I was surprised to see it was from Dr. McKnight's office.

"Uh, I've got to take this," I said to Dylan, standing up and walking out the kitchen door to the side porch. "Hello?" I answered, wondering why her office was calling me. I'd left a message canceling my previous request for an appointment.

"Hello? May I please speak with Mr. Weston?" A light and airy female voice responded.

"This is he."

"Hi, Mr. Weston. I'm Misty Larson, the receptionist for Dr. McKnight. I received your calls from over the weekend."

"Yeah, about that. I didn't mean to be a bother. I actually called and made the appointment before I realized who Dr. McKnight was. After I found out, I figured it might be some kind of conflict of interest, so I called to cancel the appointment."

"No worries. I understand, completely," Misty continued. "I was actually calling to see if you'd agree to an appointment, anyway. Dr. McKnight would really like to meet with you."

Pausing, I was unsure of what to say.

"She said if you resisted to tell you she owes you one."

I laughed, feeling slightly uncomfortable. "Tell her she doesn't owe me anything."

"Mr. Weston, if someone had saved your life,

would you want to thank them in person?"

My thoughts drifted back to Dylan's policeman brother-in-law, Chris, and Wilson, my fire-fighting partner, in Tucson. Both had played important roles in our rescue and I would always feel deeply indebted to them.

Sighing, I relented. "Yes, I would."

"Dr. McKnight would like to speak with you—in person—this afternoon, say around one? Does that work for you?"

"That should be fine. My schedule is clear until my shift this evening."

"Wonderful! I'll pencil you in. Also, she wanted me to tell you that she'd love to hear about the initial reason you called—if you feel comfortable with that—and to let you know that you won't be billed for that hour."

"I can totally pay her. That's not a problem." I didn't want to get special treatment because of this.

"I'm sure you can, but since the doctor wishes to speak to you about her own personal matter regarding the service you provided, she'd feel more comfortable not charging you. So, we will see you at one?" she continued, not giving me time to protest.

"One o'clock. I'll be there."

"Do you need directions to the office?" she asked and I smiled. Misty was very thorough.

"I'm familiar with the area. I'm sure I can find it okay."

"Wonderful. Don't hesitate to call if you need anything. See you soon, Mr. Weston."

"Okay. Thank you," I replied, ending the call

and staring out toward The Battery and the sea wall that held back the water of Charleston Harbor, beyond. Today was shaping up to be an interesting day. I had no idea what this conversation with the lady doctor would be like, but it was definitely going to put me outside my comfort zone.

Turning, I went back inside to finish eating.

"Everything okay?" Dylan asked as I entered, and I tried not to wince. I hated not being straight with him, but I didn't want to bring up anything that would remotely turn the conversation to the past events that had led the three of us to move here.

"Yeah, just a surprise phone call." Sitting down, I grabbed the butter and syrup and began slathering it on my pancake.

"Good surprise, or bad surprise?" he asked, concerned.

I shrugged. "Neither, really. I guess Dr. McKnight wants to meet me. That was her secretary. She asked me to come by her office later today." I could at least tell him that much without it seeming odd.

Dylan chuckled. "She must've seen the newspaper, too." He slapped my shoulder. "Good for you, bro. She's a hot little number from what I could tell. A few years older than you, according to the report, but that doesn't matter. A hot cougar is still a hot cougar, am I right?"

"Says the guy who robbed the cradle," I reminded him wryly.

He laughed, unfazed. "Maybe you can score

a date with her and she can thank you properly."

I groaned. "Please tell me you did not just go there."

"What?" he asked, feigning innocence. "I'm just looking out for my boy's best interest. But if things do progress in that direction, I suggest you let her take you to her house, or a hotel. The whole neighborhood would know what was going on if you bring her to that squeaky bed of yours."

"Hey, now. That bed is awesome. Think of the history those springs could tell. I figured as old as you are, you'd appreciate old things." If he was going to dish it, I could give it back just as easily. "I'm surprised a grandpa like you can even father a child at this point."

He burst out laughing. "I'm like four years older than you, dude. Old jokes aren't going to work on me."

"Almost four and a half," I reminded. "Those few extra months really count."

"Spoken like a true twenty-two year old baby," he retorted, grinning. "Speaking of robbing the cradle, if I remember correctly, the good doctor is twenty-six, so around my same ancient age."

"That seems awfully young for all the philanthropic work she's supposedly done."

"According to the paper, she's very smart—graduated high school early at sixteen and immediately enrolled in college and finished her undergraduate degree in four years. Then she enrolled in a graduate program and earned her

Ph.D. by the tender age of twenty-four. Her humanitarian work with soldiers began as part of her graduate work and has continued over the last couple of years. She really is one of the top doctors in her field."

"Dang, you've done some research! Well, that answers your question then, doesn't it? There's no chance of her having any interest in me. She's an overachiever. I'm a two-year college graduate with an Associate Degree in Applied Fire Science and Emergency Medical Technology. Shoot, someone like her would practically consider me a college drop-out." I took a bite of my food, hoping desperately we could end this conversation.

"There's not a soul on this planet who would think that," Dylan replied sincerely. "You have a good job, good skills, and you risk your life more in one shift than most people do in a lifetime. Don't sell yourself short, Russ. Even without this rescue and all the newspapers and television reporters—you're a hero." He was dead serious, staring straight at me, and somehow the conversation had ended up exactly in the place I'd been trying so hard to avoid. "I'll never be able to repay you for what you did for me and Cami."

Emotion suddenly clogged up in my throat and it was hard to swallow my food. "If anyone is a hero around here, it's you. You're the one who helped me straighten up my life. I'm who I am, today, because of you."

"You're who you are because you have an honest heart that is full of good. You can't learn that—it's born inside you, Russ. It's the kind of thing that makes you step in front of a gun and take the hit for a friend. *You* did that. *You*." His eyes watered slightly.

"I simply couldn't stand by and let that bastard hurt you and Cami anymore. It's called human decency, nothing more."

"Yet. I'd wager ninety-nine percent of the human population would've gone running in the other direction, screaming for help. You didn't. And *that's* what makes you a hero." He paused for a moment, glancing down at his fork and picking at his pancake briefly before looking back up at me. "And I'll love you forever because of it."

CHAPTER FOUR
Russ

Taking a deep breath, I entered the building and proceeded to the desk in the large lobby. "I'm here to see Dr. McKnight," I said to the young woman sitting there.

"Dr. McKnight's offices are located on the third floor," she replied with a smile. "If you take the hallway straight ahead you will see the elevators. When you reach the third floor, go to the right and you'll see it. It's well marked."

"Thank you," I replied, nodding. Turning away, I headed toward the elevators. I waited for a few moments, grateful that it was empty when the doors swished open.

Glancing down at my clothes, I wasn't sure if jeans and a t-shirt were the appropriate attire for something like this, but it was what I went with.

Why am I so nervous about this meeting? Probably because all the press surrounding this had been so uncomfortable. I didn't like being in the spotlight. I was happy being the guy behind the scenes, living and enjoying life day-by-day. Average Joe—that described me perfectly, and I wanted to keep it that way. If I could just get rid of these damn nightmares, my life would be pretty much perfect. Well, okay, a hot girl might make it a little more perfect, but I wasn't going to press that matter.

Arriving on the third floor, I went to the right, as instructed, and saw a set of heavy looking, wood double doors marked with a plaque beside them.

Dr. Evelyn McKnight, Ph.D.

Stepping inside, I glanced around the comfortable looking space and made my way to the reception desk.

A very pretty brunette, about my age, glanced at me. "Mr. Weston?" she asked, standing and coming around the desk before I could utter a word. "I'm Misty Larson, Dr. McKnight's secretary. We spoke on the phone? It's a pleasure to meet you!" She extended her hand and I shook it, smiling a bit awkwardly at how enthusiastically she greeted me. "Dr. McKnight said to show you right in. This way, please." She gestured toward a door and I followed after her.

Poking her head inside, she spoke briefly. "Dr. McKnight, Mr. Weston is here."

"Wonderful! Show him in, please," a very sweet voice responded. Searching my memory, I realized I'd only heard her talk when she was coughing and sputtering up water. I hadn't realized how melodic her voice was.

Stepping aside, the receptionist, whose name eluded me although she had just told me, gestured me into the room. I halted just inside, my eyes widening as I took in the woman before me.

She was gorgeous! My mind frantically tried to compare the image before me, against the woman I'd pulled from the lake. How could I have not recognized how pretty she was?

"Mr. Weston," she said. I barely noticed the sound of the door closing behind me as her thousand-watt smile captured me. "I'm so happy to meet you, officially."

"The pleasure is all mine," I replied, truly meaning it as my gaze traveled down her wavy, long blonde hair to where the ends rested against perfectly rounded breasts beneath her silky shirt.

I remembered enough of her rescue to know those were real, soft and supple when I'd slipped my arm around her in the water. Feeling like a prick, I quickly focused my attention back to her other notable features, doing my best to keep from gawking at the slight flair of her hips and the long graceful legs that peeked out from beneath her short, tailored skirt.

Her face didn't leave me any less mesmerized—big, bright blue eyes, high cheekbones, straight nose, and plump lips—I suddenly felt like I'd been put under a spell of some sort. I didn't want to stop staring at her. No wonder soldiers flocked to her for help, just looking at her made me feel really . . . really . . .

shit—I needed to sit down. Quickly.

"Please. Have a seat," she continued, gesturing to two comfortable chairs sitting across from each other.

Moving to the offered chair, I immediately sat, adjusting myself discreetly as she sat down—not sure if she'd noticed or not. Casually, I rested my hands in my lap, hoping to further obscure my rather obvious physical reaction to her. Thank goodness Dylan wasn't here. He'd be having a field day with this.

"How are you feeling?" I asked. "No lasting side effects?"

"I'm fine," she replied, still smiling as she stared at me, those big blue eyes looking right through me, instantly capturing all my secrets. She didn't look older than me, either. If I'd passed her on the street, I'd have thought she was, maybe, nineteen. "I've had a slight cough here and there; but other than that, nothing too bad. The doctor gave me some antibiotics, just in case I swallowed something nasty in the lake water."

"That's good. Better safe than sorry. I was surprised to hear you were back at work today, already."

She shrugged. "I feel fine, and it's not like work is a physical strain on me. I sit here and talk to people all day." A tinkling laugh escaped her and it made me smile even wider. I could listen to that sound all day. "It didn't seem fair for me to take a day for myself when I had people waiting—who needed my help."

"I'm sure they would've understood. Besides,

you, more than anyone, should be aware that there can be psychological repercussions from a near drowning. How are you, really? Have you been able to sleep okay? No nightmares?"

Laughing again, she shook her head. "Are you offering to play therapist to me, Mr. Weston?"

"Russ," I corrected her. "Mr. Weston is my dad. And yes, if you need it, I'd be happy to help. I think, in my line of work, I have enough qualifications to be a good sounding board."

"I bet you've seen a lot of sad, terrible things with your job," she stated, growing serious.

I nodded. "I have. But it doesn't make me love the job any less. I'm happy to be of help whenever possible." I smiled at her. "And every once in a while, we get a really happy ending and someone survives a tragedy—like you. Those are always good days."

"Thank you for helping me. I'm glad I was able to be one of your 'good days.'"

"Me, too," I replied. "But you evaded the question."

Smiling widely, she shook her finger at me. "You weren't supposed to notice that."

"Evasion is my specialty." I couldn't seem to get rid of this damn grin on my face. "I'm the master of it, actually."

She studied me carefully. "A hero who's a master at evasion? I'd love to get into that story."

"I'm not a hero, just a normal guy doing his job—and you're still avoiding my question." I raised an eyebrow at her.

Sighing heavily, she leaned back into her chair. "Since this is simply an informal meeting of . . . friends, and not an official session, I suppose I can answer you."

"Let's hear it." I encouraged her.

"Yes, I've had a couple of nightmares," she answered honestly. "But then, just as I'm about to die, I feel these strong arms wrapping around me and they pull me up to the top of the water. I wake up gasping for air . . . and looking for you."

"Looking for me?" For some reason this pleased me to no end.

"Well, you were the *hero* who rescued me. And, for the record, while you may not feel heroic, you are—to those people you save. Don't play down what you've done for them, and don't belittle their feelings toward you. To me, you will always be a hero."

Tapping my fingers against my leg, I allowed myself to relax a bit. She was easy to talk to and I liked it. "I never thought of it that way, I guess. To me, this is all stuff I'm trained to do. I go to work every day prepared to use that training, if needed. It's normal daily life for me— well, as normal as one can get on a job that throws the unexpected at you. But that's what I like about it. It's never the same thing twice. Each case is new and different."

"The very fact that you even chose this line of work speaks to your character."

I chuckled. "That I'm an adrenaline junky?"

Smiling, she shook her head. "You may be,

but that wasn't what I was referring to. Not everyone has the guts to do your job—to be able to stand in the middle of worst case scenarios and still have the presence of mind to try and fix things. That's very commendable, Mr. Weston."

Leaning forward, I rested my elbows on my knees. "Please, call me Russ. I insist."

Her eyes bore into mine. "Very well, Russ."

Just hearing my name on her lips did crazy things to my body. "Thank you . . . Dr. McKnight," I teased.

"Evie," she replied softly, smiling. "I think you've earned the right to call me Evie."

"Is that what your patients call you?" I asked, mesmerized with watching the way her lips moved.

"No." She was studying me just as much as I was studying her, and I was positive she felt the same attraction brewing between us. "Evie is the name I reserve for my friends and family."

"So we *are* friends, then?" I liked the sound of that.

"I'd like that, I think. If you're okay with it."

I nodded. "I'm more than okay with it, but it does leave me with one tiny little problem."

"What's that?"

"I was kind of hoping you'd be my doctor, too."

Reaching for a pencil on the end table beside her, she picked it up, tapping the eraser end lightly against her lips.

I was envious of that pencil.

I needed to get out of there and think with a

clear head. My intention was to find a different doctor, once I found out who she was. Now, here I was asking her to take me on—*knowing* I was attracted to her. If that wasn't a conflict of interest, I didn't know what was.

"What if I make an exception?" she asked.

"What kind of exception?"

"What if I was your friend who happened to be a doctor?"

I couldn't help my widening smile. I'd been grinning like a damn idiot almost since the moment I'd walked in here. "That might work."

"Only I have a little problem with that, too."

That didn't sound good. My smile faltered a little. "What?"

"I'm willing to do sessions with you, but only on one condition."

"Name it."

"I won't accept payment from you."

"Not acceptable," I said, leaning back into my chair and staring at her. "This is your job, and you're using your training and skill to help me. You need to be paid for it."

"But we just established we are friends; and as your friend, and as a thank you for saving my life, I'd like to do your sessions for free."

"And as your friend, and as your rescuer, who was on the clock getting paid when he saved you, by the way, I'd like to pay you for your work." We were totally in a negotiating war and I intended to win.

"Then how about this? I'll give you the 'hero special price break'?"

"And what's the 'hero special price break?'"

"Half off every session." She quickly leaned forward before I could protest, placing her slim hand on my knee and sparks raced straight to my groin. "Please, let me do this. Please? It means so much to me. You have no idea."

How could I refuse a request like that? "Agreed," I replied, slipping my hand on top of hers. "I really am happy you're all right."

"I'm really grateful you were there. It was terrifying."

"I'm still here for you—anytime you need me—day or night. You have my number."

"Which of us is the therapist and which is the patient again?" she asked with a slight laugh, still not removing her hand.

"Maybe we're neither—just two friends helping each other out." My eyes never left hers.

"I like the sound of that," she replied sincerely.

"I do, too."

"Shall I have Misty schedule you an appointment for tomorrow?" Evie pulled her hand away and I missed its warmth immediately.

"Sounds great. Anything before five is good for me."

"Perfect," she replied and stood up. So did I.

"I guess I'll see you tomorrow." I extended my hand but she surprised me, stepping into my arms, instead.

"Tomorrow I will be more formal, I promise. I just had to hug you today, and tell you thank you, first, while we're still just friends."

My arms went easily around her and I closed

my eyes and tried to commit everything about her to memory. I wouldn't be able to touch her like this again. It would be unethical—for both of us.

Damn. That really sucked.

SMOLDER

CHAPTER FIVE
Evie

Slipping the key into the lock of my second floor condo, I turned the knob, grateful to be home with the next few hours of quiet and solitude to myself.

Dropping my briefcase near the door, I kicked off my shoes and continued to peel my clothing off as I moved through the house—until I was wearing nothing but my bra and underwear. Making my way into the bathroom, I quickly turned on the water in the tub before digging under the sink for the bottle of aromatherapy bubble bath I kept in there.

This was my favorite part of the day, soaking in my Jacuzzi tub and letting go of all the stress and conversations that filled my mind up during the day. I made a conscious effort to keep my home life separated from my work, otherwise the burdens that my patients shared with me were sure to hang with me, plaguing me well after hours.

It wasn't that I was trying to forget them, or be inconsiderate, I simply felt the need for my own space, as well. This was my perfected ritual, a nice relaxing bath, a glass of wine, and my latest novel or autobiography. It allowed me to escape out of my own head and break away from thinking about the office. It was the only way I could casually enjoy my evenings.

Leaving the water running, I went to the kitchen to get my wine. Pausing beside the cupboard, my eyes fell on the newspaper laying there, a giant picture of a smiling firefighter, Mr. Weston . . . Russ . . . staring back at me.

Lightly, I traced my fingers over his face, thinking that even though this was an amazing picture of him, he was even more incredibly good looking in real life. Even if he hadn't been my rescuer, I had a feeling that just meeting him would've made my heart race. He was tall, and muscular, with short, thick wavy hair and bright, clear eyes. But it was his smile that captured me. It transformed his face—brightening it, shining white against the dark unshaved scruff on his jaw.

His personality had been charming, too. Yes, he was definitely the kind of firefighter a girl would consider burning her house down for—or, in my case, drowning in a lake for.

Sighing, I poured myself a glass of wine, leaving the paper where it had been on the counter. I couldn't bring myself to throw it away.

Carrying my glass, I moved through the

bedroom, glancing into the walk-in closet as I passed—seeing all of Kory's fatigues hanging there. Immediately I felt guilty for being attracted to Russ. It made me feel like I was cheating on Kory—something I'd vowed to never do.

My eyes drifted to the bed, instantly conjuring up images of all the times we'd made love, over and over again, never able to get enough of one another. Sighing, I continued into the bathroom, my gaze drifting down to the engagement ring I'd left soaking in cleaner today on my counter. Carefully, I rinsed it and slid it back on.

Moving my glass to sit on the side of the massive tub, I slipped out of my bra and panties and sank into the warm, refreshing water.

Lifting my hand, the light caught the diamond as I observed the symbol of love attached to my left hand. It winked at me, bringing back images of Kory on his knee, proposing to me.

A soft smile slid across my face as the memory washed over me, bringing all the feelings of that moment with them.

"I love you, Kory," I whispered, stroking the diamond. "You'll always be the only one for me."

Tears clouded in the corners of my eyes, threatening to spill over the edges. Kory's face had been the last thing I'd seen as the darkness of the lake consumed me. In that moment, I was ready to give up, to let go. Relaxing, I'd sunk into the vision of his face, his arms reaching for me.

The next moment I was above the water, coughing, as Russ Weston held me in his arms. For split second I thought he was Kory, his dark features shifting into the image of the face I loved so much. Then my vision cleared and I realized I was with a stranger, and not with Kory at all. For the briefest of moments, I was so terribly sad I'd been rescued.

Glancing out the bathroom door, directly in my line of sight, was the picture of Kory and I on my nightstand. He was in his BDUs embracing me as I snapped a selfie of us in the hanger after one of his returns from Afghanistan.

A sob escaped me as the grief threatened to overwhelm me, once more. Climbing from the tub, I wrapped a towel around myself and walked into the bedroom.

"Six years," I thought. *"Six years since you left, and I still feel like I can't breathe without you."* Tears streamed heavily down my face. Automatically, I leaned forward, lifting an image of Kory and my brother, Paul, my heart aching even more.

Paul. He was the one who introduced me to Kory. They were roommates in college, until Paul convinced Kory to enlist with him and let the military pay for their schooling. Paul never forgave himself for that. I never realized how hard he'd taken Kory's death—not until it was too late. I didn't know if I would ever recover from finding Paul in my parents' bathroom, lying in a puddle of blood next to a gun and suicide note, only two months after Kory had been killed.

I'd lost them both.

"But look at all the good you've done because of his death." I could practically hear my mom's words in the air—she spoke them so often. "So many soldiers have made it through their PTSD because of you and your work. Look how many lives have benefited because of our sacrifice."

It was true. Paul's death was the reason I'd delved head first into the psychiatric world of PTSD. I didn't want anyone else to experience the grief I'd known because of it. Yet I knew, in my greedy little heart, if I could rewind time and find a way to save both Kory and Paul, I would. I wanted them with me. I missed them.

My thoughts drifted once more to Russ Weston. He'd called for an appointment prior to realizing who I was. He said he was suffering from PTSD. He'd already saved my life—I owed him now. Whatever he needed, I wanted to be the one to help him find his peace.

***

I made it through the next day just fine, keeping myself busy as usual. An overworked mind didn't have time to wallow in misery and self-pity, like I'd found myself doing the previous night.

My unscheduled tears had led to too many glasses of wine and falling asleep wrapped in nothing but a towel on top of my bed, clutching the photo of Kory and Paul.

I missed them so much; and the ache in my heart continued to grow deeper, not smaller, it seemed. Staring at the same picture on my desk, I couldn't help smiling sadly back at them. Paul was my biggest regret. I'd never, in a million years, expected him to do something like that. He was always the happy, upbeat one.

And that kind of thinking was what got me in trouble. I should've realized that a combat warrior was the exact opposite of a happy, upbeat guy. All the death and killing had turned out to be more than he could handle. The nightmares had plagued him and he'd never breathed a word of it to me—determined to keep the ugly out of my life and handle it on his own.

What was the saying? Hindsight is 20/20? I definitely had 20/20 hindsight. It seemed that every picture I saw of Paul, now, I recognized the hint of sadness in his eyes.

"Dr. McKnight?" Misty's voice interrupted my musings. She sounded positively radiant—well, if it were possible for someone to sound radiant through an intercom.

"Yes?"

"Your last appointment is here. Mr. Weston?" And now I knew why she sounded that way. I was pretty sure every woman in the building had to stop and fan herself when he walked by.

Against my will, my heart rate increased and I chided myself. *It's simply because he rescued you,* I said internally. "Send him in please, Misty. Thank you."

Rising from my desk, I moved toward the door to greet him as it swung open and his larger than life presence slipped inside. It was funny, but suddenly my office seemed so much smaller with him in it.

"Mr. Weston. How lovely to see you, again," I said extending my hand and he shook it.

That incredible grin of his spread across his face, lighting the rest of his features. "Russ. I insist. I'll have to leave if you refuse."

"Fine, but I want you to call me Evie, too." I gestured to the chairs we'd sat in the day before.

Releasing my hand, he moved toward them. "But you're acting as my doctor now."

"I'm making an exception with you." He waited for me to sit down before he did, ever the gentleman. "Saving my life overrides formalities. To you, I'm simply Evie."

Still grinning, he nodded. "Okay. Evie it is." Settling back into the chair, he seemed completely relaxed with me. Slouching a little, he lifted a leg and crossed a booted heel on his other leg before propping his elbow up on the armrest and leaning his head gently against his knuckles. "So, tell me Doc, how do we start this thing?"

I was just about to correct him on calling me Doc when I recognized the pain that flashed in his eyes—the very same look that was present in all of Paul's last photos. Carefully, I studied him—taking in his comfortable pose—looking more like he was getting ready to watch a game of football than sit down at a therapy session. He seemed completely normal and at ease—but the eyes, they never lied. It was a lesson I'd learned way too late.

Behind the amazing smile, the self-confidence, and the heroics, something was eating Russ Weston in a bad way. I was determined to help him through it.

"I usually suggest that we start with whatever the current problem is and then return to the past and take the time to get to know each other a bit better. It gives me a better foundation if I know a little bit about how you dealt with things then and compare them to how you relate to them now."

"Okay, that works for me. What would you like to know? I'm pretty much an open book."

"Let's start with your initial reason for calling." I lightly tapped my pencil against my notepad. "You said you felt like you might be suffering from PTSD. Being a firefighter, I'm sure you've been trained to recognize those symptoms; so I don't doubt your diagnosis, but what is the thing that's standing out to you the most at this time?"

"Nightmares," he answered quickly. "Almost two years ago, I was involved in a hostage situation where my life, and those of my two best friends, was threatened."

Hostage situation. I wrote the words down on my paper. "That's definitely no laughing matter." I glanced at him. "How long have the nightmares been going on?"

Sighing heavily, he ran a hand through his thick hair. "Oh, I'm guessing about a year now."

"Have you ever sought any treatment for this before?"

"No." Russ gave a slight shake of his head. "I was briefly involved in therapy as part of the hiring process here, in South Carolina. The department required it of my best friend and me, to make sure we were dealing with what we'd been through. I wasn't really having any problems at that time, except for the very occasional nightmare about it. My therapist gave me a clean bill of health and I returned to work."

"And why are you seeking out a new therapist, now, if someone else is already familiar with your case?"

He didn't even blink. "I don't want the department, or my best friends, to know that I'm seeking treatment."

"I see. May I ask why?"

"My friends have already been through hell with this whole situation. Dylan, my buddy who helped with your rescue, is beside himself with grief and constantly trying to apologize to me for his part in my trauma. He's suffered with it enough. I don't want to drag things up for him, again."

"And what was his part in your trauma?" I asked, trying to follow.

"Our captor made him choose who he was going to kill—Cami, his wife, or me." His eyes bore into mine as I absorbed this news. "There was only ever one choice."

"So, basically, your best friend sentenced you to execution." I didn't miss the pained expression on his face as he shifted in his chair.

"He didn't have a choice."

"There's always a choice."

"He had to save his wife!" Now he sounded irritated with me.

"I'm not saying he made the wrong choice. I'm simply stating that the issue here is his choice. Whether or not you think he made the right choice, the fact of the matter is he could've chosen to save you."

White knuckled, he was gripping onto the arms of the chair. It was time to change tactics; this line of questioning was too tough for him.

"Let's step back a bit. Tell me a little about your childhood."

"What do you want to know?" he asked, visibly relaxing, which spoke volumes, telling me he was more comfortable with his home life.

"Were both of your parents present when you were growing up?"

He nodded.

"What was your relationship with them?"

Shrugging, he stared off as if he were recollecting things. "Both my parents worked to make ends meet. My dad was an accountant and my mom worked as a bank teller. We weren't wealthy by any means, but we lived comfortably enough."

"Did they interact with you a lot?"

"Not really. They were both tired when they got home in the evenings. Sometimes we had dinner together, sometimes we just fended for ourselves."

"Did you have any brothers or sisters?"

"No. I'm their only child."

"So what did you do to amuse yourself?"

Flashing a half grin, he continued to watch me closely. "I used the majority of my allowance getting high or drunk."

"So, you liked to party?"

"I guess. That's what I spent most of my teenage years doing."

"What about girls? Did you have any girlfriends?"

Giving a wry laugh, he shook his head. "I was kind of a late bloomer. The only girl I was with in high school wasn't even a real relationship. It was strictly for the sex."

"Are you still friends with her?" I asked, curious.

"She's dead." He shifted uncomfortably in his chair. "You should know that she, and her death, factor into the hostage situation. My best friend shot and killed her after she attempted to kill his wife."

I couldn't help it. My eyes widened a bit and I quickly tried to school my face back to being neutral.

He laughed. "Don't feel bad for being shocked. It's a pretty tangled web of events."

I could see there was much more to this story than met the eye. "Russ, why don't you start at the beginning and bring me to the present."

"Got a few hours?" he asked, giving a wry chuckle.

"You're my last appointment. Originally, I'd taken the afternoon off for a meeting, but it was canceled. We can go as late as we need to."

"I have to work tonight."

"We'll do the best we can then."

For some reason, I felt completely connected to this man. I wanted to know his story and what made him tick.

CHAPTER SIX
Russ

Glancing at the clock, I knew I was running out of time. Evie had already stayed past her regular business hours and I had about ten minutes before I absolutely had to leave or I would be late for my shift.

To her credit, she was still sitting across from me. She hadn't blinked when I told about using drugs or having sex with a psycho bitch who tried to kill one of my best friends. We'd covered everything from my childhood up to Cami's old best friend, Clay, poisoning my drink with methamphetamines and how I almost died from an overdose as a result.

Now she was staring at me, tapping her pencil against her notebook.

"So, what's your verdict so far, Doc?" I asked, shooting her a half smile. "Am I headed for the loony bin?"

She snorted. "Hardly. I'm not sure if you've

heard of my work and what I've done with combat soldiers?"

"I have, recently."

"Well, I bring that up because I feel like treating you will be very similar to treating them. You may not have been a trained soldier, but you and your friends have definitely been at war. You've had to deal with some seriously disturbed people, and you've seen people you know die as a result. That's not an easy thing to deal with."

Staring straight into her eyes, I was brutally honest. "I can't say I was sorry to see any of them die, though. I consider them being gone a blessing."

"That may be true, but even that can weigh heavily on your psyche."

I glanced at the clock again. "Hey, I'm sorry to interrupt all this, but I've really got to go to work now. I can't be late."

"No. It's okay. I understand." She smiled and laughed. "It's not like we have to try to get to everything in one day. We can take it slow. We've got time." Setting her pencil and paper on the table beside the chair, she stood, and I couldn't help letting my gaze travel over her figure.

I could think of a few things I'd like to take slow with her—or fast, or maybe right up against that wall over there.

Pull your mind out of the gutter, Weston, I ordered as I felt a certain something rising to the occasion. Standing, I extended my hand. "Thank you for your time," I replied. She slipped her hand in mine and I was reluctant to release it, continuing to grip it. "Same time next week?"

"Actually, the pace in which we go is up to you, but I'd prefer to see you sooner, if possible." I noticed she didn't try to let go of my hand either. "The sooner you can tell me all your story, the sooner we can get on to the therapy part."

Still holding her hand, I nodded. "That works fine for me. When would you like me to come back?"

"I had a late cancellation for tomorrow. Say around four? That way if we need to run over we can."

"Sounds perfect." I smiled. "It was nice seeing you again today, Evie. I hope you're still feeling okay after your . . . swim." I winked at her.

"I think you mean my lack of swim." She laughed lightly and I joined her. "I'm doing fine, thank you."

"Well, my advice to you is don't be afraid of the water. You know, that whole 'if you fall off a horse, get back on and ride' thing." I shook my head. "I should just shut up now, you're the therapist. You know better than I do."

"No, I appreciate your concern. It's heartwarming."

Both of us glanced down to our still clasped hands and I couldn't resist rubbing my thumb over the back of hers before glancing back into her eyes. "Who's your therapist?" I asked softly.

"Excuse me?" She seemed flustered, and I wasn't sure if it was from my question or the fact that we were still holding each other's hand.

"Who do you go to for help?"

She stared blankly at me.

"That's what I thought. You help all these people, but you don't seek help for yourself." I continued to slowly brush my thumb over her skin. "If you ever need to talk to someone, you have my number. There's no reason this street can't go both ways."

Seeming to regain some of her senses at this point, she straightened and pulled her hand free. "Actually, there is. It would be considered an unethical practice for me to call you or associate with you outside of this office."

I shrugged. "Then I guess I'll just have to fire you." Her jaw gaped at my suggestion and my chuckling as I headed for the door. "I'm serious. If you ever need anything, just call me. I'm happy to help out. It's what friends do. See you tomorrow."

"So, you aren't firing me?"

"Hell, no. Why would I fire the best doctor in town?" Resting my hand on the doorknob, I turned to glance at her. "I may instigate that old legend though."

"Old legend?" She looked completely lost.

"You know, the one that says if someone saves your life you become beholden to them until you've repaid the debt." I grinned widely and she smiled back at me.

"I'm definitely beholden to you, Mr. Weston."

Raising my eyebrow, I stared at her. "You better not be beholden to my dad for anything."

She practically giggled. "Russ. I'm sorry. It's

something that's been engrained into me for many years."

"You're not old enough to have anything engrained in you as far as I'm concerned."

Laughing, she moved forward, waving her hands in a shooing motion. "Out you go, *Russ*, before I succumb to your flattery and want to keep you here all night."

This time I was the one who was shocked. "Oh, I'm all for that," I responded quickly.

Shaking her head, she practically pushed me out the door. "I meant to continue our session."

"Well, damn. You got my hopes all up." I kidded.

"Goodbye," she said.

"Goodbye," I answered and she shut the door.

Chuckling, I shook my head and turned to walk away.

"Mr. Weston?" her voice called after me and I turned to find the door open just a crack, enough for me to catch a glimpse of her plump lips and a hint of her sparkling eyes.

"Yes?"

"I just wanted you to know, that in my professional opinion, there's nothing wrong with your libido." The door quickly shut, again, and I laughed heartily, shaking my head.

"I didn't think there was, Doc," I replied to the closed door, knowing full well she could hear me. "But thanks for the assessment."

A slight giggling sound was heard to my left and I turned, spying Misty staring at me with twinkling eyes. "You caught all of that, didn't you?" I asked smiling, and she nodded. "Well, I hope it didn't scar you too badly." I winked at her.

"Not at all, Mr. Weston. I find the whole thing to be quite romantic, personally." Her green eyes sparkled as she spoke.

"Romantic?" I asked, placing my hands on her desk and leaning in so close I could smell her sweet perfume. "Don't you know? It's unethical to date your therapist."

Smiling, she nodded. "Yes, I know. I'm simply hoping you might be able to convince her to date you instead of being your therapist. I hate seeing her so alone all the time."

"I don't know about that. Your boss is a pretty stubborn woman. I'm not sure I'm up to the task."

"Oh, I don't know. I can totally see you rising to the occasion." Briefly, her gaze dropped lower before returning to my face. She was obviously flirting with me, and I didn't hate it.

Laughing, I pointed my finger toward her. "I need to stay away from you." Slowly, I backed away, moving toward the door.

"And why is that, Mr. Weston?" she asked, clearly teasing me.

"Because you're one of those girls who could get me in a lot of trouble," I stated, resting my hand on the door. "And please, like I told Ev – Dr. McKnight, please call me Russ."

"Certainly. Have a great day, Mr. Weston."

Leaving her office, I couldn't stop chuckling and feeling confused. It was too damn bad Evie was my therapist, because I liked her. And damn it all to hell, I liked Misty, too.

I was looking forward to seeing them both at my appointment tomorrow.

***

"Where have you been?" Dylan asked as I sauntered into the fire station. "I've been trying to call you for hours."

"Shoot!" I reached into my pocket and retrieved my phone. "Sorry, bro. I forgot it was turned off. Thanks for reminding me." I quickly turned it back on.

Glancing back at him, he continued to scrutinize me.

"What?" I asked, still trying to avoid his initial question.

"Where've you been? Chief wanted us to come in early for a briefing. You missed it."

"Shit. What was it about?" I asked, deflecting the question once more.

"The last couple of fires we've run on have been ruled as arson. They match the M.O. of some of the fires Department Two has run on, as well."

I considered this information. "So, if they started in Department Two's area, and they've branched into Department One, then whoever is doing this is expanding their threat zone."

Dylan nodded. "The police have asked us to be hyper aware of any fires we're called out to and on the lookout for any early evidence that might be considered arson. They want to catch whoever this is before it gets any worse. So far it's been abandon or vacant buildings, but they're all close to residential areas, so that's a cause for concern."

"I agree. Is the chief still here?"

"No, he left right after. I told him I'd been unable to reach you and he said to fill you in on the details."

"Okay, thanks. I would've been here had I known."

"Which brings me back to my original question. Where were you?"

Damn. He was like a hound dog on the scent and wasn't letting this go. "I was meeting with someone," I said evasively.

"Someone?" He raised his eyebrow and folded his arms. "Is this someone of the female variety?"

Sighing, I nodded, knowing he was heading in the completely wrong direction with this; but that was fine with me, as long as he didn't discover the real reason.

"Awesome!" He clapped me hard on the shoulder. "Do I know who this someone is?"

"You've met her, yes."

"Then come on, give me the deets. I can't have my bro out there getting lucky and me not knowing a thing about it."

I chuckled, shaking my head. "I didn't say I was getting lucky. Hell, I just barely met the girl." Going over to the turnout wall, I routinely began inspecting all my gear, like I did at the beginning of every shift, making sure everything was ready to go at a moment's notice. "I'm fast, but I'm not *that* fast," I added.

Dylan laughed. "So, who is it?"

By all that was holy, why wouldn't he give

this up? "Evie." I waited.

"Evie? Evie as in the woman we rescued from the lake? Doctor Evelyn McKnight?" he asked skeptically.

"One and the same," I replied, trying to sound nonchalant.

"How'd that happen?" I could tell he was totally interested now.

"Her office called me and asked if I would come in and meet with her. She wanted to thank me, in person."

"Well, that was nice of her."

"I thought so, too."

"And?"

"And what?"

"How did it go? Was she nice? Did the two of you hit it off? Will you see her again?"

"You've turned into a girl, you know that right? I swear, spending all that time with Cami has turned you into some romantic fool."

Dylan burst out laughing. "Is that so bad? And is it bad that I want the same for you, too?"

I simply grunted in reply, wishing to avoid this line of questioning. I didn't want to mislead him, but if that was what it took, then I wasn't above lying to him about it. He couldn't know the real reason I was seeing her. It would hurt him too badly, and I was done seeing my friend hurting.

"Come on. Give me something, Russ."

Standing, I forced a grin. "She's hot; and I mean really hot. And she's very nice."

"Hot as in you'd like to date her hot?"

Shaking my head, I stared at him. "Yes, that

kind of hot. There's definitely some chemistry going on."

"Will you see her again?"

"I already have. Today was the second time I met with her."

"Oh." He grinned widely. "You do move fast."

I shrugged. "What can I say?"

"I just want to know why you're holding out on me?"

"Maybe I wanted five minutes to see how things would work out before I start bringing her around to meet the family." I rolled my eyes. "One meeting with Cami and her and the next thing I know you all will be helping her pick out wedding gowns or something."

Dylan punched me the shoulder. "We aren't that bad."

Eyes widening, I stared at him. "Really? This from the guy who has practically tutored me on how to make babies with all his public displays of affection?"

"Whatever."

"Yeah, ask any guy on this crew. We could walk in here and find you doing Cami against the wall and no one would even blink an eye, we're so used to it."

Dylan shook his head, grinning. "You're so full of shit."

"Just like you, huh?" I smiled. "Two peas in a pod."

"Well, I hope you will bring her by sometime. Cami and I would love the chance to get to know her."

"We'll see how it goes," I replied, frustrated.

It seemed I'd just dug myself into an even bigger hole.

CHAPTER SEVEN
Evie

For the twelfth time in ten minutes I glanced at the clock, my hands subconsciously running over my clothing to make sure everything was still straightened. Sighing heavily, I rolled my eyes. He was late, and I was acting like some nervous schoolgirl about to go out on a date. It wasn't like patients hadn't missed appointments with me before. Russ didn't seem like the type that would miss and not call, though. I hoped everything was okay.

"Dr. McKnight, Russ Weston is here," Misty's voice came through the speaker and I immediately relaxed.

"Send him in, please."

The door opened and I couldn't help smiling as he stepped inside, looking much the same as he did yesterday, sporting a navy blue fire department shirt and EMS cargo pants of the same color, except where a few reflective strips of material were sewn on them. The uniform made him look even sexier, I thought.

A smile broke out easily across his face and I didn't miss the way his eyes roamed over me, looking pleased. I guess the four times I changed outfits this morning had actually paid off.

"Sorry I'm late. I got a flat tire."

"No worries," I replied with a smile, and gestured toward the chairs. "Have a seat." Moving around my desk, I quickly settled into the chair across from him. "How are you, today?"

"I'm good; but before we get started, I need to confess something."

That caught me off guard. "Okay. What's that?"

"Well, Dylan has been quizzing me about where I've been going lately. I told him I'd been meeting you and he naturally assumes we are dating. I'm sorry, but I let him think that."

For some reason it made me very happy to hear that. "Oh, all right. How does that make you feel?"

Chuckling, his eyes traveled over me, again. "It makes me think it's a damn shame that it's not true. I think I'd like dating you." His eyes shifted to the ring on my hand. "But it looks like some other lucky guy has already snatched you up."

Glancing down at my ring, I rubbed it lightly. "His name was Kory."

"Was?" he said, catching that immediately.

I nodded. "He died six years ago in

Afghanistan."

"I'm sorry for your loss."

"He survived a helicopter crash and fired on insurgents covering the rest of his crew so they could make their escape. Unfortunately, he didn't survive the insurgents."

"Now, see? There's a real hero," Russ said. "That must've been awful for you."

"Extremely. My brother, Paul, was in his unit. They were best friends. Paul was one of the guys Kory saved that night. Sadly, Paul never recovered from the incident. I didn't even know he was having problems. I went to visit my parents after class one night and found him and the suicide note he left." I didn't know why I was telling him all this. I wasn't usually so free with information about myself—especially with a patient, but Russ didn't feel like a regular patient.

"So that's why you got so heavy into this line of work?"

I nodded. "I was already going to school for all this. I should've known—I should've seen the signs that something was wrong. I've often wondered what kind of therapist am I if I can't see someone suffering right in front of me?"

"Hey, don't go there." Standing, he moved beside me squatting down and taking one of my hands. "He was responsible for himself. Not you. If he knew something was wrong, he should've known he could come to you about it. You aren't responsible for his death."

A half-quivering sob escaped me. "I feel responsible though. Looking back, I see little hints that should've been red flag warnings to me. I ignored them all."

Russ's arms wrapped around me, enveloping me in their strong warmth, and the scent of his aftershave flooded my senses. I sank into his embrace, relishing the feel of him and the comfort I found there.

Sighing heavily, I closed my eyes, one of my hands slipping to rest on his large bicep, as his lips brushed lightly across the top of my forehead.

What the heck am I doing? Immediately I straightened and he released me. "I'm sorry. That was totally inappropriate."

"No, it wasn't," he argued. "Sometimes doctors need some compassion, too."

I simply stared at him. "Are you for real?"

He laughed, putting much needed distance between us as he returned to his chair. "I'm very real. And that may be exactly what's upsetting you. I know there are rules regarding conduct between doctor and patient, but you should also know I don't pay a whole lot of attention to rules. If I see something that needs to be done, I do it, consequences be damned. You needed some comfort—so sue me."

I couldn't stop smiling. "Somehow I think the world would be a whole lot better place if there were more people like you in it."

"I'm just a regular guy, Doc. No need to go setting me up on a pedestal."

Forcing myself to look away from him, I gathered my notebook and pencil, briefly going over the notes from our last session. I wasn't sure what it was about Russ, but he was quickly turning into the most difficult patient I'd ever dealt with—not that I thought he was being that way on purpose, but still, he constantly distracted me in a completely unprofessional manner. This was something I'd never dealt with before, and I'd treated many handsome men. Russ was even a few years younger than me, but my heart and head didn't seem to mind that, either. He acted mature for his age.

I was attracted to him. A lot. But I wanted to help him, too—and helping him find peace was more important to me. I needed to set my attraction for him aside and help him. That was the greater thing to do.

"So, in our last session, we left off with you accidentally being poisoned by a drink that was meant for Dylan." I glanced at him. "How did that make you feel? Knowing that you'd taken the fall for him."

He shrugged. "It made me want to bash Clay's face in when I found out what he'd done, but Dylan's quick thinking and actions are what saved my life. I felt like I owed him. It was also a big wake up call for me to get out of the drug scene. I don't think I realized exactly how much I wanted to live until that particular moment when it was all almost taken away."

"But it would've never happened to you if Dylan hadn't been in the picture to begin with."

"True, but then none of this would've. I'd probably be off stoned somewhere, wasting away my life right now, and Cami would be some scarred basket case because Clay raped her or something." He stared pointedly at me. "You would be at the bottom of a lake. Our lives are better because Dylan came into them. Nothing will convince me otherwise."

"You love him a lot, don't you?"

"More than my own life," he answered without hesitation. "He's my brother, just the same as if he were born that way."

"So what happened after Clay?" I encouraged him to continue.

"Well, Cami and I graduated from high school and we followed Dylan back to his hometown of Tucson, Arizona. She and I both enrolled in school there and Dylan continued doing undercover work as a police officer, infiltrating a car theft ring. For the most part, I was on the outside of that case, though there were a couple scary close calls for Cami and Dylan. They ended up getting married during all that, which didn't really surprise me." He paused and grinned, showing me he was truly happy for his friends before his smile faded. "It was after that case wrapped up that they started having problems again."

"What do you mean by problems?"

"Dylan decided to change careers and become a firefighter. Cami was always worried about him getting shot, so he became a firefighter; and so did I. Weird things started happening and it soon became apparent that someone was harassing them. Their dog was slaughtered on their back porch and then someone set their house on fire and burned it down. Dylan and Cami were put in a protection program and sent away while the police tried to figure out who was behind it."

"And this is where," I glanced back at my notebook. "Where Gabby came in. The girl you'd previously been sleeping with?"

"Yeah, I sure know how to pick them, don't I?" He ruffled a hand through his hair. "Gabby always wanted Dylan, from the very beginning. She was sleeping with Clay, too, while the two of them were trying to split up Cami and Dylan in high school. She had no clue Dylan was an undercover cop until Dylan arrested her. Apparently jail time didn't stop her delusions. After she found where Cami and Dylan were hiding, she went to the cabin and shot Cami in the stomach." Pausing, some heavy anguish passed over his features. "Cami was pregnant and the baby died as a result. Cami almost died, too."

"So was there a manhunt for her?" I continued to prod him along before he got too caught up in the emotions.

"Yes, but Dylan found her first, at a store across the street from the hospital that Cami was in. Gabby attacked him and he shot and killed her. We thought that was it. We all thought it was over—that it was done."

"But you were wrong."

"So wrong. Derek came out of left field. None of us knew that he was still in touch with Gabby and that the two of them had planned this elaborate scheme. He blamed Dylan for his brother's death because Dylan sent him to jail and cut off their family revenue. We had no idea that when he was selling drugs in high school that it was to help pay for cancer treatments for his little brother. Why didn't his family just say something? Hell, we could've organized a benefit for them or something."

"Sometimes when people are under that kind of pressure, they don't act rationally."

"Well, he was certainly beyond rational. He kidnapped both Dylan and Cami. I think he intended to kill them both, too. He just wanted to make Dylan suffer as long as possible. And he did."

His face got a pained faraway look and I knew he was reliving those events.

"When I walked in on that scene, I didn't even recognize Cami—she'd been beaten so badly. The color of her hair was the only thing that hinted to her identity. And Dylan . . . I've never seen him so afraid in his life. I could taste his fear—it was that strong."

"I bet that was hard for you, knowing that he was *your* personal hero, someone that you looked up to. What were you thinking at this point?"

"I was thinking I needed to stall for time long enough for my shift partner in the truck outside to figure out something had gone wrong." He shook his head, giving a wry grin. "It sure as hell took him long enough."

"Did you think you were going to die, Russ?" I asked the hard question, point blank.

Staring straight at me, the grin faded and tears filled his eyes. "Yes. I knew it the moment I sat down in that chair and began tying myself up with Derek holding a gun on me."

"And you made the choice to stay anyway? You could've run."

"No," he choked out, almost in a whisper. "He would've killed them right then if I had."

"But at least you might have escaped and been safe. Why not do that? Why not protect yourself?"

"Because I wouldn't have ever been able to look at myself in the mirror again, knowing I ran."

"People come and go, Russ. It's okay to try and save yourself."

"I wouldn't want to live in a world that they're not a part of."

"But when it came down to it, Dylan picked you to be the one who died anyway."

"He had to. He had to save Cami. He had no choice."

"He did have a choice, Russ. And he didn't choose you. I think this is why you're having the nightmares. Your subconscious feels betrayed because it knows you would've done whatever was necessary to save him, but the street didn't go both ways for you."

"So how do I fix it? How do I make it stop feeling that way?"

"I honestly don't know that there is a way. At least there's no magic switch that will make it all better. It's something you're going to have to learn to come to peace with somehow. What would you have done if Dylan chose you over Cami?"

"I'd have shot Dylan, myself. I love Cami."

"Are you in love with Cami?" I asked, noting the way his face softened every time he spoke about her.

"No. Not in the way you mean. She's like my sister—my best friend. I'd do anything for her."

"Even die?"

"Yes, even that."

"Why? She never rescued you from anything."

He stared at me, his eyes almost pleading for me to stop. "She's my family—they are my family. They've been more family to me than my biological family. I love them. Would you die for your family, Doc?" he asked, turning the question around on me.

"I would."

"And could you choose one of them to die so that others might live?"

He made his point.

"I don't know if I could."

"I don't know if I could either."

There was the key. "Let me ask you this, Russ. If the shoe had been on the other foot and Derek would've made you choose between Cami and Dylan, who would you have chosen to live?"

Tears dripped over the rims of his eyes, but he never looked away from me. "Cami," he finally choked out.

"Why?" I asked.

"Because I know Dylan would never be able to live in a world without her."

"Well, there's your answer. Apparently he felt the same way, too. You just happened to be caught in the crosshairs of a very tragic and dangerous situation."

"I know all this. How do I get the nightmares to stop?"

"You need to find a way to feel like you have control, again—that you aren't sitting helplessly at the whims of others. I think once you can find that place, you'll find the memories and dreams hold no power for you anymore."

"So, how do I do that?"

"One day at a time, Russ. One day at a time. But I'll do my best to help you out with that."

CHAPTER EIGHT
Russ

Evie had given me a bunch of positive mantras to recite whenever I found myself being plagued with thoughts of the past. She was very much about replacing negative energy with positive energy. I often found myself reciting things like, "My family is alive today because of me" and "I deserve to have peace and happiness in my life."

I'd felt rather silly when I'd first started doing it, but after a week, I began finding I kind of enjoyed all the positive little catch-phrases. It improved my attitude every time I thought of one, and I could definitely see the value of using them.

"You are looking more and more like the cat that swallowed the canary every time I see you," Dylan commented casually, as I entered the kitchen after returning from my jog along the waterfront. "What's got you so happy lately

. . . or is it a who?" He raised an eyebrow, staring pointedly at me.

I shook my head. "Just happy to be alive and enjoying life." Grinning, I winked at him, setting my water bottle down on the counter and doing a few after-run stretches.

"Are you still seeing Evie?" he asked, and I nodded, some of that happy fading a little inside me. I hated misleading him about her.

"You should invite her over for dinner sometime this week, since we have the next few rotations off."

"Uh . . . ." *Shit. Now what should I do?* "Um, her schedule is pretty busy. I don't know if she'd have time," I stalled, panicked.

"Call her up and ask her."

"Right now?"

"Yes, right now. Ask her if she'd like to come here for dinner tomorrow night with Cami and me, too. It's about time we got to know her a bit if you're going to keep seeing her. Or are you keeping her to yourself for other reasons?" His smile widened suggestively.

"No, no, nothing like that. We are still just getting to know one another."

"Well, give her a call and we'll all get to know her."

"Shouldn't we ask Cami first?" I was literally grasping at straws. "She may not be too happy about having a dinner party without us even telling her."

"Whatever. You know she'd love it. That girl is constantly in matchmaker mode when it comes to you."

"I'd feel better about it if we asked her first."

"Fine," Dylan replied, dragging his phone out of his pocket.

"Wait!" I almost shouted, still trying to stall him. "Didn't she go to the Firemans' Spouse's meeting? You don't want to interrupt her."

"That was over thirty minutes ago. She called to say she was stopping by the grocery store and then she'd be home."

Damn. I waited, knowing exactly what Cami's answer would be; so it didn't surprise me one bit when Dylan hung up sporting a Cheshire cat-like grin.

"Cami says to see if Evie can come tomorrow. She'll make Italian for dinner. She's buying the stuff as we speak."

Damn. Damn. Damn. Retrieving my phone from my running shorts, I brought up her information. Thankfully, she'd given me her private number, telling me to call her if I ever needed to. Somehow I didn't think she meant for me to use it to ask her out.

"Hello?" Her sweet voice answered on the second ring and, in spite of everything, I couldn't help smiling. Flashing a look at Dylan, I moved outside onto the porch, not wanting him to overhear this conversation, feeling relieved when he didn't follow.

"Hey, Doc, it's Russ."

"Russ, is everything okay?" I instantly heard the tension in her voice.

"Yes, no—I'm, yeah, everything is fine with me, but I need your help."

"Anything. What can I do?"

"Remember how I told you that Dylan is under the impression you and I are . . . dating?"

"Yes," she replied hesitantly.

"Well, he asked me to invite you to dinner tomorrow night. I'm not sure how to get out of it without clueing him in."

She sighed. "I see."

"Any chance you'd mind playing along just this once? Cami is making Italian food, which is always good. And it would give you a chance to officially meet Dylan, since he helped in your rescue, too." All of a sudden, I realized I really wanted her to come.

"This is very unorthodox," she replied— hesitant, but it wasn't a no.

"Under normal rules, yes, but you have extenuating circumstances. Surely there's no law about a therapist having a nice thank you dinner with her rescuers."

She laughed slightly. "You weren't kidding when you said you like to bend the rules, were you?"

"Not even a little." I was grinning from ear to ear.

"All right." She relented. "What time is dinner?" I glanced to where Dylan was watching me through the window, realizing we hadn't set a time. "How about five thirty? You can come here straight from work."

"Okay, that works for me."

"It's a date," I replied, still grinning.

"It's *not* a date!" she stressed, and I laughed.

"All right. It's a non-date."

"Yes, it's a non-date. See you tomorrow."

"I can't wait," I replied, hanging up and stepping back inside.

"I'm guessing from your smile she said yes."

"Yep. I told her dinner at five-thirty, so she can just come by on her way home from work. I hope that's okay."

"Sounds great to me. Wait! Shoot!"

"What?"

"I forgot I have my evaluation tomorrow with the chief from five to six."

"So you'll be a little late. We can wait thirty minutes for you to get home. It'll be fine."

"You sure? I don't want to make everyone wait on me."

"It'll be all right," I said. "I'm going to go hit the shower."

***

I'd been restlessly helping Cami with food preparation and cleaning things up as we worked. Staring out the kitchen window, I noticed immediately when the silver compact car turned into the driveway. Glancing at the clock on the wall, I saw it was only five fifteen.

"Hmmm. She's early. That's a good sign," Cami said, bumping slightly into my shoulder.

"Is it?" I asked, reaching nervously for the glass of wine I'd already poured myself in an attempt to calm my nerves.

"It means she's anxious to be here, I think. It's a good sign she likes you. No girl rushes to a date she isn't excited for."

"Either that or she's trying to get it over with as quickly as possible." I tossed back the rest of the contents of my glass before heading to the door to greet her, thankful that Cami stayed in the kitchen. Swinging the door open, I caught her just as she was raising her hand to knock. "Gotcha!" I said with a laugh, gesturing for her to enter.

"Oh, hi." She smiled and made a sound suspiciously like a short giggle.

Eyes traveling over her, I would've never believed she was a well-revered therapist. Her long blonde hair hung straight down her back and she was wearing a short creamy-colored sundress with tiny flowers on it. The neckline scooped, showing just a small peek of cleavage—and the way the fabric gathered underneath her breasts made them look huge. Dragging my eyes from that spot, I continued my perusal, noting the short length accentuated her long tan legs down to her strappy sandals.

"You look amazing," I said, forcing my mind and thoughts to return to her face. Her make-up was light and fresh and I thought she didn't look a day over eighteen. She totally looked like the kind of girl I normally found myself going for, that whole hot, college age, coed vibe coming off her in waves.

"Thank you." She smiled. "I decided to change into something more casual after work. I didn't want to look too stuffy. Oh, this is for you—or Cami and Dylan, or whoever." She held out a bottle of wine and I liked that she seemed as nervous as I did.

"Follow me. Cami's still cooking. Dylan is running a little behind. He forgot he had his evaluation today, so he'll be here closer to six." Placing my hand lightly at the small of her back, I guided her down the hall toward the kitchen.

"I'm sorry if I'm too early."

"No, it's perfect." I lowered my voice. "Thanks for even agreeing to do this."

"It's not a problem, really. I know how important this is to you. I'm happy to help. Anything for a friend, right?"

Friend. I knew that was all we could ever be, but it still felt like the kiss of death on her lips. "Right," I said, trying to keep the smile on my face and not show my disappointment as we entered the kitchen. "Cami, I'd like you to meet Evie," I said, using her casual nickname since calling her Doctor McKinley would seem especially formal.

Cami immediately left the stove, extending her hand and smiling widely. "It's such a pleasure to meet you, Evie." They clasped hands warmly. "I was totally shocked when Dylan told me Russ and you are dating now."

"That makes three of us," I whispered, mostly to myself, but Evie heard and laughed.

"Yes, it did happen kind of suddenly," Evie said, playing along.

"Well, have a seat and you can tell me all about it while Russ pours you some of that wine. I'd have some with you, but as you can see . . . ." She gestured to her huge stomach.

"When are you due?" Evie asked, and I was glad she'd managed to divert the subject from the two of us and back to Cami. I retrieved another wine glass and poured some for both

Evie and myself.

"Next week," Cami said, rubbing her baby bump fondly. "I swear it seems like next year though. It will never get here. I've been to the hospital three times with Braxton-Hicks. It's been downright embarrassing. I'm sure the OB department thinks I'm nuts. Here comes the crazy lady again, thinking she's having a baby."

"I doubt that," Evie said sympathetically, as I placed a glass of wine in front of her. "In fact, I'm certain they deal with such things on a regular basis. Hopefully it won't be too much longer for you. Do you know what you're having?"

"A little girl." Cami beamed. "We are so excited."

I took another hefty swallow of my wine as I watched the two women banter easily back and forth, almost like they'd completely forgotten I was there—which, in truth, was just fine with me. It helped to avoid awkward conversations.

"Have you picked a name?"

"Dylan likes Noelle, since that's my middle name, but I like the name Piper. I'm not sure if he's sold on that though."

"Piper Noelle would be adorable," Evie said, testing it out.

Cami nodded. "I agree. I just need to convince her daddy."

I snorted and they both looked over at me. "You know full well Dylan will give you whatever you want. There's nothing too good for you."

"Says the man who Dylan would do anything for." Cami smiled. "He loves you just as much as he loves me."

"He better not," I replied with a grimace. "I refuse to do the things you do for him."

She laughed. "You know that's not what I meant."

"Yeah, well, I just want that to be clear. He definitely loves you more."

Evie was scrutinizing the exchange between us and I could practically see the doctor wheels turning in her head as she sipped her wine.

"Cami, do you need any help right now, or do you mind if I show Evie around the place?"

"Go right ahead. I'm all set here. I'll call you if I need anything."

"Would you like to see the house?" I asked Evie.

"I'd love it. I'm a big history buff and I find these old houses fascinating. Do you all live here together?"

"Sort of. Technically, I live on the third floor. I've been remodeling it to be my own apartment. It's still a pretty good size on its own. Three bedrooms, two baths, with its own living room, kitchen and dining room." I pointed out the window to the side door. "It has its own entrance from the side of the house there. Just take those exterior stairs right on up." I didn't know why I was telling her all this—it wasn't like she'd ever have a reason to come over after this. "These go up, as well."

"So did you buy the house together?" Evie asked, as we started up the interior stairs to my quarters.

"Yeah. The bottom two floors are Cami and

Dylan's. They've got most of their remodeling done already. Mine has been going a little bit slower, but it's getting there."

We reached the top and I opened the door, allowing her to step inside.

"Oh, I love the dark stain you put on the floors. They're beautiful."

"Thank you. I thought they turned out nice."

"Have you been doing all the work yourself?" she asked, looking at me with admiration in her eyes.

I nodded. "I have. Now that the floors and walls are finished, most of the work I have left is in the kitchen. I have the refrigerator, but I still need to finish all the cabinetry and put in the stove and whatnot. Cami and Dylan have basically been keeping me fed, since I don't have a way to prepare stuff yet."

"Cami seems really nice. I can see why you hold her in such high regard."

"She's the best." I watched as she meandered on toward the hallway, peeking into some of the other rooms. Following closely after her, I enjoyed knowing that she was moving closer to my bedroom.

"Your room?" she asked, pausing in the doorway and I nodded.

"Yeah, it's bigger than the others and I was able to make a doorway so one of the bathrooms became an en suite."

"It looks very . . . inviting," she said, softly, glancing at me.

"It is. You should try the bed."

Arching an eyebrow, she looked a bit

surprised.

"No seriously. Go sit on the bed. Give it a little bounce."

She continued to eye me, but eventually moved forward, slowly sinking to the edge of the bed. The springs protested wildly and she laughed. "You seriously sleep on this thing?" She bounced again and again, making the bed squeak repeatedly.

"I do. I actually requested to keep it. It's original to the house."

She was still bouncing on it. "How can you get any rest at all? It's so loud."

Smiling, I shrugged. "I've gotten used to it. Though Cami and Dylan seem convinced they'll be able to tell if I ever entertain anyone of the female variety." I stared at her pointedly. It took a second, but as soon as she caught my meaning, she instantly stilled.

"Oh, because they'd hear you . . . uh . . . ."

"Going at it?" I supplied with a grin and she blushed heavily. "Maybe Cami thinks I'm up here getting lucky right now."

Her mouth dropped open and her gaze lowered, landing somewhere in the vicinity of my zipper. She flushed, again, when she realized where she was staring and immediately stood. "I'm sorry. Is it hot in here all of a sudden?" I couldn't help my continued grin as she pushed past me into the hallway. "Maybe we should go check on Cami."

Stepping in beside her, I happily followed along. "You looked good on my bed, Doc," I said, not caring if it was appropriate for me to say so or not.

Pausing, she turned to stare at me, and suddenly the hallway felt really small.

"You know you can't say things like that to me, right?"

I stepped closer and she moved back, leaning against the wall. "Yes, I'm aware of that." I stared down at her lips. They were so close. It would be so easy to capture them.

"Russ, I . . . ."

Immediately a loud crashing sound came from downstairs, diverting our attention.

"Cami?" I hollered, backing away instantly and running down the stairs.

CHAPTER NINE
Russ

The high-pitched wail made my heart rate accelerate as I raced into the kitchen, finding Cami on the floor with a pot of noodles strung out beside her.

"Are you burned?" I asked, fear shooting through me as I knelt beside her.

"No. I think . . . ." She panted, a look of desperation in her eyes. "I think I'm in labor."

Now I was panicking. "In labor? You can't just start labor like this."

"Well, I've had this backache and some tightening all day. I just figured it was another false alarm." She tightened a fist in my shirt. "Ahhhh!" she hollered. "Russ, you need to check me. You're trained for this."

"Cami don't you dare do this to me. Let's try and get you to the hospital."

"It's too late," Cami screeched, her eyes wild. "I need you to help me, now."

"Dylan will cut off my body parts if I look at you down there, let alone touch you." I was desperate to avoid this.

"And I will cut them off if you don't," Cami growled through her teeth. "Follow your training steps!"

Her saying that popped my head immediately into gear. Helping her slip her panties off had me trembling. Dylan was not going to like this at all. I lifted her skirt, staring.

"Can you tell anything?" Cami huffed out.

"Um, you're a natural redhead?" I felt completely out of my element. Red tinged water leaked from her, suggesting her bag of waters had already ruptured.

"Russ! Now is not the time to tease me."

"Evie call 911 and tell them we need an ambulance for a woman who is crowning. Then go into the hallway and grab some towels out of the bathroom."

"Second door on the right," Cami squeaked out. "You can see the head?"

"Yes." I quickly began ripping the lace out of my shoes.

"What are you doing?"

"We need something to tie off the umbilical cord. Do you have any scissors?"

"In the drawer behind your head."

Quickly turning, I snatched them out, cutting my shoelace in two. Then I grabbed a pair of latex gloves from the box Dylan always kept in the kitchen, slipping them on.

"Here you go," Evie said, tossing several towels at me. "The ambulance is on the way."

My phone started ringing and instantly I knew it was Dylan. "Answer that for me, Evie." I gestured to my pocket and she slipped her hand inside, but I didn't get the chance to enjoy it. "Put it on speaker," I ordered. Dylan needed to at least hear his child being born.

"Russ! Russ, what's going on? Cami is in labor? I heard the call come in," Dylan's frantic voice came through.

"The baby is crowning, Dylan. I'm prepping for delivery."

"Tell her to hang on. I'm on the rig. We will be there in less than five minutes."

"Here's another contraction," Cami said, her voice tightening.

"Remember Lamaze," Dylan shouted through the phone. "Use your breathing, push low." His instructions did seem to comfort her.

"Pull your knees to your chest, Cami, and if you feel like you need to push then do whatever you need," I told her. Evie slid behind Cami, helping to cradle her body forward as Cami bore down.

"Ahhhhhh!" She gasped, sucking in a deep breath as a partial sob escaped her. "I can't do this!"

"Yes, you can, Goody" Dylan said, calling her by his pet name for her. I recognized the sounds of sirens coming from the outside. "I'm almost there. Just a couple more blocks."

"Tell me when you feel another contraction," I said, reaching up and quickly flitting through a utensil draw until I found a small turkey baster. That would have to do if I needed to suck the airway.

Carefully, I placed it on the edge of the towel I'd spread beneath Cami.

"Ok. It's starting again." Cami groaned as she clenched her muscles. I heard the rig pull up outside and doors slam.

"Cami?" Dylan practically slid across the wood floors trying to get to her side, tossing an open birthing kit toward me.

"Here comes the head," I shouted, grinning as it popped out in a gush of blood and water. Rotating the baby, the shoulders came through easily, followed quickly by the rest of the body.

"I need the time of birth," I said to no one in particular.

"Eighteen hundred and twenty hours," came a reply.

Tying the cord off, I quickly grabbed the hand suction and began removing debris and vernex from the mouth, encouraging the baby to cry as I stimulated her, rubbing her with the towel, vigorously.

"It's a girl," I pronounced, and everyone cheered.

"Ready to cut the cord, Dad?" I asked, staring at Dylan.

Hand shaking he lifted the pair of sterile scissors and cut.

"Congratulations," I said, handing the baby to Cami.

Standing, I stepped away and let the on-call crew take over providing care. Cami and the baby where quickly transferred to a gurney together, while I gave the report.

Dylan glanced at me. "Dude. I owe you so much. You have no idea."

"Get out of here. Go take care of your wife and baby. I'll clean things up."

"Man, you're the best. The best, Russ." He pointed over at Evie and maintained eye contact with her as he pointed back to me. "The best. I mean it."

Laughing, I watch him walk down the steps, following his wife and baby into the back of the ambulance. Turning, I quickly grabbed a garbage bag, and began stuffing all the towels inside.

"Surely you aren't going to throw all those away?" she asked, horrified.

"Yes. Cami and Dylan are plenty rich and they can afford to buy new towels. I am not washing these things." Thankfully, all the mess had been contained to the towels, making clean up easy. Tossing my gloves into the trash, I washed my hands thoroughly at the sink.

"Wasn't your turkey baster and scissors in that stuff, too?"

"I didn't need them once I had the Birthing Kit, but again, all replaceable. I'm sorry. I could never use those scissors again without thinking where they'd been. That's something I need to forget, immediately." Glancing down, I caught a small spot that looked like it might be blood on my shirt. "Well, damn. I liked this shirt, but I guess it's got to go, too." I quickly unbuttoned and slipped out of it, glancing over at Evie as I did so.

Her mouth was slack jawed, eyes roaming

over my chest and abs. My body reacted instantly. "See something you like, Evie?" I wanted her to like it. Rules be damned.

"You really are like this, aren't you?" She stared at me wide-eyed.

"Like what?" I was completely confused, but that didn't stop me from stalking toward her.

"A hero. This is all just second nature to you, isn't it?"

I loomed over her. "I have no idea what you're talking about. But I'm no hero."

She was out of space, her back against the wall and I pressed in as far as I could go without actually touching her. Her eyes burned into my chest. "You are to those that need you." Her breath got shorter and she slowly dragged a hand over my pecs. "People like me," she whispered.

It was all the encouragement I needed. Capturing her mouth with mine, my hands reached lower, scooping her up so her back was against the wall and her legs wrapped around me. She held my head in her hands, kissing me frantically, as if everything we felt needed to be shoved into this one particular moment.

"Evie," I murmured against her lips. "I want you." Arching her back, she simply moaned in reply. Everything was moving too fast, but I couldn't take the tension between us anymore. I wanted her. Even if it was only one time—I wanted her.

Fumbling at my waist, I managed to undo my pants and then pushed up her dress, tugging the scrap of lace covering her to the side and entering her in one swift thrust. Breathing heavily, we both panted and shouted, her hanging on to me as I drove heavily into her—until we both cried out with release.

For several moments I simply held her, my face buried in her neck as we tried to catch our breath.

"I'm sorry," I finally spoke. "I didn't mean to lose control like that. There's just been something between us that's been driving me crazy. I have the hardest time staying away from you."

Sighing heavily, her warm breath filtered through my hair. "Russ, I can't be your doctor anymore. I could lose my license for this."

Still I held her, unwilling to move away and relinquish her. "I understand. I don't want you getting into any trouble because of me." I kissed her exposed collarbone, knowing reality was causing her to cool quickly, but wishing I could somehow convince her to spend the night.

"I . . . I need to go, Russ." Her voice was nervous and she sounded scared. Carefully, I pulled back, my body groaning in protest at the loss of her warmth, and I helped her back to her feet. She swiftly straightened her dress, which just made me want to peel it off her even more.

"Don't be upset." I stared at her, not even attempting to adjust my pants. "Stay the night. Don't go."

Her eyes traveled lower before shooting back to look in mine. "I have to." She scurried toward the door. "I'll call you and we will talk this out. Just give me some time. Okay?"

"Okay," I replied, knowing there was nothing I could do. Pressuring her would only make it worse. "Try not to take too long."

Unmoving, I watched her hurry to her car and drive away. I had no idea how long I stared, only at some point I realized my pants were still hanging open and I was in front of the window. Quickly, I adjusted myself before grabbing my phone and dialing her number. It went straight to message.

"Don't feel bad, Evie. We both had wine, and then we were feeling celebratory. Things like that can happen. I don't want you to feel ugly about this." I paused, considering my next words. "If it helps at all, it was something I really wanted—really wanted with you."

CHAPTER TEN
Evie

I managed to make it all the way home and into my hot shower before I burst into tears. "Oh my gosh! What have I done?" I said aloud as I slumped against the wall, sliding to the floor. Unmoving, I let the water rush over me as I gripped fistfuls of my wet hair.

Had I really just had sex with Russ Weston? That couldn't be possible, could it? One minute everything had been fine and the next . . . I was just totally overwhelmed with how incredible he was. Watching him help Cami give birth—he just seemed more than human to me; and then he ripped off his shirt . . . .

Really? What kind of girl could've resisted all that? I'd been completely mesmerized. And then it was over before it even started. Not that I was complaining. It might've been fast, but it was good. Oh, so good. I blushed remembering the sounds I'd made in his arms and the way I'd devoured his mouth like a woman starving.

I had been starving. That was the whole point. I hadn't been romantically involved with anyone for six years—not since Kory. *I cheated on Kory*. Fresh sobs wracked my body.

"I'm so sorry Kory," I said, and it echoed off the shower walls. I'd promised myself that he was it for me—that I would never move on with anyone else. And it was working just fine, too, until this farce of a date, tonight. "Oh who are you kidding?" I kept talking to myself like I was a nut job. "You've practically been salivating over him from the first time he stepped into the office." What was I doing? He was only twenty-two for crying out loud. He was practically a boy. *He's no boy*. I contradicted myself, remembering that body and what he was packing. No man in existence had ever made me burn as hot as I had been back there.

I cried louder. That only made it worse—made me feel like an even bigger slut. I liked it. In a few short moments, Russ had completely obliterated all my previous sexual experiences. It wasn't fair. He hadn't even been trying. Neither of us had been prepared for it. He hadn't even used a condom for crying out loud.

Immediately I stiffened, counting off days in my head, relieved when I realized it wasn't time for me to ovulate. I hadn't been on birth control since Kory died. I didn't see the need, since I planned to remain celibate for the rest of my life.

What a mess. I was going to need to report myself, or leave my job, or something. I just had sex with a patient, a firm line I'd never come close to crossing, despite the men who'd flirted with me in the past.

Russ was different, I realized. I'd never truly considered him my patient. He was my rescuer—my friend. I'd been attracted to him from the start. This was my fault. He'd been ready to find another therapist, but I wanted an excuse to see him again, and a chance to help him with whatever problem he was having. His easygoing nature was so much like Kory's. It allowed me to start falling for him without even fully admitting it to myself.

Eventually, I got back to my feet, finishing my shower and drying off before slipping into a fluffy white robe and heading back into my bedroom. Pausing, I glanced to the foot of my bed where my purse and briefcase lay strewn across the bed where I'd thrown them.

Slowly, I sat down and reached into my purse for my phone, seeing I'd missed a call. There was a message. I knew immediately who it was from. Hitting the playback button, I listened to Russ's voice—just hearing it filled me with both longing and regret.

"Don't feel bad, Evie. We both had wine, and then we were feeling celebratory. Things like that can happen. I don't want you to feel ugly about this." There was a short pause. "If it helps at all, it was something I really wanted—really wanted with you." The voice message ended and I played it back again, closing my eyes and simply listening.

Had it only been an hour since I was

wrapped in his arms? I'd been in such a hurry to leave that his words, then, hadn't really registered with me. "Stay the night. Don't go."

Remembering those words actually forced a little laugh out of me. If I had stayed, we'd be going at it on the squeaky bed of his right now. Just the thought of the sounds it would make beneath us made me blush.

Being honest with myself, I knew I was completely in control of the situation— completely capable of saying no. I just didn't want to. I'd wanted him as badly as he wanted me. When had that happened? Yes, there had always been some chemistry there, but when did it sneak up to this level of attraction?

Now I was torn with what I should do. Did I stay away from him and move on with my life, letting this be a lesson to myself to not become so involved with a patient? He'd given the impression that he was okay with what happened. At least he wanted me to spend the night. But did that one episode warrant a relationship? I wasn't dumb enough to think hot sex automatically meant a commitment. And I knew enough about Russ's past to know he'd never been in a long-term, committed relationship. His sexual experiences had been casual, simply a means to an end, a way to slack his lustful needs.

I didn't do casual. I never had. My heart became too easily invested because I wanted a relationship. I wanted the dream family, the monogamy, the marriage, the children—all the things I should've had with Kory.

Russ, he was still several years younger than me, out sowing his wild oats. He didn't need to be tied down to someone.

That made my decision for me. It would be hard, but I needed to make a clean cut and walk away. We both needed to move on with our lives.

It was sound reasoning, but it sure didn't seem to help my heart feel any better. Yes, I definitely became too invested too quickly. It was time to put the brakes on hard.

**

The intercom buzzed on my desk.

"Yes, Misty?" I answered.

"Mr. Weston is here to see you."

Panic welled inside me. He was here. I didn't think he'd come to my office, not after everything that happened. What was I going to do? Glancing around, I suddenly wished I had some issue that needed my attention immediately, so I could avoid this confrontation; but my workday was through.

"Dr. McKnight?" Misty's voice came through the speaker again, reminding me that I hadn't replied.

"Uh, send him in, I guess." I wondered if she heard the tremor in my voice. The door opened and Russ stepped inside. It didn't escape my notice that he locked the door behind him.

I stood, petrified, behind my desk, gripping the edges for support. "I can't be locked in here with a patient." I protested weakly, grasping at straws.

"I'm not your patient anymore, remember?"

His gaze traveled up and down my body before settling on my face. Strolling slowly through the space as if he owned it, he plopped down in one of the leather chairs and gestured to the one across from him. "Have a seat, Doc. Let's chat."

"I can't do this with you, Russ. It's unethical for you to be here." I didn't move.

"The only reason I'm here is because you've been ignoring me for three days. You haven't returned any of my calls or texts. You've completely shut me out. I've given you plenty of time. You were the one who said we'd talk things out later. Well, I'm tired of waiting, so I came to the one place I knew you'd be. So sit down and let's talk."

I could hear the frustration laced in his voice and I figured I deserved it. I'd been acting the total coward with this whole situation, hoping that if I ignored it, it would go away. Russ, however, seemed to have a different opinion.

Sighing, I made my way over to the chair and sat down in front of him. "What do you want to know?" I asked bluntly.

"Well, first, I'd kind of like to know if you're okay?" He sounded exasperated. "Regardless of what conclusions you've come to about me, I am actually a decent sort of guy. I understand that what happened between us wasn't planned, but I wasn't just out for a good fuck and have that be the end of it."

Glancing down, my hands were trembling. "I'm sorry if I handled things wrong. I just decided a clean break would be the easiest for us both."

"You decided. So I don't get any say in this?"

"I . . . I . . . what is there for you to say?" I hated feeling so emotional over this. "That you're sorry? That you know we made a mistake and it can't happen again? I know all that already."

"Now you're putting words in my mouth, Doc." Groaning in frustration, he ran a hand through his hair. "Look. I don't have much time before my shift, but I want you to know the only thing I'm sorry about is that this seemed to hurt you so badly. I, personally, can't stop thinking about it and how much I'd like to have a repeat performance." Heat filled his eyes as he stared at me.

"And then what?" I asked. "We become hook-up buddies? I don't do that kind of stuff, Russ. I can't."

"I'm not asking you to," he replied defensively.

"Then what are you asking?"

"I'm asking to date you! Am I that bad at showing you my intentions, Doc? You're right. You can't be my therapist, but why does that mean you have to leave my life completely?"

My jaw gaped open and I realized he was sincere. I allowed a second of joy to kick through my heart before squashing it down. "I did something terrible with you. Don't you understand? I broke trust with you. I was your therapist, a person you should be able to trust absolutely, and I crossed that line—a line that should never, ever, be crossed. I failed you." I stared at him sympathetically. "Every time I look at you, I'm going to be reminded of my failure to protect my client."

"Since we are obviously back to the client thing, I'd like to see my bill from you, please. I'd like to pay it while I'm here." His eyes never left mine, and I felt like they were drilling holes through me.

"I, uh, don't have one for you," I confessed.

"Why not?"

"I didn't want you to have to pay, because you saved my life—because we said we were . . . friends."

"So, you never charged me for my visits?" He leaned forward, looking determined. "Even after I asked you to?"

I shook my head. "No."

"Then, technically, I can say I was never your client. Money never exchanged hands for services rendered."

"But I have a chart on you—with notes and treatment suggestions," I argued.

"Do you like me?" He asked point blank.

"Wh . . . what do you mean?"

"Do. You. Like. Me?" He carefully enunciated every word. "It's not a difficult question, Evie. Yes or no, it's a simple as that."

But it wasn't as simple as that—not for me, at least. Saying yes to him would be like saying no to Kory. I'd been true to him for so long, clinging to his life and memories with all my heart, never wanting to give them up. Tears welled in my eyes and I tried to rapidly blink them back.

Russ's penetrating gaze never left me.

"You're still in love with him, aren't you?" he said quietly.

I hated hurting him—hated shooting him down. "I am," I whispered. "I know he's gone, but it's so hard to let go."

Sliding from the chair, he knelt beside me, slipping one of his large hands over mine. "Liking me doesn't mean you have to love him any less. You realize that, don't you? It just means you like me."

A wry laugh escaped. "You make things sound so simple."

He smiled softly. "That's because they *are* simple. You're the one making them difficult."

"I don't know if I will ever be ready for another relationship."

"And how will you ever know unless you try?" His words hung in the air between us and he glanced down at his watch. "Damn. I wish I could stay longer, but I have to go." Leaning forward, he placed a tender kiss near my hairline and then he stood, striding toward the door.

I watched him, wishing I had the words to call him back, but I couldn't. He stopped when he reached the door and glanced back at me.

"See you around, Evie." He flashed that devastating grin of his and left.

I sat silently, wondering if I'd made the wrong choice; but my biggest worry was that this would actually be the last time I ever saw him.

CHAPTER ELEVEN
Russ

Dylan caught my attention and motioned for me to follow him. Rising from the recliner I was kicked back in, I made my way into the crew bunkroom we shared at the station.

"What's up?" I asked as he settled onto his bed, which looked just like mine but on the opposite side of the small room.

Sitting down, I sent a puzzled glance his way. "What do you mean?"

"I mean what's going on with you? Ever since Cami had the baby you've been all . . . melancholy. You mope around at home and any time you see us with the baby, you disappear."

I smiled. "You have a baby now, Dylan. I'm not avoiding you. I'm simply trying to give Cami and you some private Mom and Dad time while you adjust to being parents. I don't want to intrude on your family or your bonding time with little Piper. She's beautiful, by the way."

Dylan's face lit up. "She is, isn't she? I swear, every time I look at her, I just get this feeling. I don't know how to explain it, but it's like . . . wow. Instant love. A *lot* of instant love—like, I can't remember what life was like without her." It was easy to see how smitten he was.

"Well, she's a beauty, a perfect blend of you both."

"Her momma's beautiful features with my coloring. Though I wouldn't have minded another cute redhead running around the house."

Laughing, I stood and strode over to him, clapped him on the shoulder. "Give it time, man. Your knock up ratio with Cami runs high. At the rate you're going, you'll have a dozen little kids running around before Cami keels over from exhaustion. One of them is bound to be a redhead." Casually, I headed toward the door, hoping I could make a clean getaway.

"Where do you think you're going?"

Damn. "To make a sandwich. Want one?" I was totally going for clueless.

"Shut the door and sit down." He gestured to my bed. "I'm not done talking to you."

Raising an eyebrow, I stared at him pointedly. "Is that an order, *Captain*?" I replied, throwing his rank in his face.

He grinned. "Yes, if it'll get you to sit still for a minute."

Moving back to my bed, I plopped down. "What do you want to know?"

"I want to know what's going on with my

best friend. You're acting weird. Even Cami has noticed. So spill it."

Leaning forward, I rested my elbows on my knees and silently wished for a massive fire alarm to save me. After several moments, it was clear that wasn't going to happen. Slowly, I rubbed my palms together, thinking of how to explain things and still avoid his knowing I'd been going to therapy.

"Well," I began. "You know I've been seeing Evie." That was the truth at least, without defining the real reason behind my seeing her.

"Yeah. Is there trouble in paradise, already?"

I snorted. That was the understatement of the year. Glancing up, I locked eyes with Dylan. "Are you familiar at all with her past?"

He shook his head. "No. Why?"

"I thought maybe it was mentioned in one of the newspaper articles on the rescue. Evie was engaged six years ago, to a soldier in Afghanistan. He was killed in action saving her brother. I guess her brother, Paul, suffered with PTSD after the incident and he killed himself. Evie had no idea anything was wrong until she found him and his suicide note."

Dylan sighed heavily. "Man, that's rough. I'm guessing that's what got her so heavy into working with returning soldiers?"

I nodded. "Yep. And in all that time, she's never dated anyone else. Her heart is still wrapped up in this Kory and mourning the loss of both him and her brother."

"Now wait. You said she contacted you and wanted to meet you. So why is she dragging her feet if she started it?"

I gave a wry laugh. "She never intended anything to develop between us. There was definitely this instant attraction, but she's been . . . resistant. I've been trying to accommodate that, and failing miserably."

"You like her. A lot." It wasn't a question.

"I do. But I'm afraid I pushed her too fast and scared her off."

"What happened?"

A nervous chuckled escaped me now. Time to own up. "I, uh, had sex with her . . . in your kitchen."

Eyes going wide, he stared at me in complete shock. "How'd you manage that?"

Rolling my eyes, I sighed again. "There was the whole excitement of delivering the baby, and we were cleaning up everything together. When we were finished, I noticed a small spot of blood on my shirt—,"

"And so you used it as an excuse to take it off and show her the goods, didn't you?" He was grinning.

"I did. And it all went downhill from there."

"Downhill? Sounds like uphill to me. Was it that bad?" Of course he had to ask.

Snorting, I shook my head. "The sex was great—hot, fast, against the wall. But as soon as it was over, reality hit her hard. She practically ran out of the house, promising to talk to me later. I haven't been able to get her to return my calls or messages for three days, so I dropped by her office before work and spoke to her."

"And?"

"She told me she's still in love with the other guy." I shrugged it off. "How about that sandwich, now?" I stood.

"Sit," he ordered again, and I did.

"What?"

"If she had sex with you and didn't try to put a stop to it, then she's obviously attracted to you."

"I never said she wasn't attracted to me. I know that she is."

"Then go after her, idiot." He stared me down.

"I don't want to pressure her into something she doesn't want."

"Then *make* her want it," he countered.

Leaning back on my elbows, I stretched my legs between the beds and crossed my ankles. "You're the Mr. Casanova around here, not me."

Shaking his head, he chuckled. "If she's nervous, you need to start small. Do little things to reassure her. Send her flowers to perk up her day, or send her chocolates, even. Just start doing nice little things for her that will catch her attention and help her respect for you grow. It will keep her thinking about you . . . in a good way. It doesn't have to be elaborate. Sometimes the small things are what women appreciate the most. At least that's the way it is with Cami." He smiled. "I can give her an expensive piece of jewelry and she loves it. But she totally freaks if I ever do the dishes for her. Lands me straight in bed. Every. Single. Time."

"And that's the only reason you do them,

isn't it?" I grinned and he laughed.

"The only reason." He shrugged. "A guy's gotta do what a guy's gotta do. That's my advice to you. If you want her, don't walk away. Be the guy she can't live without."

It was solid advice; and just the thought of doing nice things for her made me feel better. "Thanks, man."

"Any time," Dylan replied. "I got your back, bro. Now let's go make those sandwiches."

"I didn't really want one. I was just trying to avoid all the questions."

"I know you were." Dylan smiled. "Doesn't mean you still aren't going to make me one."

I laughed. "Becoming a dad sure has made you a pushy guy, you know that?"

His laughter joined mine. "Just trying to practice being tough for the future."

"You're gonna need it. Piper's going to have guys crawling all over her."

Dylan grunted. "I'd appreciate you rephrasing that comment. I swear if I see one guy within twenty feet of her before she's thirty, I'm gonna run them off with a shotgun."

"All I'm saying is you better buy some more guns. I don't think you have enough."

Dylan stared at me, rubbing a hand across the back of his neck. "I have two handguns and two rifles. You know that."

I nodded. "I do. And like I said before, I don't think you have enough."

"You aren't helping my nerves any."

I squeezed his shoulders and shoved him away as we entered the kitchen. "At least you have a few years to prepare for it. Just keep her close. It'll be okay."

"Yeah, I keep you close and you just had sex in my kitchen."

"Like that kitchen hasn't seen sex before. There's not a surface in that house that's safe from the two of you."

He grinned. "And apparently they aren't safe from you either, are they?"

"Touché, bro." Grabbing the bread out of the cupboard, I set it on the counter. "What stuff do you want on your sandwich?"

"The works. Lay it all on there. I'm starving."

Several sets of tones crackled through all the radios, piercing the air. "Department One, Engine One and Ambulance Rescue. We have reports of a structure fire at 2201 Penny Drive. Multiple 911 calls state there are children trapped inside."

"Shit!" Dylan and I both said at the same time, leaving the food where it sat as we ran to the turnout rack. My hands shook with adrenaline as I quickly donned my gear. I hated calls with kids. They plucked at my heartstrings.

As soon as I was ready, I headed toward the truck, the first one to climb aboard so I fired it up. The ambulance bay opened and I watched the unit pull out into the street, lights and sirens wailing. Immediately, the rest of the crew began boarding the vehicle.

Carefully, I eased out the bay door and onto the street, flipping on the lights and siren. Dylan grabbed the chart and the radio.

"Dispatch, Engine One and Ambulance

Rescue enroute to structure fire at 2201 Penny Drive. Copy children still in the structure. Rolling Code Three."

"Roger, Engine One. Enroute time Twenty Fifteen."

"Dispatch, do you have any more info for us regarding this call?"

It wasn't far away. I could see orange glow from the flames and the heavy black smoke billowing up. This did not look good.

"Engine One, please switch to secure channel 4."

"Copy, Dispatch. Switching to channel 4." There was a slight pause as he clicked the radio over. "Dispatch, this is Engine One on secure channel 4."

"Roger, Engine One. We are receiving multiple 911 calls on this fire. Police are enroute for crowd control. The information we've been given is that one child has escaped the structure, but two children are still missing."

"Copy, two children possibly inside the structure. Is this confirmed? And do we know the ages of the children we are looking for?"

"Please standby for one moment Engine One." The line was left open and we could hear the dispatcher speaking with an officer who had just arrived on scene. "Engine One, officer on scene reports the house is nearly fully engulfed at this time. The children missing are ages two and five. They were last seen in their bedrooms inside the structure."

Damn it to hell! We rounded the corner, the horrific site filling our view. People were running up and down the street screaming hysterically. This was a nightmare!

"Copy, Dispatch. We are on scene. Dropping line now at the corner hydrant."

"Roger, Engine One. Prayers are with you. On scene time is twenty-twenty."

"Send me in," I said to Dylan as I parked the truck.

"Are you sure?" he asked me seriously, taking a quick glance down the street. "The odds aren't good."

"I know, but I can't sit out here waiting, either."

He only paused for a moment. "Suit up. Camden, you're going in with him."

"Yes, sir!" Camden replied.

"The rest of you start attack procedure, now."

I ripped off my small Velcro nametag and handed it to Dylan. He slipped it under the heading "Interior, search and rescue" on his command board before grabbing the radio.

"Engine One to Dispatch. Please roll Engine Two and Engine Three to this location. Also, put a chopper on standby on the off-chance we have successful retrieval."

"Roger, Engine One."

A second set of tones filtered through the radios as the new page went out. Glancing toward the house, I saw Tony and Wayne with hoses rolled out attacking the side door with water, where the fire wasn't quite as bad, knocking it down even more.

Sliding   my   self-contained   breathing

apparatus over my face, I locked gazes with Dylan through the mask.

"Be careful, Russ," he said, worry evident in his eyes, and I knew he wanted to be inside with me.

"I will be. Save the world."

"Save the world," he replied softly, repeating the catch phrase we'd developed between us.

I took off running, full sprint toward the building.

SMOLDER

CHAPTER TWELVE
Evie

Staring at my television screen, I was completely mesmerized by the scene developing in front of me. A local camera crew was capturing live footage of a house fire not far from here, and the brave and daring rescue of— not one—but two small children pulled from the burning structure and rushed toward a waiting ambulance. The camera followed the firefighter as he exited the building—both he and the children sprayed with water as he ran toward the ambulance. Waiting paramedics quickly took the children and put them in the ambulance, while the firefighter was pulled to the side where the department had both oxygen and water ready for him.

Ambulance doors closing, the camera crew zeroed in on the hero, trying to catch more of this breaking news story. The firefighter removed his helmet and mask and I briefly saw it was Russ before an officer stepped in front of the camera and ordered them away.

My heart rate escalated by a thousand percent. "Russ!" the words tumbled from my lips and my hand went to my throat. Was he okay? How bad were the children?

The media obviously was curious about this, too, the reporter shoving a microphone into a police officer's face. "Officer! Can you tell us the state of the children?"

"The children are being tended to by the best medical care available at this time. They're being prepared for transport by helicopter to the Center for Burns."

"So they are burned? Can you tell us how badly?"

"I only know the firefighter who found them said they needed immediate medical attention. I have no further information."

I thought the man very composed for how pushy the reporter and camera crew were; but like every other person guiltily watching this, I wanted to know what was happening.

"And what about the firefighter who rescued them? Is he okay? We see he is receiving medical attention, as well."

"The recovering firefighter is Russ Weston. He appears to be okay and is receiving routine care—hydration and oxygen, which is standard after doing an interior search and rescue."

"Where did he find the children?" The reporter continued to push for more answers.

"I believe they were found in the bedroom they shared."

"Do they have smoke inhalation?"

The officer gave the camera a look that clearly said, "Come on, really?" But instead, he answered politely. "As I said before, I don't have all the details. I would imagine there has been a good chance for smoke inhalation considering the current state of the house. That'll be all the questions for now. If you could please take your crew back behind that barrier so these emergency teams can work, that would be appreciated."

The field camera was suddenly cut off and the studio news crew instantly reappeared, swiveling away from the screen behind them to face the camera in front of the news desk.

"So, there you have it." The anchorwoman picked right up. "Obviously a big emotional scene developing out there on Penny Drive, tonight. We'll stay on it as much as possible and bring you the latest coverage and up-to-date information we have on this story. As of right now, it looks as if this house is a total loss, but the good news is that two young children have been rescued from this horrific blaze. That, in itself, is a miracle!"

"And I didn't fail to notice the name of the rescuing firefighter, did you?" The extremely good looking anchorman asked radiantly, and immediately confirmed my longstanding suspicions about him.

Yep, he's gay—another loss of a hot guy for the female population.

"I did." The co-anchor needed no more encouragement. "It looks like not long after saving renowned Doctor Evelyn McKnight from drowning, Russ Weston has stepped up to the plate again. I'm sure we will be hearing his name everywhere over the next few days as this story unfolds more."

"Until then, keep tuned right here on Charleston Ten News!"

I clicked off the television and stood, pacing around helplessly in my condo. First, I went to the window, wondering what I thought I could possibly see, since it faced the opposite direction of the fire. Next, I went to my kitchen and got a glass of water, staring aimlessly at the sink as I drank it, my mind running constantly over every memory I had of Russ.

The idea that he'd jumped into a lake after me, and he'd rushed into a burning building, and even the fact that he'd tried to sacrifice himself to save Cami, spoke loads about his character. At least it did to me. True, he was trained to do these things, but it still seemed very heroic to me.

I've had spontaneous sex with this guy. The thought appeared unbidden, making me groan. And how had I treated him? I'd ignored him for three days. So, maybe he wasn't perfect—I certainly wasn't either, but would it really be that bad to get to know him better?

You haven't thought of Kory since Russ left your office today. This realization made tears leak slowly down my face. Moving quietly through my house, I made my way to the nightstand. Lifting his picture, I stroked a finger lightly over his features.

"I love you, Kory," I whispered. "I miss you so much." Lying back on my bed, I held the picture against my chest, hugging it, as I wanted to hug him. "I think I'm starting to forget things about you," I added, continuing my lonely discussion. "I don't want that, but I don't know how to stop it."

Lifting the image, I lovingly touched it, again. "Would you hate me if I fell in love with someone else? I promised I'd never move on after you."

There was no reply, just as I knew there wouldn't be. But I would've given anything to hear him.

***

"Hero Firefighter at it again! Saves Two Children From Burning Structure!" The headline of the morning paper was practically screaming at me along with an image of Russ running from the blazing building with a child in each arm.

Quickly, my eyes scanned over the article.

Hero firefighter, Russ Weston, still remains elusive this morning after rescuing two children, ages two and five, from their burning home on Penny Drive last night. When trying to contact the station for a phone interview with Mr. Weston, the press was given a statement from Fire Chief Daniels, saying, "Mr. Weston is grateful for his opportunity to serve the community and we are lucky to have him as part of the many men and women who serve and protect this city. In order to show respect

for his colleagues, who also put their lives on the line every day, Mr. Weston would like you to please refrain from asking him for interviews. Thank you."

A similar statement was made by firefighter Weston just a short time ago, after he rescued Doctor Evelyn McKnight from a near drowning. He was adamant then about not speaking with the press, either.

The children, whose names and gender have not been released because they are minors, are currently hospitalized at the Center for Burns, where they are both listed in stable condition. The hospital has released a statement saying they are "both being treated for second degree burns around their hands, feet, and knees, as well as for smoke inhalation; but they are in good spirits and surrounded by the rest of their family."

A fund has been set up at South National Bank for the Trent family. Donations may be made by calling the following number, donating online, or going into the bank."

Releasing my grip on the paper, I folded it and tucked it under my arm, carrying it back into the house with me and setting it on the counter while I made myself some coffee.

My eyes kept straying toward the image of Russ holding those two kids. Suddenly, I had the urge to throw my arms around him and hug him as tight as I could. Walking into my room, I glanced at my phone, still sitting where I'd left it charging on the nightstand.

I did have his number. I could text him and make sure he was okay, couldn't I?

Just as quickly as I got the idea, I dismissed it. I couldn't be giving him false hope, especially not after our previous conversation. It would come off as being inconsistent—or worse, like I liked him simply for his heroics.

No, it was definitely better not to call. The paper had said he was okay. That was good enough for me. As long as he was safe, I could be happy.

Rolling my eyes, I didn't even want to analyze what that statement might mean. "I'm happy regardless of what Russ Weston is doing," I said out loud, managing to make myself feel like an even bigger idiot.

Setting my coffee down, I went and got in the shower before deciding I was going completely crazy and in need of therapy myself.

***

"What is this?" I asked, my confusion completely apparent as I halted in the doorway to my office.

"You got a special delivery this morning," Misty said, smiling widely. "Aren't they gorgeous?"

"Who are they from?" I asked, still refusing to step into the room as I stared at the giant bouquet with roses of every color, artfully arranged. It was easily three dozen, at least.

"I don't know. I didn't read the card. It was addressed to you."

"There's a card?"

"Yep. It's on the side facing your desk chair."

Glancing briefly back at Misty, I could tell she was as anxious as I was to find out what this card said. "That'll be all, Misty. Thank you." I didn't wait to see her disappointment, instead slipping inside my office and closing the door behind me.

Slowly, I approached my desk—and the arrangement for that matter—with the same stealth one might have when sneaking up on a bomb.

Not that I'd ever actually snuck up on a bomb.

Or knew anyone who had.

But they totally did it this way on TV.

Skirting around the side of my desk, I set my briefcase down and reached for the tiny envelope with my name on it, which was supported in the arrangement by a plastic prong. I plucked it out, opened it and drew out the small rectangular floral card inside.

Thought these might brighten your day.

It was clearly scrawled out in a man's handwriting, but there was no name. Flipping the card over, I checked for a signature on that side, too, but it was bare, as well.

I pressed the intercom. "Misty, did these come with an invoice?"

"Yes, ma'am," she replied.

"Does it say who the sender is?"

"No, ma'am. It didn't." I really hated when she called me ma'am. It made me feel so old.

"The card is unsigned."

"Would you like me to call the florist and see if they will tell me who sent them?"

"No. That's not necessary. I'm pretty sure I know who they're from." I clicked off the intercom before she could reply, bending to smell the beautiful flowers. Inhaling deeply, I closed my eyes, allowing the fragrance to wash over my senses.

I couldn't deny it. I was pleased and definitely wanted them to be from Russ. But since he didn't sign the note, I wasn't going to go hunting for the answer. If he wanted me to reply, then he needed to leave his name.

Russ Weston, what are you up to? I thought. I was ninety-nine percent sure it was him who sent the roses. It made me wonder when he'd ordered them. This morning? Surely he was too tired after their big fire last night. It must've been after he left my office, but wouldn't the florist have been closed by then? Sighing heavily, I realized I was allowing this to occupy way too much of my time.

Sitting down, I slid the vase over to a nice vacant corner of my desk, smiling at them a moment longer before buckling down to work.

CHAPTER THIRTEEN
Russ

"How's our little plan going?" Cami asked, giving me a sly look before glancing back down at Piper and smiling. She continued to rock her gently, but returned her gaze to me.

"I honestly have no idea. I haven't heard a word from her."

"Which was the plan at this point. We want her to think it's you, but to not be sure. That's keeping her thinking about you, and guessing. Without even trying, you're now occupying her thoughts twenty-four seven."

"You're sure about that?"

"Positive. Something like this would drive me crazy. Not knowing who to thank, thinking, you know, being too embarrassed to do it in case you have the wrong person." She giggled. "It gets me tied up in knots just thinking about it."

"Well, thank you for your help. I appreciate it."

"Even if it doesn't work?"

"Even if it doesn't work." I responded with a smile, staring at her. I had some pretty strong emotions for this girl. "I'm just happy to have you in my life; and have I told you what a beautiful mother you are?"

Blushing, she shook her head. "No, but thank you. You and Dylan need to stop with all the compliments, though. They're going straight to my head."

"Can you blame us? Look at you? You're perfection. I don't think I've even heard that kid cry once since she was born. And you don't even look like you've had a baby."

"You're too sweet."

"Nope. Not sweet at all. Just telling it like it is. Dylan got all the luck when he decided to sneak in and sweep you up."

"You'll have all that too, someday. I just know it. No woman in her right mind would pass on you."

I laughed. "Are you saying Evie isn't in her right mind?" I asked jokingly.

"That's exactly what I'm saying. She's a fool if she passes you up."

"Whatever. Hand me my kid."

She laughed and leaned forward, handing me the baby. "You've got to quit calling her your kid. People are going to get the wrong idea."

"Hey, they can just get their minds out of the gutter. I'm the one who pulled this kid out of your . . . ." I paused, blinking, and she cocked her head, clearly waiting to see how I was going to finish this. "I . . . uh . . . out of your down there." I briefly glanced toward her legs before looking away. "That means I get to claim partial ownership."

Leaning back, she folded her arms against her chest, grinning. "Does it now? I'll have to explain that to Dylan, so he knows."

"It's probably not best to remind him that I've seen you, uh, there. He's pretty possessive of his playground."

"His playground?" She snorted, shaking her head.

"Don't even try to get around this. You know that's his favorite place to be, so don't even try to say otherwise."

"Hmmm." She eyed me warily, so I stared at Piper to avoid eye contact. "Remind me what we've done so far?"

I was grateful for the shift in subject. "Flowers the first day. Hot bakery muffins the next, and spa basket the day after that. Yesterday was the relaxing music CD."

"And today is the painting of the lake where you first saw her, by that local artist, Jean Perry."

I nodded. "She will know for sure it's me when she gets that."

"We want her to. We've teased all her five senses—smell with the roses, taste with the muffins, touch with the spa basket, hearing with the music, and now sight with the painting. Now she's thinking of you while doing all those things. I wonder if, as a therapist, she will catch onto our mind game?"

"Your mind game," I reminded her. "There's

no way she'll ever believe that I was this smart. This evil genius is all you. Guys are dumb. We're lucky to remember our way home at night and how to put the toilet seat down before getting distracted."

Cami's laughing outburst made the baby jump. She quickly sealed her lips, holding her index finger over them.

"Why are you telling me to be quiet?" I whispered. "You're the one being obnoxiously loud. Can't you see my kid is trying to sleep?"

"Whose kid?" Dylan's voice interrupted as he suddenly appeared, leaning on the doorjamb and smiling as he stared at me. "I don't recall you being there when this baby was made, Russ."

Cami giggled. "He's claiming since he pulled her out, he gets part ownership."

"Is he now?" Dylan stared pointedly at me. "Go make your own baby. This one is mine."

Laughing, I shook my head. "I have no problem doing that, but I need a willing partner . . . unless you're gonna let me borrow Cami?" I was totally teasing, but I didn't miss how he stiffened. I knew immediately I'd overstepped with that one. "Of course Cami would never work out, seeing how she's so into you and all. I get jealous, you know?"

Dylan visibly relaxed. "I know exactly what you mean. I feel the same. By the way, you should definitely get your own wife, too, while you're making your own baby."

Cami laughed. "Russ isn't going to need me, anyway. We're getting ready to reel a fish in for him right now, aren't we?"

"I'm glad you're confident this whole thing is going to work," I mumbled.

"Trust me, Russ. I'm a woman and I know what women like. Evie is going to eat all this up. Before long, you'll be trying to remember the days when you were single."

"I highly doubt that, but I hope you're right."

"I am. You'll see."

***

Cami told me to trust her, but I was beginning to get nervous. The painting had been delivered yesterday morning, along with a short simple note that read, **Meet me where I first saw you tomorrow at noon.** I didn't sign it. There was no need. She knew exactly who it was from.

Yet, as I stood here, staring at the now very quiet and seemingly deserted lake, I saw no other signs of life. Glancing at my watch, I saw that it was now twelve thirty.

Evie was late. Did this mean she wasn't coming? Was this my answer once and for all? Cami and I had just assumed the thoughtful gifts would work to soften her. Maybe they just annoyed her instead.

I was such a damn idiot. She'd made it pretty clear she was in love with her boyfriend still—and everyone on the planet knew it was freakishly hard to compete with a dead guy. What was his name? Kory? He'd always be on a pedestal with her. Was I willing to live with that? Was I willing to constantly be measured against a corpse? There was no way I could ever win that battle. Kory would always remain perfect, and all she would see of me was my very obvious flaws.

Plus, there was the whole age thing. Maybe she just felt I was too young for her, but I hoped not. I never even once thought of our age difference when we were together. To me, she was simply a beautiful, accomplished woman. It was easy for me to talk to her, and I like being in her company. Hell, I friggin' missed her, for crying out loud, just from the small amount of time we'd spent together. If that wasn't an attraction with some potential, then I didn't know what the hell it was.

Unless. Unless it really was all one sided. Maybe she really didn't have any interest in me.

Immediately, my thoughts drifted back to that day in the kitchen. Her body had been soft and pliant—ready for me. And the sounds she made as I pressed against her. Damn, I was getting turned on just thinking about it. No. She wanted it just as badly as I did. She was definitely attracted to me.

So why wasn't she here?

Glancing around the lake again, I saw no signs of life. Sighing, I briefly checked my watch, again. One o'clock. She was an hour late, now. I had my answer, but I still sank down on the grassy bank. Absently searching for smooth pebbles, I began carefully throwing them out into the water, skipping some and sinking others. The sun continued to travel across the sky.

"Don't you know that this is the worst time

of day to be out in the sun?" Evie's voice broke into my silent ponderings and I smiled. Continuing to throw my pebbles in the lake, I didn't even look at her.

"You're late."

"I am not. I've been here since before noon."

This revelation had me turning to stare at her. "What?"

She smiled widely. "I parked my car just out of sight over by that hill." She pointed. "And then I sat over on the picnic table in the trees there and watched you."

What was going on? "How very . . . stalkerish . . . of you," I replied. "I would've never pegged you as someone who silently follows people around." What kind of game was she playing with me? Was she happy to be here or not? I was having a hard time reading her and it was making me feel on shaky ground.

"I'm not, usually, but you're special."

"Am I? How so?" Picking up another rock, I chucked it into the lake.

"You can learn a lot about a person by watching them. I wanted to know how long you'd wait for me, and if you'd get angry when you thought I wasn't coming."

"And?" I encouraged her to continue, wondering if I'd passed her little test.

"You waited, and never got angry."

"Is that a good thing?"

"That's a very good thing." She sat down beside me. "Thank you for all the sweet gifts you sent me this week. It was very thoughtful of you."

"I wanted to do something nice for you. I can't take all the credit, though. Cami helped me plan a lot of it."

"That Cami's a doll."

"Yes, she is," I replied.

"How's the baby?"

"Piper is an angel. You really need to come see her. I've never seen such a pretty baby. I tried to tell Dylan I get to claim rights to her since I delivered her, but he's having none of it. He refuses to share. He told me to go out and get my own wife and baby."

Evie laughed loudly, the sound echoing around the silent lake, and I liked hearing it. "Is that what you're here trying to do today? Get your own wife and baby?"

I grinned, shaking my head. "Right now I'd just settle for dating someone."

"Dating *someone*?" She threw a rock into the lake and I watched the ripples for a moment before turning to stare at her.

"Dating you," I replied honestly. "I'd like to date you."

Staring at me, she didn't answer right away and I'd have given anything to know what was going on in that head of hers. She wasn't smiling—she wasn't frowning—she was simply blank.

I didn't look away, but then neither did she.

"If I agree to date you, you have to promise me one thing."

Elation coursed through me. She was considering it. "What's that?" I tried to reply nonchalantly, not really sure if I pulled it off or not.

"We need to go slow." Her eyes seemed pleading. "I mean painfully slow, Russ. Before you, I'd made up my mind to never be involved with another man again. It's been hard for me to get past all this. It's forced me to deal with certain things I've been avoiding. I've had years of conditioning myself to the idea that I would be alone for the rest of my life. Then you came along and everything started . . . changing. I don't really know how to deal with all that."

"Slow, I can do. But I need you to promise me something, too." I scooted closer to her.

"What's that?" Lifting a hand, she pushed a stray lock of my hair away from my eyes and I couldn't help leaning into the gesture.

Nuzzling her hand, I stared at her. "You need to judge me on my own merits. I don't want to be the guy who is always being measured against your fiancé. I'm not him, Evie. I never will be."

"I know you aren't, Russ. And I don't want you to be. I like you."

I smiled, her words thrilling me. "I like you, too."

We both sat there, smiling at each other like idiots. I wanted so badly to lean in and kiss her sweet lips, but I'd just promised her slow—and I intended to keep my word.

"Cami made this really amazing picnic for us to eat here. Are you hungry?" I gestured over to where the picnic basket sat on a large blanket spread out under a shady tree.

"I'm starving," she replied. "That sounds

wonderful."

Standing, I held a hand out to her and immediately noticed the sparks between us when she slipped hers inside mine. I helped her up, but didn't release her, continuing to hold her hand as we walked toward the blanket together. Thankfully, she didn't try to pull away.

"I'm really glad I came today."

I smiled at her and she squeezed my hand. "I am, too. I've missed you." Was it too early to say that? Oh well, it was out there now.

"I tried to miss you, but I couldn't."

That did not sound good; and I quickly glanced over at her. "Why not?"

"You were everywhere, that's why!" She laughed. "You were in the flowers on my desk, the soft music playing in my office, my Jacuzzi tub with all the spa products. I even thought of you every time I walked past the bakery by my office and smelled all those delicious muffins."

"And what about the painting?" I asked.

"The painting is in my bedroom."

"Your bedroom?" I raised my eyebrow.

"Yep."

"Why?"

"So it's the first thing I see when I wake up and the last thing I see when I go to sleep. It reminds me of the day I got a second chance at life." She glanced briefly down at her feet before looking back up at me. "Thank you for that."

A soft breeze stirred her hair, lifting some of the strands to blow about her face and she absently reached up and tucked them behind her ear, smiling at me. She was so beautiful. I really wanted to forget the food and lay her down on the blanket and kiss her until she was screaming my name, but I couldn't. Right now she was still as nervous as a newborn filly. I wasn't about to scare her off again, like I did before. It was too much, too fast. I was lucky she was giving me another chance as it was.

"Maybe we can swim later?" I suggested. "Get you back in the water."

She laughed. "I didn't bring a suit."

"Then we will definitely be swimming later, "I teased and she blushed.

"You're incorrigible, you know that?"

"Yes, I consider it one of my most endearing qualities."

She laughed. Laughter was good.

"Let's eat." We both settled on the blanket and I opened the basket.

CHAPTER FOURTEEN
Evie

"So you've already dredged all my dark and dirty secrets from me. I say you start spilling the dirt on yourself," Russ said, a wicked glint in his eyes that made my heart rate accelerate.

"I don't have any dark and dirty secrets," I replied with laugh.

"I can think of at least one that you have." His eyes never left mine and I blushed furiously.

"Hmmm. There is *that*."

He chuckled. "*That* was amazing."

I stared at him seriously.

"What?" he asked, looking surprised.

"It doesn't bother you? That you're my dark and dirty secret, I mean?"

"Hell, no," he replied shaking his head and grinning. "I'm hoping all this may lead to a bunch more dark and dirty secrets with you— just being honest."

He was always so straight to the point. I

loved it, and it embarrassed me at the same time. I kind of liked it though. With Russ, I never seemed to really know where I stood, but in a good way. It kept me guessing.

"I . . . I'm not sure how to respond to that."

"No need for words, Doc. That pretty blush of yours is doing plenty of talking for you." He winked.

Dammit. I blushed harder. Eyes dropping to the sandwich in front of me, I tried to focus in on my food instead of him, but I could practically feel his heated gaze following me everywhere. He was going to burn holes through me at this rate, but I liked it.

Six years alone and suddenly my hormones were all lit up like I was a sixteen-year-old girl, again. The strange thing with that was I'd never really been a sixteen-year-old when I was sixteen. I was so focused on overachieving that I'd missed out on discovering a lot of things other teens took for granted. I hadn't gone to many dances or football games, or any extracurricular events, for that matter. Unless they had to do with academics—then I was there for sure.

Now I found myself having a serious, sixteen-year-old girl crush. That's exactly what this was—hero worship, plain and simple. I'd fallen for my rescuer. This happened to people all the time. It was totally normal to transfer emotion to someone you shared a traumatic experience with.

Unfortunately, a lot of those relationships never lasted. Once the trauma passed, couples often realized they didn't have much in common but the trauma. Is that where I was headed right now—for more heartache?

"You're doing it again, Doc," Russ's voice filtered into my head.

"Doing what?" I asked innocently.

"Over analyzing things."

"And what makes you such an expert on me?" I asked, half-teasing, half-annoyed that he was spot on with his assessment.

"Hours of close scrutiny," he replied wryly, taking a bite of his sandwich and leaning back against the tree behind him.

"Hours?" I narrowed my eyes at him. "Are you spying on me when I'm not aware?"

He snorted. "I'm not a dang stalker, Doc. I meant from our sessions together."

"Interesting. I guess I never realized patients might be scrutinizing me."

"Why not? I'm just as curious about you as you are about me."

"You and I are different though."

"How so?" he asked, and I felt a little hurt that he didn't recognize it.

"Because . . . because we are connected." I waved a finger back and forth between us.

Smiling widely, he nodded. "Glad you can finally admit it out loud."

"You're incorrigible."

"So I've been told." Just staring at his boyish grin made my insides melt. I could stare at him all day and never get sick of it.

"How are those kids you rescued doing?"

He smiled widely. "They're doing great. I've

been by to see them every day this week. Both of them seem to be handling it all okay. They were released this morning to go home."

"That's wonderful news. Does the family have a place to stay?"

"Right now they're staying in a spare room with some family, while they try to get funds together to rent a new place. They've received a lot of financial support from the community and people wanting to help out, so that's good. They lost everything they owned."

"They made it out with the most important stuff, though, thanks in large part to you." I was so proud to know this man.

"Thanks, in large part, to an entire fire department that works together like a well-oiled machine. I keep getting all the credit for these things, but the fact of the matter is I couldn't have done what I did without the support of a great team of co-workers. They deserve just as much credit as I do."

"That may be, but it doesn't dilute the fact that you were the one who rushed into the burning building."

"And Camden," he replied, his voice darkening.

"Who's Camden?" I asked.

"Exactly my point!" He waved a hand toward me. "Camden was right beside me, helping me break down the door to get into the bedroom and attacked the fire while I dragged the kids out from under the bed. Those kids and I wouldn't have survived that fire if it hadn't been for Camden. But no, the news sees one story and they run with it, elevating one person without giving any thought to all my other brave heroic peers." He leaned forward, pointing a carrot at me as he continued speaking heatedly. "Do you have any idea how many people those men and women have helped? I'm the newbie of the department. Yet, I'm getting all the credit for their heroics. It takes all of us—every one of us—to make things work. Either everyone gets credit or no one." Releasing a great breath, he settled back against the tree. "Sorry, didn't mean to rant on like that. It just chaps me a bit."

"I understand better, now that you've explained it." Taking a bite of my sandwich, my eyes never left him, watching as he stared out at the lake. "I'm glad Camden was with you," I added after several long moments.

"Me, too." Staring at me, he lifted his water bottle to his lips, taking a long swallow before recapping it. "You want to know what I was thinking about while I was in there, Doc?"

"What?"

"You." He didn't move at all, simply continuing to stare at me.

"Why me?" I asked, my pulse rate picking up.

He shrugged. "Fires are dangerous; and while I'm always careful, I know accidents can happen. I wondered if you'd be sad if something happened to me, or if it really wouldn't matter to you."

A knot tightened in my throat, but I didn't look away from him, wanting him to see the honesty in my eyes. "If anything ever happened to you, I'd be devastated."

"Why?" His heated gaze was burning through mine.

I faltered, not knowing how to put what I wanted to say into words without admitting things I wasn't ready to admit to myself, let alone to him. He waited for my reply though, unspeaking as he studied me.

"Because I want to know what this is, too." I gestured between the two of us and he smiled.

"I'm happy to hear that, Evie."

Smiling back, I was too, the words having lightened me somehow. I kept hoping he'd lean forward and kiss me, but he seemed to be holding true to his promise to go slow. Suddenly, that made me feel very sad and I realized I wanted him to kiss me. I didn't want him to wait, but I was scared to make the first move.

Glancing out at the lake, I gathered my courage to ask him some questions. "Do Dylan and Cami know what happened between us?"

He nodded. "Well, I assume Cami does. Dylan tells her everything and I told Dylan about it."

"Because that's not embarrassing at all."

"What's embarrassing about it?" he asked, seeming genuine.

"We had sex in their kitchen!"

He laughed. "Trust me. It's not the first time that kitchen as seen sex. Cami and Dylan are constantly going at it like rabbits. Besides, there was nothing embarrassing about it. It was fuckin' hot, if you ask me. Of course, maybe I was the only one who felt the earth move." His eyes narrowed as he studied me.

"The earth didn't move for me," I replied honestly, and his expression immediately showed disappointment. "It shattered. Completely." That was the total truth. My world had been broken apart and turned on its side at that moment in time.

Russ looked relieved; and this time he moved closer, pushing the food out of the way. "I'd like to have the chance with you again." He brushed several loose flying tendrils back behind my ear. "I'd like you to let me do it right—in a bed with a couple of days set apart for me to get very intimately acquainted with you and your body."

His words painted an image that set me on fire. "And what about time for me to get acquainted with you and your body?" I asked boldly.

Grinning widely, he leaned in even closer. "You're right. Sounds like we might need to escape for a week, then. We don't want to rush these things."

"Yes, that would be a shame," I agreed, shifting closer to him, my eyes trained on his lips and imagining how wonderful it would feel to have them brushing across my heated skin for days.

"We'll definitely have to plan for that—when you're ready." Placing a quick kiss against my hairline, he moved away, settling back against the tree.

"Wait a minute. What just happened here?" I asked, blinking wide eyes at him.

Winking, he smiled wider. "We're taking it slow, remember? 'Painfully slow', if I correctly recall."

"That was pretty painful," I said, slumping to my side and propping my head up on my hand, continuing to stare at him. "You like driving me crazy, don't you?"

"Most definitely. But there are some ways I prefer over others."

"Like?"

"Like anything that might end up with sex." He lifted an eyebrow suggestively, his gaze traveling over me.

I shrugged. "At least you're honest."

He shook his head. "I'm not honest. If I were being honest, you'd already be on your back and I'd be hard at work driving you crazy."

His words sent heat shooting straight to my core. "You'd do me right here? In the middle of the park?"

"And not even think twice about it," he replied, staring hungrily at me.

"What if someone saw us?" His words both frightened and excited me because I could tell he was totally serious.

He shrugged. "They'd be really jealous, I guess."

I laughed. "You're so . . . confident."

"Is there a reason I shouldn't be?"

"No," I replied quickly, remembering the exact size of the confidence he was packing around. "You have every reason to be . . .

confident."

Now he laughed. "And you tell me . . . exactly how much 'confidence' have you had experience with? Am I being measured against several guys, or just a few?"

I snorted. "Several," I replied, loving the way he seemed to get totally jealous about it.

"Wow. Several." He absently picked a few blades of grass out of the ground before looking up at me. "It doesn't surprise me, really. You're very beautiful. It's only natural that lots of guys would want to be with you like that."

I totally giggled. "I didn't say I'd slept with them. I just said I'd seen a lot."

Now he looked completely confused. "How do you see a lot if you aren't sleeping with them?" he asked.

Sighing, I couldn't stop grinning. "It was at a frat party my college roommate dragged me to. I shouldn't have even been there since I was still underage at the time. Everyone was drunk— except me because I refused to drink—but it was a toga party. All the guys there decided to flash what was under their togas to all the girls present. Since you can imagine what might happen when a bunch of girls are staring at a certain part on a guy . . . let's just say things were very . . . erect. And, since I was sober, I have the misfortune of remembering everything in pretty great detail."

Russ snorted, laughing. "I can't even imagine you at a party like that."

"It wasn't really my scene, but I did have a good time for the most part. I didn't relax much when I was younger, always pushing myself to get done faster and be at the top of my class. I think I maybe went to three socials during all my years of school."

"So, you didn't sleep with any of those guys that night?" Russ asked, obviously still stuck on that part of the conversation.

Sighing, I shook my head. "No. I left shortly after that because the party turned into an—,"

"Orgie?" he supplied and I laughed and nodded.

"Yeah, I didn't need to see all that." Dropping my gaze, I rubbed my hand lightly over the blanket. "Kory is . . . was . . . the only guy I've ever been with—until you."

Eyes widening, he leaned his head back against the tree. "Wow."

I knew what he was thinking. He knew I was in love with Kory. Now finding out Kory was the only other person I'd been with, he was wondering how, or if, he measured up in comparison. It was only natural.

"Knowing that helps me to better understand why you were so upset after we . . . ." Letting his voice trail off, he left it to me to fill in the blanks.

I wished I could tell him how he'd made me feel that day. How it broke my heart that one very casual sexual experience with him had completely obliterated my past sexual experiences with Kory.

And I hated the way it made me feel. For six years, my memories of being with Kory were what kept me warm at night. He was an incredible lover, so considerate of my needs. He was strong and steady, always trying to please me. Kory knew every part of me, intimately. He knew my secrets, my fears, what made me burn with need and how to satiate it. I loved our physical relationship.

But Russ . . . everything with him had been quick, hot, and fast. It was like riding a shooting firework straight to its peak and having this massive explosion that repeatedly sent shock waves rolling through my system. I'd never experienced anything like it before—ever.

I'd be lying if I said I didn't want to experience that again. If that was what crazy frantic sex was like with Russ, what would it be like if he was taking his time? Biting my lip, I attempted to keep the moan inside at this thought. I wanted to know what that would be like; but at the same time, I was terrified to find out.

"What's wrong?" he asked.

"With you, everything is so quick. We crossed so many lines so fast. I wasn't looking for this. I didn't want it."

He was silent for a few moments, brushing at an imaginary spec on his jeans. "You said you didn't want it. Do you now?"

He was so direct. I both loved and hated it.

"You realize I'm older than you, right?" I asked, deflecting the question with another.

"So?"

"That doesn't bother you?"

"Not even a little. Does it bother you?"

I shook my head. "No, it just makes me

wonder why you'd want me and all my baggage when you could have any girl you wanted."

"You *are* the girl I want," he replied, eyes never leaving me. "And maybe I like baggage."

I chuckled. "Sure you do."

Scooting away from the tree, he stretched out beside me, propping his head on his arm, mirroring my position. He continued staring at me. "I think a guy could deal with lots of baggage if he got to wake up every morning looking at this." His eyes traveled heatedly over me before returning to my face.

He hadn't even touched me and I was already burning with need for him. I wanted him to forget his promise, rip my clothes off and make sweet, hot, passionate love to me.

"Are you going to kiss me today?" I asked, tired of waiting for him to do it.

Smiling widely, he made no advances toward me. "No. I'm not. Ask me again tomorrow."

Disappointment flooded through me. "What's tomorrow?"

"Our second official date."

I smiled. "You miscounted. It'll be the third."

"No. This is our first date. The dinner before this was a non-date, remember?"

"Hmmm. A non-date with sex?"

"Yep. It was a sucky non-date with great sex. Wait until we have an awesome 'real date' that ends in even greater sex. That's the date that's gonna blow your mind."

"Greater sex? I can't even imagine that. Last time was pretty great." I couldn't believe I was talking this candidly to him about it.

"Doc, that was just the tip of the iceberg. I have a lot more I can't wait to show you—if you'll let me." He was grinning wickedly at me.

"Let's go. Right now." I challenged him, suddenly wanting nothing more than to be lost in his arms.

"I'd love to, but I can't," he replied, looking truly regretful.

"Why?"

"Because I promised someone I'd take it slow."

Groaning, I rolled onto my back, letting my arms flop to my sides as I stared at the overcast sky. "I'm going to regret ever saying those words, aren't I?"

"Probably, but it's all for the best." Moving closer, he leaned over me, draping an arm across my waist and I was so happy to have some sort of physical contact with him. His eyes bore into mine seriously. "I want you to be one hundred percent sure that you want me. I want to be the only face in your mind when I'm moving inside you and the only name screaming from your lips as you fall over the edge."

Paralyzed by the vivid imagery his words created, I wanted to tell him—reassure him—that his was the only face in my mind that day, but I couldn't speak—unwilling to break the mood.

"I want you to crave me the same way I crave you," he added, brushing a thumb over my lips. "I don't care if you think I'm too young, or you're too old—none of that matters to me. It's just a number. I simply want to be with you."

Rolling onto his back, he stared at the sky, too, neither of us speaking. I felt his hand slide closer and he linked his pinky finger with mine. Sparks shot through my body at the simple contact, making my heart sing.

It was enough. For now, that simple, tiny touch was enough.

CHAPTER FIFTEEN
Russ

"Are you seeing Evie again tonight?" Dylan asked as I came down the stairs.

"Nah. I just thought I'd get dressed up and do some dishes for you," I replied, rolling the sleeves of my dress shirt part way up my arm. I wanted to look nice, but not like I was trying too hard.

"You look great," Cami said, cuddling baby Piper in her arms. "Perfect for dinner and a movie."

"Oh, where you taking her?" Dylan asked, reaching over and stealing the baby from Cami.

I smiled. "To the backyard."

"Excuse me?" Dylan raised his eyebrows and glanced between the two of us.

"Cami came up with this romantic movie night idea."

"Well, actually I got the idea off Pinterest," Cami interjected and Dylan groaned.

"You and your dang Pinterest. I swear you're addicted."

Cami simply smiled, not denying it. "All my pinning is working out good for Russ."

"We rented a movie screen and projector and set up this nice little lounge area with cushions and pillows," I told him.

"And we added white Christmas lights everywhere." Cami's eyes were all lit up. "You have to go see it, Dylan. It's so romantic."

Dylan stared wryly at me. "Warn me now. Are you going to be having sex in my backyard?"

I snorted, shaking my head. "I can safely promise you there will be no sex happening tonight."

"You sound very sure of this. Is everything okay?" Dylan asked.

"Everything is great. She asked for things to go painfully slow, so painfully slow is what I'm giving her. And trust me when I say it is, indeed, *painfully* slow. I'm actually afraid I might die from blue balls or blue everything, for that matter. I barely touch the girl these days."

Dylan laughed. "Sadly, I remember days like those." He glanced at Cami, winking. "I don't miss them at all."

"Well, if you're suffering that bad, then I promise you she is, too," Cami said, returning Dylan's look. "I remember what it felt like—hours of making out. Dylan running his hands everywhere, touching all the places he could without actually touching the places I wanted him to. It was torture."

"Hey. I was kinda trying to keep from landing my ass in jail with you," Dylan said, staring heatedly at Cami. I knew that look. I needed to get out of here before they started going at it. "Trust me when I say, it was not an easy thing to do."

"But it was fun." Cami smiled invitingly.

"Yes, it was that," Dylan replied, sidling up next to her. Shifting the baby to one shoulder, he reached out with his free arm and pulled Cami against him, his hand sliding down and very obviously squeezing her butt.

"Maybe I should take Piper on my date with me," I said, reminding them I was still there. "I would hate for her to see certain . . . things."

Cami popped up on her toes, wrapping her arm around Dylan's neck and kissing him. Sighing, they both pulled away from each other.

"Stopping already?" I joked, leaning against the stair railing. "I'm shocked."

Cami giggled and brushed past us, heading into the kitchen, and Dylan stared after her wistfully.

I glanced at my watch. "Seriously, bro. I've got time. Give me the baby and go get yourself a little somethin' somethin'."

"I can't." He sounded positively mournful.

"Why not?"

"Women aren't supposed to have sex for up to six weeks after having a baby. It's only been two weeks."

"What the hell?"

"Recovery time."

"Hmm. I never actually thought of that . . .

like ever."

"You were just gonna have your gal pop out a kid in the morning and in the sack again that night, weren't you?"

I laughed, elbowing him. "I'm not *that* bad. I would've given her a night off."

He laughed harder. "That's my boy. Always thinking with his head."

"You know it." I glanced at my watch again. "I need to go pick up dinner."

"What are you eating?"

"I ordered Chinese."

"Well, have fun. Carry some condoms, just in case."

Shaking my head, I laughed and hurried out to my truck. Dylan's comment stuck with me and gave me a sinking feeling. I hadn't used a condom last time. I didn't have one with me when it happened. Pretty much every girl I knew was on the pill, anyway. Surely Evie was, too? Unless she was thinking about her dead fiancé for six years and basically sentencing herself to celibacy. Then there would be no reason for the pill.

Damn. I needed to try to find a nice way to bring this up, tonight. If we were going to be together, we needed to take better precautions and be safe.

***

"You look amazing," I said, opening the back gate for her. She stepped inside, wearing a short black dress that hit about mid-thigh, again accentuating her long legs, which looked even longer because of her high heels. The dress scooped low, revealing a good deal of cleavage, and she wore her blonde hair straight. It practically glowed against all the black. She was a knockout. Already my head was imagining all kinds of things it shouldn't be, and my body was at complete attention, ready to follow those orders.

"So do you." She gave a quick laugh. "We match tonight."

Glancing down at my black shirt, pants and shoes, I nodded. "True, but trust me when I say, no one is noticing what I'm wearing with you standing in the room."

Giggling, she moved closer and I could smell the gardenia scent of her perfume. "We aren't standing in a room, Russ," she whispered, drawing a finger lightly over my chest. "We're outside, remember? And you should trust me when I say, I notice you just fine."

Shit. It was going to be one of those kinds of nights. I wanted to forget the movie, forget dinner, and carry her over to the cushions and then peel that dress off her gorgeous body and have hot, naked sex with her all night long.

"If you keep dressing like this and touching me like that, my promise to go slow is going to be a lot harder to keep." Staring down at her legs, imagining them wrapped around me, I so wanted to feel that again.

"Maybe I changed my mind." Smiling, she continued to touch me.

"Maybe you should quit teasing me before you land flat on your back with your legs in the air." That mental picture made me really happy.

"Sounds fun," she replied, licking her lips, and I groaned.

"Yeah, it does." I needed to change the subject right now. "Are you hungry? I got us a bunch of Chinese take-out."

Sighing, she dropped her hand away and nodded. "I'm famished, really. I promised my mom I'd come over and help her weed her flowerbeds and vegetable garden today, and it turned into a bigger project than we initially thought it would be. I haven't eaten since breakfast."

Taking her by the elbow, I guided her over to the cushions and throw pillows. "You just sit right here and I will get you some food. Is there anything particular you like?"

"I'm not too picky, but I do love sweet and sour pork."

"Coming right up!" I loaded her plate with sweet and sour pork, noodles, and fried rice, along with a fortune cookie. Placing a pair of chopsticks on the side, I carried it over to her. "Here you go."

She stared at the plate for a moment before glancing up at me from her seat. "I suck at using chopsticks."

"Do you now?" I grinned. "I think I'm looking forward to watching this."

"You aren't going to take pity on me and bring me a fork, instead?" She took the plate.

"Now what makes you think I'm willing to ruin all my fun just to make it easy on you?" Quickly, I hurried back to dish my own food before returning and settling down beside her.

"Do I need to feed you?"

"You might have to. I'm that bad at it." She continued to stare at her plate.

I took a bite, moaning as the flavor burst into my mouth. I hurriedly finished chewing and swallowed. "You really should try it. It's amazing."

Picking up one chopstick, she stabbed a piece of the pork and ate it. Laughing, I shook my head.

"That's one way to do it, I guess. Whatever works."

"Not very graceful, I imagine."

"Hey, you're eating dinner with a firefighter. Don't you know we eat like pigs?"

She smiled. "Whatever."

"I'm being totally serious. We never know when a call is going to come in. The result is that we've learned to shovel our food in as quickly as possible and then we sit around and visit. If we go slow, and get interrupted, who knows when we might get to eat again?"

"I could see how that might be a problem. But, thankfully, you're not on call tonight, so you can go slowly."

"Hmmm." Her words conjured up something totally different for me. "I have no problem going slow, either. In fact, I've been looking forward to it." My eyes drifted over her gorgeous figure, immediately wanting to strip her bare.

"I don't believe I put out on the second date," she said, slightly stabbing another piece of pork and eating it.

"Oh, yeah, I forgot. You only put out on first

non-dates."

Laughing, she rolled her eyes. "That's right."

"We need to have another one of those then. Do you put out on second non-dates?" I asked, eyeing her and she totally choked on the bite she was chewing. Reaching over, I patted her on the back, lightly, as she continued coughing. "I can see you're wanting to move straight to mouth-to-mouth. You should've just said something. I would've accommodated you, I know you're dying to kiss me."

A strangled laughed escaped her amid more coughing sounds and I quickly dragged out the bottle of wine chilling in a bucket of ice and poured her a glass. With a grateful expression, she accepted it and downed the entire contents, swiftly.

Taking a deep breath, she smiled, only a couple small coughs escaping her as she handed the glass back to me. "Thank you."

"More? Already?" I asked, staring at the empty wine goblet. "At this rate you're going to be drunk as a skunk here, shortly; but if you insist." Pouring her another, I handed it back.

"I wasn't asking for more," she replied with a laugh, accepting it. I was totally surprised when she slammed the contents and extended her hand again.

"Let me guess? You're a closet alcoholic?" Still, I couldn't resist refilling her drink. I was enjoying seeing this side of her. She always seemed so controlled.

"Are you going to have some?" she asked, gesturing to my still empty glass.

"Honestly, I'm having too much fun watching you. I completely forgot about it."

"Well, I'm not drinking this one without you."

Grabbing mine, I quickly filled it and held it out toward her. "To tonight." I toasted and she clinked my glass and downed hers again. Chuckling, I did the same. "So, let me guess. You were a champion drinker in college?" I refilled our glasses, noting the end of the bottle. I quickly slipped the spare into the ice.

"Were you planning on getting me drunk tonight?" she asked, eyeing the second bottle suspiciously.

"Not at all," I assured her with a laugh. "I just like to be prepared, you know, in case a champion drinker stops by for dinner."

Giggling, she snorted and shook her head. I could tell the alcohol was taking affect already. "I wasn't old enough to drink in college. Well, at least I wasn't when most kids around me were into all that. In fact, I never even tried a drink until I was twenty."

"Why twenty?" I asked, unable to imagine going that long without ever trying alcohol.

"That was when Kory died. I didn't care if I was too young then. Plus, I had plenty of college friends who sympathized with me and were very happy to buy for me. I didn't drink enough to affect my schooling; but at night, when the day and my homework were done, I got wasted." Glancing at me, I could see the sadness radiating from her eyes. "I couldn't sleep without it—too many nightmares." Staring at me, she raised her finger and shook it. "This is not me advising you to drink to get rid of your nightmares."

"I didn't think you were. Besides, I've already tried that. It didn't work."

"When did you have your first drink?" she asked, thankfully steering the conversation away to safer subjects.

Smiling, I thought back to my childhood. "I never set out with a desire to be a bad kid or to break the rules. That being said, the party scene was totally where I wanted to be. My first beer was one my dad had chilling in the refrigerator. There was always beer in there, and he drank enough that he never seemed to notice when I took one or two for myself—or if he did, he never said anything to me about it."

"You didn't tell me how old you were," she said.

I chuckled. "I was twelve."

"Twelve! Oh my gosh! Do you even have a liver left?"

Laughter erupted from me. I loved how she always caught me off guard. "I didn't become an instant alcoholic, you know. My beer sneaking ratio averaged about one a week. I'm fairly certain my liver is fine."

"What about later? You said you were into the party scene."

"I preferred marijuana. If there was anything I really abused, it was that."

"So you never got drunk?"

"I didn't say that. I've been plastered more times than I can probably count, but it wasn't near as much as being stoned."

"You mentioned in your session you tried a lot of other drugs, too. Did you use them regularly?"

"How did this become a discussion about my past substance abuse history?" I asked with a laugh. "Is this a therapy session, Doc? Because I was under the impression that part of our relationship was over."

"Sorry. It's training that's ingrained in me." She bit her lip, cocking her head to the right as she stared at me. "I'm just curious about your past and getting a clear picture of how you ended up here, like this."

"Like what?" I asked, curious to what label she'd put on me.

"Perfect," she said with a sigh, and I laughed, reaching over and taking her glass and setting it beside mine.

"I think we've had enough to drink."

"I'm not drunk," she said, leaning closer. "I can handle my liquor very well."

"Can you now?" I asked, enjoying her close proximity. My gaze dropped to her plump, glistening lips. "Then what's going on here?"

She leaned in closer. "I'm going to kiss you because you're taking entirely too long to do it and it's driving me insane."

I shook my head. "Sorry. I can't kiss you. You're under the influence and that would be taking advantage of you, and breaking my promise to 'go slow.'"

Giggling, she moved a hairsbreadth away from me, her lips almost touching mine. "What if I'm doing all this because I want you to break your promise and take advantage of me?"

I swallowed hard—hell, everything was hard, but I continued to play her game. "I still couldn't do it."

She pulled back slightly. "Why not?"

"Because kissing you would automatically lead to sex and I promised Dylan there would be no sex in his backyard tonight."

"Oh." The way she said it followed by the disappointment in her eyes made me want to throw all caution to the wind and kiss her anyway. Immediately, her expression brightened. "So let's going up to your apartment. We can always make out on your squeaky bed."

I groaned loudly. "You can't say things like that to me."

"Why not?"

"You know why."

Smiling, she placed a light kiss against my lips. I didn't move. In fact, I didn't respond at all. Well, that wasn't entirely true. Other parts of me were responding just fine. Still, I didn't move, trying very hard to stick to my resolution.

"From the moment I showed you that bed, I've been imagining you in it."

"Really?" She smiled even bigger. "I was pretty sure I was the only one who imagined that."

"Now I'm positive this is the alcohol talking," I said.

"Why?"

"Because you're pretty good at keeping me at arm's length. I'm fairly certain you haven't been imagining yourself in my bed."

"You know what they say . . . ."

"Um, no, I don't. What do they say?" I was thoroughly enjoying this conversation.

"Alcohol loosens the tongue, so the truth can finally come out."

"Is that what they say?" I asked, my pulse picking up speed.

"It is."

"So what are you trying to tell me, Evie? Say it plain—no games." I brushed my hand over her hair, our food and drinks completely forgotten.

"I'm asking you to take me to bed, Russ. To your bed."

Everything inside my body begged for me to give in to her request. "And what happens later, when you regret asking me to do this?"

"I can't regret doing something I want."

"And what about Kory?" I asked, knowing this question could possibly derail everything.

She was silent for several moments. "You were right. Liking you doesn't mean I have to love Kory any less."

"I don't want to be the guy who is on standby for you, Evie. I want more than that from you."

Sidling against me, she placed her hands on either side of my face. "Russ, I don't want you to be that either. I'm so tired of crying. I'm so tired of being lonely. I'm so tired of waiting for . . . something. All I know is you're the first guy I've even noticed since Kory died. I like you. I enjoy being with you. Whenever you're around, I'm happy; and when you leave again, I'm not."

Staring at her, I continued to finger the silky strands of her hair. "That sounded surprisingly lucid."

She laughed. "I told you, I'm not drunk. A little mellow maybe, but I'm not drunk."

"So, if I take you to bed, you aren't going to scream at me later for taking advantage of you?"

"I never said there wouldn't be screaming," she said, smiling briefly before pressing her lips to mine. Fire shot straight through me at the contact and I scooped her up, carrying her to the exterior stairs that led to my apartment, unwilling to waste one more second.

CHAPTER SIXTEEN
Evie

With an exhausted, satisfied sigh, I plopped back onto the mattress, its squeaky springs protesting wildly. "How many times has that been now?" I asked breathlessly.

Russ fell beside me, panting just as badly as I was. "I don't know. I've lost track, but it was still amazing. Let me know when you're ready to go again."

I totally snorted. "You're kidding me, right? I didn't even know it was humanly possible for a guy to keep going like this."

"Some guys are lucky," he replied with a grin. "And since I have no idea when you might decide you need me again, I intend to take full and complete advantage of what you're offering as many times as you'll give it to me."

I couldn't help my blush, or my laughter—not that I was actually complaining. Russ was amazing in bed, and I jealously thought back to his therapy session and his revelation about the girl he'd slept with in high school. He'd said there was no relationship and it was strictly for sex. I was starting to think that the girl had been born stupid. I couldn't imagine anyone sleeping with Russ and then wanting anyone else after that. I was pretty sure he'd just ruined me for any other guy out there. He was that incredible.

Right now, in this moment, I totally felt like the cougar I was. Russ could probably screw laps around me. It was all I could do to keep up with him; yet, for some reason, I couldn't seem to keep this damn grin off my face.

He was grinning, too. "It's fun, huh? And despite all my worries, the bed makes it even better."

Catching me by surprise, I laughed, thinking of the insane amount of loud squeaking it had made underneath us—except for the time we did it on the floor; oh, and that other time against the wall, and the one time bent over the chair. But the rest had been on the very squeaky bed.

"Do you think they heard us?" I asked, staring into his beautiful eyes in the lamplight.

"Cami and Dylan?" he asked and I nodded.

"Well, I have been sound proofing this part of the house to keep the noise from traveling between the two places."

Instantly, I was relieved.

"Of course, I'm pretty sure I left the interior door open between my house and theirs; so yeah, they've probably heard the bed and a whole lot more."

Covering my mouth, I stared at him in horror. "Oh, my gosh! Go shut the door! I'm so embarrassed."

"They know how to close the door if they needed to." He grinned, seemingly unconcerned. "Besides, I consider it payback for everything I've had the pleasure of witnessing between the two of them."

"That bad, huh?"

"You have no idea. I swear they never lock a door, like ever. I can't count the times I've walked in on the two of them going at it."

"And they still don't lock the doors?"

"They don't know about it," he replied with a chuckle. "I've never told them."

"Well, then I hope you've learned to knock or call out before entering."

"Always. Always, always." Shaking his head, he grinned. "I've learned to listen, too. They aren't exactly quiet either. Hence the need for sound proofing."

"And here I thought you were doing it so you didn't have to hear the baby crying."

"Nope. It's so I don't have to hear those two screaming each other's name."

"And the truth comes out." I snickered against the pillow. "But good for them. It's nice to know that they found love like that with each other."

"They're perfect together. I've never seen two people who were made for each other as much as those two." Trailing a finger over my nose, he continued to smile. "Except for maybe you and me."

My heart jumped at his words, but I had no idea how to respond to that comment, so I simply leaned forward and kissed him. Groaning, he dragged my body against his, deepening it. In a matter of moments, I was on my back and he was leaning over the top of me, the sound of the squeaking springs matching his rhythm.

Staring up at him, my eyes traveled over the strong, masculine planes of his face before traveling down his sculpted body to where it disappeared beneath the tangled sheet. Trailing my fingers up and down his back, I closed my eyes and simply enjoyed the sensations he was causing inside me.

"Open your eyes, Evie. I want to see you," he said, and I immediately looked at him, and he groaned. "You're so beautiful. I swear I could stare at you for days, doing nothing else but watching you, and I'd never get tired."

His words made me melt inside. "Do you think so? You could stare at me and do nothing else?" I teased.

"Uh, yeah. I may need to rephrase that a little." Bending, he captured my lips, never breaking his tempo. I wrapped my legs around him and was rewarded with another groan. "Let's both quit our jobs," he added suddenly and I laughed.

"What brought that on?" I managed to spit out unevenly as my breathing increased, matching his.

"I want to just stay home and do this all day."

I couldn't help the smile. "That does sound

fun—though I doubt having sex all day will pay the bills or feed us."

"Details," he replied, grinning.

"I have one request if we decide to stay home and do this all day," I panted out.

"New bed?"

"Definitely," I agreed. "This thing is loud."

"Shut up and kiss me again," he said. And from that moment on, he had my complete and undivided attention.

***

The week that followed was a blur. Russ monopolized every spare second I had—taking me out every night he was off or inviting me to eat with him at the fire station. He consumed even the moments I didn't spend with him, because I couldn't stop thinking about him. I couldn't count the times people had to call me back to reality because I was staring off into space, daydreaming about the time we'd spent together.

Giving a slight snort, I stared at myself in the mirror, running my hands over my casual, yet flirty, outfit. Yes, it was true. I, the woman who was determined to remain celibate the rest of her life as she clung to the memories of her broken heart, was in love. Not only was I in love, but the celibacy thing was definitely long gone. Russ dropped me in the sack at every possible opportunity. The two of us should have bedsores by this point; we'd spent so much time in bed. Of course, there were the times when a bed wasn't around, either. Blushing, I remembered our encounter at the fire station, locked in one of the bathrooms. I was as red as the truck by the time I left there.

Russ made me do things I would've never considered doing before, too. I didn't even think about them twice either. I simply loved his carefree approach to life and experiencing it with him. He made me feel like a girl . . . a young, carefree girl. I didn't realize, until now, that I'd skipped all of that. In my rush to push through my education, I'd never taken the time to smell the roses along the way.

I liked smelling roses. I liked smelling roses with Russ—and tonight was the night I was going to tell him I loved him.

Yes, I was a little nervous, but he hadn't been shy about showing his feelings for me, even though he'd never spoken the words. That, along with a few minutes of visiting with Dylan one night at the station, boosted my confidence. Dylan said he'd never seen Russ so happy before, and he was glad I was hanging around more.

I was there more often because Russ told me he liked it when I spent the night with him, because he didn't have nightmares while I was there. Naturally, I had to do my best to spend every night with him after that. But there was no way I could fill Dylan in on that.

There was one place we'd never been though; and that was here, at my house. I'd hesitated about bringing him home. Kory's stuff was here, and his pictures were still set out. My memories of him were like ghosts, cluttering every surface I looked at.

All of that changed today. I called Russ and asked him if I could make dinner for him tonight, and he readily agreed. After I hung up, I went into my closet and carefully, and lovingly, began removing Kory's belongings and packing them.

It was so hard. I still loved him. I would always love him, but it was time to put this part of my life away and bring my new life home with me. When it was all said and done, I placed my pictures of Kory in a special album, so he would always be there if I ever needed to look at him and just smile and remember.

Kory wasn't as spontaneous or carefree as Russ. He was definitely more methodical and liked to weigh things out before committing to anything, but we still had lots of fun together.

A sharp pang filled my heart as I closed the photo album, hiding his smiling face. It was extremely hard for me to do this—to officially let him go. He'd been my world.

Placing the photo album on the bookshelf, I glanced around my condo. Everything seemed so bare now. Half of my closet and dresser were empty. There were empty drawers in my bathroom. Blank spaces stared back at me from where his pictures used to be.

Honestly, it was a little unsettling. It made me feel—alone.

"Suck it up, Evie," I said out loud. "It's just stuff. You will survive this."

Returning to the kitchen, I checked the pot of boiling water I'd put on and saw it was ready for the spaghetti noodles to go in. As soon as I did that, I stirred the meat sauce that was simmering and checked the garlic bread in the oven. Glancing at the clock, I realized it was getting close to time for Russ to arrive, so I quickly began setting the table, placing out my best dishes and a couple of taper candles. I wanted the first night we spent together in my house to be perfect.

As soon as the table was arranged, I turned on some of the music Russ had given me, sighing at the nice peaceful touch it added to the ambience of my space. This was perfect—everything set just right for an amazing dinner, some cuddling, and hopefully some hot sex in a bed that didn't creak.

I couldn't help laughing at that memory. Dylan and Cami had both been awake and taking care of the baby when I made the walk of shame from Russ' front door and down the stairs to the driveway.

"Hey, Evie!" Dylan poked his head through the screen. "It's a beautiful morning, isn't it?"

"The best," I replied, keeping my eyes glued to the stairs as I self-consciously ran a hand through my bed-tangled hair.

"Can I get you to do me a favor," he asked, not allowing me to ignore him.

"What's that?" Lifting my gaze to meet his, I briefly saw the humor in his eyes before he spoke.

"Can you please convince Russ to get a different bed?"

My humiliation was complete. "Don't worry! He's already working on it."

"Awesome. I'm so glad to hear it . . . or not hear it, in this case." A fevered blush had continued to spread across my face. As soon as my feet hit the ground, I practically raced toward my car. "Glad you both had fun last night!" He hollered after me, and I waved before slipping inside my car and leaving as fast as I could.

Yes, that was truly mortifying. Glancing around my apartment, I was happy that sound had never really been an issue here. My bedroom was in the middle of an exterior wall that had two separate rooms on either side, so I never heard the neighbors when I was in my room. Plus, there were a lot of older, retired people living in this community, so it was rarely rowdy.

The loud doorbell sounded, causing me to jump a mile. Glancing at the clock, I saw that Russ was almost thirty minutes earlier than he said he would be. Smiling, I went to the door, knowing this most likely meant he was super excited for tonight, as well.

Once again, I quickly checked my appearance in the mirror, pinching my cheeks and pressing my lips together to plump them and redistribute my lip-gloss.

Grabbing the doorknob, I turned it, smiling as I opened it—only to have the smile slip from my face, a shriek replacing it.

"Hey, Evie," Kory said, looking quite the worse for wear. "I finally made it home, baby."

Springing forward, I threw my arms around his neck, sobbing hysterically. His arms wrapped tightly around my waist and he squeezed me, burying his face into my hair.

"Man, I've missed you so bad, Evie," he whispered, his voice choked. "You have no idea how many times you've saved my life during the last six years. Thinking of you, and about coming home, where the only things that kept me going."

"Where were you?" I asked, pulling back slightly and shaking him. I could tell he'd lost a lot of weight. "Where have you been? We were told you were killed in action."

"Almost. I was almost killed in action. My wounds were serious, but the insurgents nursed me back to health so they could torture me. I've been in a prison camp all this time. I'm so happy the rest of my team escaped. How's Paul?"

My hand went to my throat as I realized this miracle had just thrown my entire life into a complete tailspin. I had no idea which direction was up and which direction was the right way to go. Having Kory here brought all my feelings flooding back, as strong as they'd ever been. But I loved Russ, too.

"Paul," I repeated, trying to push past the onslaught of equal parts joy and horror at Kory's return. "Paul . . . died."

Kory staggered backward as if struck by a heavy blow. Immediately, I took his arm, guiding him into the house and closing the door. Leading him to the couch, I encouraged him to sit. "When? What? How?" He finally managed to get out.

I toyed restlessly with my fingers, not

wanting to tell him the truth. Not right now. He'd just barely come home. Lifting my head, I stared sympathetically at him. "It wasn't long after he returned, only about two months. He never got over seeing you die and not being able to save you," I said. Pain flooded his features. "I found him in my parents' bathroom with a gun beside him. He left a note."

"No, no, no!" Kory said, running his hands over his short hair as he rocked back and forth. "This can't be happening. It can't be. I shot at those men so Paul could escape and come back to you."

"Apparently he couldn't get past it. I take the blame. I should've seen the signs, but I didn't."

Kory didn't speak, continuing to hold his head and rock with his grief.

The doorbell rang again, and I immediately knew it was Russ. "Wait here. I'll be right back," I said, dread filling me as I made my way to the door.

Quickly, I stepped outside and Russ immediately noticed my distress.

"What is it?" he asked, moving closer; but I stepped way, raising my hand.

"I'm going to need some time, please," I asked, wishing my voice wouldn't shake so badly.

"Time for what?"

"To think." Staring at him, I wondered if he could see the battle waging inside me. "Kory is alive, Russ! He's alive! He's been held prisoner this whole time we thought he was dead."

Russ's face blanched and he ran a hand

through his hair. "When did you find out? Are they sure it's him? There can be mix-ups, you know. When is he supposed to come back?"

"It's him, I'm certain. He's sitting on my couch right now. I just broke the news about Paul to him. I don't think he can handle hearing about us tonight, too. You need to leave."

He nodded, his jaw clenching as he shuffled his feet. "Where does this leave us, Evie?" I could hear the tension in his voice as he tried to hold it together.

Lowering my eyes, I couldn't meet his. "I'm not sure there even is an 'us' anymore, Russ."

"Damn it, Evie. I know you care about me. Doesn't that count for something?" He placed his hand on my shoulder and squeezed.

"It does. I love you, Russ." I snorted. "I intended to tell you that tonight. I guess I just did."

Instantly, I was in his embrace. "I love you, too, Evie. Please don't . . . I know it's hard . . . but don't. Don't leave me."

"I . . . I . . . ." I fumbled for my words, not knowing what to say. Finally, I stared up at him. "I need time, Russ. Lots of it. To try and sort things out—both in my heart and my head." Tears streamed down my face, but I couldn't stop. "This is his home. He lived here with me. We were getting married. I owe it to him to see if any of this will still work. He put his life on the line to save my brother. I owe him, Russ. I owe him so much. Please try to understand."

"But do you still love him, Evie?" he asked, lifting both hands to the sides of my face.

"I never stopped loving him." Russ's hands dropped away from me. "Now I just need to know if things are the same between us."

"A lot can happen in six years. You have no idea what he's gone through over there."

"On the contrary, given my line of work I know a lot more about what has gone on over there than most other people do. I may be just the person to help him."

Russ was silent, staring at me for several long hard moments. "All I can say is I love you, Evie. When you're ready—if you ever are—you know where to find me."

I couldn't think of anything else to say, so I simply stood there and watched him walk right out of my life.

CHAPTER SEVENTEEN
Russ

I couldn't stop shaking. Climbing into my vehicle, I stared at my hands, noticing the slight vibrations as I gripped the steering wheel, my emotions a total mix of horror and self-loathing. I should be happy that Kory was alive and able to come home. Sure, I didn't know the guy, but I knew enough about him. He was a real hero, the kind who stood up in the middle of battle to save his companions. I didn't need to know anything else about his character. That spoke volumes.

The gut kicker was this super, amazing, hero happened to hold the heart of my girlfriend. Yes, everything was new with us, but I'd easily begun thinking of her as mine, my heart laying claim to her. If it weren't for me, she wouldn't be alive. That formed a connection. That meant something. Didn't it?

Casting a glance toward the window of her

condo, it killed me to know she was in there with another man—another man she loved with all her heart. There was no way I could even compete. All that was left to do was to stay busy and let her come to terms with things on her own.

Reaching for the key with my shaky hand, I grabbed it and started my truck, slowly pulling out of the parking lot. I wasn't whole, though. My heart had been left back there with her.

Numbly, I made my way home, avoiding Dylan and Cami as I entered my apartment from the outside of the house. Everything was quiet. I tossed my keys on the coffee table and went straight to the fridge, pulling out not one, but two beers. Slouching into one of the leather chairs in my living room, I stared out the window at the night sky, trying to drink enough to fill the hollow section of my chest.

"This is ridiculous," I said softly, swallowing another large swig.

A knock sounded at the interior door between my apartment and the floors below. "Can I come in?" Dylan's muffled voice came through the wood.

"It's open," I said, which he probably knew anyway. I rarely locked that door, trusting Cami and him implicitly.

"What's going on?" he asked, his face a mask of concern as he stepped inside, coming to sit in the matching leather chair across from me. "I thought you were having dinner at Evie's house? We weren't expecting you home."

I stared at him, a knot forming in my throat.

"Six years he's been missing. Six years she waited for him. I finally find her and get her to come around, and he comes home." I snorted, wry laughter escaping me. "What are the odds?"

Dylan looked horrified, at least what I could see of his face in the dim light from the windows. "You're shittin' me?"

"Oh, how I wish I were," I said, sighing deeply.

"When did all this happen?"

"Just now. Apparently he arrived at her place right before I did, I guess." I snorted, again. "Except it's his place, too. He lived there with her before he deployed. It's a good thing he arrived when he did or he may have walked in on something he never wanted to see."

"Is she going to tell him about the two of you?" Dylan asked.

"I have no friggin' idea. All she said was she needed time to think and to find out if he still loved her like she loved him. But she did manage to throw an 'I love you, too' at me before I left."

"I can't even imagine what this must be like for her right now." Dylan ran a hand through his hair. "But what about you? What can I do to help you?"

"Just take me out back and shoot me." I knew I was being melodramatic at the moment, but it was truthfully how I felt.

"It probably wouldn't hurt you any worse," Dylan said, understanding my feelings completely.

"How do I even ask her to consider me?" I

asked Dylan. "She's been pining for him—pining—for six years. She practically took a vow of celibacy to remain true to him. I'm the one who talked her into more. I'm the one who messed up her plans. How can I ask her to forget the man she's been dying to have all this time in the hope that I can have a chance, too? He's had her heart for years. I've merely been given a sliver of it for a few weeks, and I had to fight for that sliver."

Pausing, I stared at him, misery filling my chest because I knew—I knew—there was no way I could ask for her to stay with me. Yes, I loved her. And the only way I could prove that I loved her was to let her go.

"If I would've had more time, maybe there would've been a chance, but now—I'm not even trying to fool myself."

"You need to let her go," Dylan said, giving voice to the words that threatened to end me. "I know it's going to be hard for you, but you've got to let her work through this on her own."

"Except she won't be on her own. She'll be living with the guy she's been longing for. It's kind of hard to get past someone you're actually living with." Again, I downed more beer, wishing I could just forget everything.

"So, let me ask you this. Would you want her to be with you knowing she still had unresolved feelings for someone else? Or do you want her to come to you because you're the only person she wants."

I sighed in exasperation. "You already know the answer to that."

"Then all the advice I can give is that you need to step back and give her all the time she needs. If she chooses you, then you'll know you're meant to have her. If she chooses him, then you know there's someone else meant for you. And if that's the case, don't miss out on the girl who was meant for you because you want to wallow in misery over the girl you can't have." Leaning forward, he placed a hand on my knee. "It may not seem like it right now, but this is all going to work out somehow, I promise."

"Can I ask a favor of you?" I stared seriously at him.

"Anything. You know that."

"Can you stop trying to help me feel better and just get plastered drunk with me instead? I think that's what I really need right now, a good old fashioned stone-cold drunk session."

Dylan grinned. "Do I need to go downstairs and get more beer?"

"I have a case in the fridge. Let's see what kind of damage we can do with that first." I took another swallow.

"Nah, I think you need to go out instead. Come on. Let's go down to the South Bend Bar. We'll drink, eat bar mix, throw some darts."

"Start a bar fight?" I asked, only halfway joking.

He shrugged. "If that's what you really need, I got your back."

"What I really need is to be eating dinner with a pretty blonde and making love to her all night long. But, instead, some other guy is there, eating my dinner and most likely doing my girl." The thought made me completely nauseated. I stared at Dylan. "Do you think she will sleep with him, too?" I could hardly spit the words out.

Dylan shrugged and glanced down at the floor. "I don't know, bro. But I'd like to think if I'd been missing for six years that my fiancée would happily welcome me back into her bed. I know that's the first place I'd want to be. If she hasn't told him about you, well, it would seem she's holding out on him, wouldn't it?"

"Shit." I said, hating that he so readily confirmed my own worries. "And if she does sleep with him, I can't blame her. Not without coming off like a complete prick."

Dylan stood, grabbing the beer beside me and settling back into the chair. "On second thought, it might be best if we stay here instead. I think you need a little down-time."

I didn't say anything, simply continuing to drink as I stared blankly off into space, knowing Evie was going to sleep with someone else and there wasn't a damn thing I could do about it.

***

It had been a week and I still hadn't heard from her, but the news of Kory's rescue was splashed all over every newspaper and television station across the country. Everyone was touting his return as a miracle—even Evie, her happy, teary face appearing beside his on more than one occasion, as she was repeatedly interviewed. Kory was being hailed the hero, even given a Medal of Honor.

While I was truly happy he'd been found and

returned home, I couldn't help staring at all the images of Evie. I studied them all in detail, thinking she looked happy, but there was also a hint of sorrow in her eyes. It was the only clue I had that she might be suffering as well.

Staring at my phone, I quickly typed out three words, but I didn't hit send; instead, I stared at them, pondering the very short time we'd shared together. Her face was constantly in my mind, remembering the day I'd saved her, the first time I'd met her in her office, and how attracted I'd been to her.

Thoughts of her draped languidly across my bed after hours of losing ourselves in each other threatened to tear my heart to shreds. I hated knowing that she was wrapped up like that in someone else's arms now.

True, I had no actual proof of that, but the more time that went by without any word from her seemed to be sending me a certain message.

"Text her," Cami said, coming into the kitchen and finding me aimlessly staring at the unsent text.

I grappled for something to say, but it didn't matter, she'd caught me. "I'm not sure she wants to hear from me. I'm thinking her silence is her answer."

"It might be," Cami snapped, catching me by surprise. "But she owes it to you to tell you in person, not to just leave you standing here guessing. If you ask me, this behavior of hers comes off as blatantly rude. She knows how serious the two of you were. She can't just dump you like this."

"Maybe she wasn't serious," I said, my heart aching. "Maybe it was only ever me. She tried to push me away on more than one occasion, you know."

"Then she's stupid," Cami said, meeting my stare eye to eye. "Anyone who would let you go for someone else is too stupid to have you to begin with."

I couldn't help chuckling. She was really upset. "Tell me how you really feel, why don't you?"

She didn't laugh; instead, she placed Piper in her swing and wound it up. Coming to me, she placed her hands on either side of my face. "I love you so much, Russ, and so does Dylan. You're our *family*, and I can't stand to see anyone in our family hurting the way that you are right now."

Gritting my teeth, I struggled with my emotions. "Am I that obvious?"

"You've always pinned your heart to your sleeve. It's obvious to everyone who knows you that you're hurting." Popping up on her toes, she kissed my cheek. "Get hold of her. I'm serious. It's time the two of you got everything out on the table between you. She owes that to you." Releasing me, she moved about the kitchen gathering things to make dinner.

I wasn't sure if Evie owed me anything, but I did really want to talk and see what—if any—resolution had been made on her part. Glancing at my phone, I stared at the three words I'd typed.

I miss u.

Hitting send, I waited, wondering if she would reply at all or just ignore me. A few seconds later, my phone buzzed.

I miss u 2. Can we talk?

Name the time and place. I will be there.

Your place? Now?

My heart raced at her words and I couldn't deny I was hopeful. I'll be waiting, I replied.

CHAPTER EIGHTEEN
Evie

I was shaking so badly I hardly managed to get my keys out of the ignition. Slipping them into my purse, I exited the car and stared at the tall narrow staircase that went up the side of the grand house to Russ' apartment.

Truthfully, I'd been relieved to get his text, not knowing how he was feeling or how to approach this subject with him, again. It seemed so difficult a thing to do; but, once again, he made the difficult easy with just three simple words.

I miss u.

And those three little words nearly tore my heart to pieces. I had no idea when my life had become so dramatic, but I hated it. I longed for the simple days of living in one happy relationship with one happy man. I knew I could find that spot again, but the question that remained was which man would I be with?

Suddenly the door to Russ' apartment opened and he was standing there on the landing, looking as handsome as ever in a pair of worn jeans, boots and a white wife-beater.

"You coming up, or you just gonna stare at the door all day?" he asked. The sound of his voice rippled through me—just hearing him caused goose bumps to rise on the surface of my skin. He didn't wait for me to answer, instead disappearing back inside and leaving the door open for me.

That didn't bode well. I expected he'd be upset—it was only natural. I'd left him hanging far too long while I mulled everything over. I needed to own up to my decisions.

Slowly, and carefully, I made my way up those steps, not really knowing what was waiting for me at the end of them. I found him sitting in one of his leather club chairs, rubbing his forehead as if he were in pain. Quietly, I shut the door behind me and slipped into the chair, across from him.

"You look nice," he said finally, his gaze traveling over me and I could easily see the desire in his eyes. "I wasn't really expecting you to answer me. At least not right away, since you're normally at work right now."

"I cancelled my afternoon appointments when I got your text. I decided this was more important."

He nodded. "And this way he doesn't know you're here either, does he?"

"No. He doesn't."

"Does he know about me at all?" he asked,

pain radiating through his voice.

I shook my head, feeling every bit like the awful woman I was. "I don't know how to tell him about you." There had been many opportunities, but somehow I couldn't seem to utter the words. Even when Kory had asked me about the dinner I'd been preparing the night he came home, I'd brushed it off as a fun evening of pampering with a friend. I knew Kory thought I was talking about a girlfriend, and I didn't do anything to change his assumption.

"He's been missing for six years! Does he really think you just sat around twirling your thumbs while you waited for him?" He was angry. I didn't blame him. He should be angry.

Tears filled my eyes. I hated hurting him. "He didn't realize the others in his unit thought he was dead when they left. He's been hoping for rescue this whole time, so yes, he believed I was waiting for him."

"And you didn't correct him?"

"It was true! Why would I correct it? I have waited for him . . . the whole time he was gone I was praying for this very miracle. If I would've had any idea that it was going to come true—."

"You would've never jumped into bed with me," he supplied, looking sick. "I get it, Evie. I really do. I just want you to do me the justice of telling me it's over to my face."

Letting the tears fall over the rims of my eyes, I stared at him, shaking my head. "I haven't called you because I don't want it to be over. I don't want it to be finished between us. I wasn't lying when I said I loved you. I do love you. I love him, too, though. I don't know how to fix this." The words escaped me, almost a hysterical sounding. "I have no idea what to do. I'm completely and totally in love with two different men. I want you both."

Russ stared at me for several long moments. "Have you slept with him?" he asked, causing my heart to come to almost a full stop.

"I haven't. Because I need to figure out what is happening with you before I make that commitment to him, again." Dropping my gaze to my skirt, I picked off a stray hair that had landed there. "Kory hasn't even been sleeping in the same bed with me. That's been his choice. He has nightmares, and he's clearly suffering with some form of PTSD, which is totally to be expected. He's afraid he'll hurt me, so he won't sleep with me. He's been on the couch since he came home."

Russ' face was a combination of both relief and frustration. "Don't sleep with him, Evie. Please. I'm begging you. I know you have a past with him, but I believe you and I could have a future together. I don't want to lose you."

Sobs escaped me and I didn't know how to answer him. "I know I prayed for this, but I never really expected it to happen. I miss you so much. I was enjoying discovering our new relationship and seeing where it would go. I'd be lying if I said being with you didn't start a healing process for me. But I have no idea where to go from here, Russ.

"I planned a future with him. We dreamed about the things that were in store for us—

careers, children, and a house of our own. We had a future together, and we were both excited to live it.

"My future with you is uncertain. We never discussed those things because we never had the opportunity to get that far. What if you and I fizzle out after a couple months? Just because we are getting along good now doesn't mean it will last. We barely even know each other. Don't you see? I'm torn between what is a possibility and what was a sure thing for me. How do I risk that?"

"I don't know what to tell you, Evie, except that I love you. I don't want to be your second choice. If you stay with me, I want it to be because you believe we might have a future together."

"I love you, too." He loved me. My heart soared and then crashed again. When did the world become so complicated?

Rising, I went to him, settling myself on his lap and taking his face in my hands. He slipped his hand behind my neck and pulled me toward him.

Kissing me deeply, I could feel both the tension and the relief in him as our mouths tangled together. I didn't protest when he pulled the pins out of my hair, sinking his fingers into it.

"I've missed you so much," he said, staring intensely into my eyes. "You have no idea."

"I've missed you, too," I replied, my eyes never leaving his face, all the love in the world captured in his gaze. I didn't doubt his words.

They were apparent every second he was with me.

He kissed me again, and it was hot and intense, his hands roaming over my body familiarly. I wanted to lose myself in him. I wanted to let him sweep me off my feet and carry me off to bed, but I couldn't. Doing that wouldn't be fair to Kory or him.

Pulling away, I tried to hide my tears as I straightened my clothes and gathered my purse and keys. I needed to leave before we crossed a line I would regret later.

Russ didn't say anything, not even trying to stop me or force me to change my mind. Part of me was angry with him for it. I wanted him to fight for me. I wanted him to tell me that he couldn't live without me and that my leaving would destroy him. But it never happened. He never said that.

"Goodbye, Russ," I said, my words coming out forced, leaving a hole in my chest as I looked at him.

"You're choosing Kory, aren't you?" he asked, the pain evident in his voice as he stared at me. I wanted so badly for him to pull me back to him and make love to me, but I knew he had too much honor to do that. He'd respect my choice whether I wanted him to or not.

"I am. He's the innocent victim in all of this. It's not fair for me to leave him over something he had no control over." I felt like the worst person on the planet, and my heart was breaking into so many pieces I was sure it wouldn't ever be found again.

"I love you, Evie," he said, his eyes full of intense sorrow and I wanted nothing more than to kiss away his pain.

"I love you too, Russ. I'm so sorry. Oh my gosh, I'm so sorry." Quickly heading out the door, I knew this would be the last time I ever saw him. I hurried to my car, starting the engine. I couldn't help myself, glancing one more time at Russ' apartment. He was standing on the upper wide porch that ran across the entire length of the house, leaning against the railing.

"Don't go." He mouthed to me.

"I have to." I mouthed back, allowing the tears to streak down my face as I put the car in gear and backed out of the driveway.

CHAPTER NINETEEN
Russ

"Mr. Weston? Is that you?" I vaguely recognized the voice that called to me, but I couldn't quite place it. Glancing around the bar, I tried to find who was speaking. A pretty brunette girl waved at me, and I smiled widely.

"Misty! What are you doing here?" I asked, turning to throw my dart at the board before facing her.

"I meet with some of the other secretaries once a week for drinks. I never thought I'd run into you, here," she replied, smiling.

"My buddies and I come here sometimes because it's close to work," I replied, again making note of how hot she was. "You want to come play with me?" I asked, not caring that I was totally plastered drunk and playing a game with myself at the moment.

"I don't think I've ever played darts," she said, glancing at the woman she was sitting next to.

"No worries. I'll teach you," I said, staring at her invitingly.

"Okay." She seemed hesitant at first, but she got up and joined me. Her friend smiled as she watched the two of us, and I winked at her. She was cute, too.

"You want to learn?" I asked. "I have two sides. Plenty of room for you both."

The woman laughed and shook her head. "No thanks. I'm just an observer when it comes to darts. Besides, I'm still waiting for some others to arrive."

"Suit yourself, but if you change your mind, you know where to find us. By the way, I'm Russ." I held my hand out to her.

"Marie," she replied, taking my hand and shaking it. "It's a pleasure to meet you. How do you know Misty?"

I laughed, glancing at Misty. "I was sort of dating her boss—kinda. At least I thought we were dating. She might have just been passing the time." I knew Evie wasn't just passing the time with me, but the hurt words bubbled out of me before I could manage to stop them.

"So, it didn't work out then?" she asked, sympathetically.

"Not even close." I didn't want anyone's sympathy.

"I'm sorry to hear that."

"Me, too; but hey, there's other fish in the sea, right?" I glanced back at Misty, thinking she was a pretty gorgeous fish. "You ready to play some darts?"

She blushed and I liked it. "I'm ready."

"So, you just hold the dart like this, between your thumb and forefinger. Aim at the board and throw."

"That doesn't seem too hard," she said, mimicking my movements. "Oh my gosh! Look! I almost got a bull's-eye!"

I laughed at how excited she seemed. "See! I knew you were a natural," I exclaimed, gathering her into my arms and placing a kiss near her ear.

"You're drunk," she said, pulling away from me.

"I am. But that's not going to stop me from having a good time with you." I replied, running a hand down her back.

"Is it me you really want, or my boss?" she asked, her bottom lip moving into a pout. "I know she turned you down."

"Which leaves me all nice and open for you," I explained, wanting nothing more than to bury my sorrows. I hated the hollowness I was feeling.

"What if she still wants you, too?" she asked, trailing her finger over my pecs.

"She's made it pretty clear who she wants," I said, pulling her closer.

"Sometimes the mouth and the heart speak two different languages."

She'd lost me. "Huh?" I tried to follow what she was saying.

"I'm saying that she may have made her choice, but she looks miserable." Her eyes traveled over me. "Almost as miserable as you.

I think she's missing you. She's not happy—not like you'd expect her to be over finding out her fiancé isn't dead. He doesn't look too happy either, for that matter."

Releasing her, I went over to the board and picked out all the darts while I pondered her comments. I wasn't going to lie, it made me feel great knowing Evie was miserable. Not that I wanted her to be that way, but it was a whole helluva lot better than the scenario that had been playing out in my head for the last week since I'd spoken with her. I kept imagining her wrapped up in his arms as he made passionate love to her. I could hear the soft sounds and the moans she made as he touched her intimately.

Suddenly I needed another drink. I signaled the bartender and he poured me another mug from the tap and slid it down the bar toward me.

"Don't you think you've had enough?" Misty asked, eyeing me with concern. "I can give you a ride home."

I snorted. "I'm fine." I handed some of the darts to her. The last place I wanted to be was home. I hadn't even been able to sleep in my own bed. Every time I looked at it, I could see Evie there, her hair spread over my pillows and her beautiful body draped languidly across my sheets. I could still hear her laughter over the squeaky springs—laughter that had turned into moans of pleasure for both of us. I hated that bed, now. The first thing I'd done when she left me that day was to order a new bed. Hopefully it would arrive soon. The couch was damn uncomfortable and not nearly long enough for me to stretch out comfortably. And then there were those damn nightmares. Ever since we'd called it quits, they'd come back with a vengeance—but often Evie was in Cami's place now. I did everything I could to stay awake as long as possible each night.

Throwing my dart, I stepped aside, drinking a large portion of my beer while she took her turn. "Are you sure you've never played this before? You seem damn good for a beginner. You're kicking my butt."

"I'm not drunk, and you are," she replied with a laugh. "This is all an illusion, one I'm betting you won't remember tomorrow."

My laugh mingled with hers. "You might be right, but that's fine by me. Just point me in the right direction to find oblivion and I'll happily go there."

Sighing, she stared at me. "It's pitiful seeing you reduced to this, Russ. Catch a cab and go home. Sleep it off for a while."

"I can't go home. I see her everywhere." Angrily, I threw my next dart and it hit the board loudly, bouncing off and clattering to the floor. I stared at the dart before turning to Misty. "She was only at my place a few times, but that was enough. All I see are my memories with her. They keep playing over and over again in my head, and I can't make them stop."

"Have you told her this?" Misty asked, and I saw her signal the barkeep to cut me off and he nodded. I was too soused to care.

"No. She made her choice. Besides, there's no way I can compete with Mr. Hero without looking like a first class jerk."

Carefully, she removed the darts from my hands and placed them on the bar. "You're a hero too, Russ. Everyone knows that. You saved Evie, and you saved those kids from that fire."

"Yeah, but he's a decorated war hero. He stood in the line of fire and sacrificed himself for his platoon. There's no comparison between his heroics and mine."

"You walked into a burning building, risking your own life for those kids. I'm sorry, but I bet their parents would claim your heroics are just as good as his. It's not a competition. You're both good men."

"That might be, but we are both good men in love with the same woman. Unfortunately for me, that woman loves him more. Did you know she hasn't even told him about me?"

Misty guided me over to a stool at the bar. "Come sit by me." She gestured to the seat and I sat. "No. I didn't know that, but it surprises me. Dr. McKnight has always been very forthcoming. She's not one to keep secrets."

"She told me to my face that he didn't know about me. I was supposed to meet her for dinner at her house that night. She was cooking for me when he showed up. And she even came outside to talk to me when I arrived. He had to have asked who I was. Why didn't she tell him? Did she lie about me then?" Reaching into the bowl of nuts, I pulled out a peanut and began crushing it on the bar in front of me.

Misty placed a hand over mine, stilling me. "I don't have the answers to that. All I can tell you is that when you started coming around, she was happier than I'd ever seen her. And now that you're not around anymore, she's the most unhappy I've ever seen her." She paused for a moment and I stared at her hand that was covering mine. She continued, "I didn't know her before—you know, when Kory was declared dead—so I can't compare this with that, but I do know she's hurting and barely holding it together."

I didn't reply, instead just sat there lost in the haze of my own mind. My vision was blurry and the room shifted heavily, causing a wave of dizziness to come over me.

"I need to go home," I mumbled, feeling like I was going to pass out. Standing, I dug my keys out of my pocket and Misty grabbed them.

"Oh no you don't. You're way too drunk to drive."

"I know that. I was going to ask you to drive me home."

"Do you even remember how to get there?" she asked, laughing.

"Of course I do. I'm not *that* drunk."

"Are you sure? You're swaying and slurring your words."

"I am?" I asked, paying special attention to my speech. "I don't notice anything different."

She laughed, again. "I'm sure you don't." Standing, she reached into her purse and threw a few bills on the table. "Sorry to ditch you," she said, looking at the other girl . . . what was her name? Sybil? Sherri? It definitely started with an S.

"Nice meeting you . . . ." I trailed off.

"Marie," she replied, smiling. Damn. I wasn't even close. "Nice to meet you, too. I hope you have a better night."

I waved a hand in dismissal. "Nah, I'm fine. Nothing a good nap won't cure."

"Come on," Misty said, slipping her arm around my waist and guiding me toward the door.

"Dang, you're short," I said, clutching her as I tried to maintain my balance. "When did you get so short?"

The sound of her laughter tinkled through the room right before we stepped outside. "I'm the same height I've always been."

"Really?" I replied, finding that odd. "You must've been a really tall child then."

She laughed and I did, too, though I couldn't remember why we were laughing.

"Which car is yours?"

I pointed to the far end of the lot. "That big black truck over by the fence."

"There are two black trucks by the fence," she pointed out.

"Mine is the cool one."

Chuckling, she continued in the direction of the fence. "And what exactly makes it cool?"

"That awesome fire department sticker in the window," I replied. "I work for the fire department. Did you know that?"

"Yes, I knew that. We talked about you rescuing Evie and those kids earlier, remember?"

"Oh yeah." I heard my truck beep; signaling

she'd unlocked the doors from the key fob. "That was scary, you know."

"What was?" Opening the door, she waited patiently for me to climb inside. I leaned my head back against the headrest and she shut the door, suddenly appearing at the other side and climbing in. I couldn't remember what we were talking about. "Where's your house?"

"Across the street from the Battery by White Point Garden," I said, knowing I didn't need to give her any other directions. Everyone in Charleston knew where the historic Battery was and the role the defensive seawall had played in the Civil War.

"Wow. You live in one of those houses?" Misty asked, clearly impressed.

"I do, along with my two best friends. They live in the bottom two floors of the house and I live on the third floor."

"That must be awesome. I'd love to live in a place like that. I've toured a couple of the homes they have open to the public. They're incredible."

"They are," I agreed, closing my eyes as another wave of nausea threatened me. I'd definitely had too much to drink. "How are you going to get back if you're driving me?"

"I can call a cab. It's not a big deal. I just wanted to make sure you got home safely."

"Oh. Okay. Well, I'll pay for the cab." Opening my eyes, I stared at her while she drove. Either she didn't notice or she was pretending not to. She was really pretty. "Do you have a boyfriend?" I asked.

Glancing at me, she laughed. "Now there's a random subject change if I ever heard one."

"Well, do you?"

She shook her head. "Nope. The last guy I went out with was a first class asshole. I decided to take a break from men for a while after him."

"Hmmm. So you're trying women out now?"

Loud laughter burst through her lips and I couldn't help but smiling. "No. I'm not into women either. I'm just doing the solo thing for a while."

I nodded. "You're smart to do that. No sense rushing into something else that might end up the same way."

"This is true."

I continued to stare at her. "You and me, we should form a club."

Raising an eyebrow, she cast a sidelong look at me. "What kind of club?"

"A loser's club. You have to be dumped to join. I don't want none of those happy romantic people in our club."

Laughing again, she nodded. "I hear you on that one."

"It could be fun. We can all hang out together, no reason to hook up with anyone, and we can just kick back and enjoy life."

"Actually, I have a very nice group of platonic friends. We often go out and do stuff together. We're going to the lake this weekend if you want to join us."

"Are you going to *the* lake?" I asked, referring to the one Evie had nearly drowned in.

She nodded. "We are. Is that a problem?"

Yes. I was tired of seeing things that reminded me of Evie. "No, but you might have to remind me again, later. I'm a little drunk right now."

"Just a little," she replied, smiling.

"Turn right here," I said, gesturing to my street. "It's the third house on the right, the one with the black Camaro in front of it."

"I love Camaros. Is it yours?"

"No. It belongs to my best friend, Dylan, and his wife, Cami. This is actually their second black Camaro. He traded in his old one for a newer model. Who does that? Usually people like to mix it up a bit, or at least change the color. Not Dylan. He's a die-hard black Camaro guy."

"Well, I think he has great taste."

"Yeah, he has a truck, too, plus Cami has another car."

"Three cars? For the two of them?" Misty asked as she pulled in front of the house and parked.

"Yep. They're loaded."

"What do they do to make all this money?" she asked. "I know these houses are expensive."

"Actually, Dylan is a firefighter with me. He got a big inheritance from his dad and he invested a lot of it into some very lucrative projects and made a bundle on his own. He doesn't have to work, he does it because he wants to. Cami is a stay at home mom. She just had the most beautiful baby."

"Sounds like they're great people. I'd love to meet them sometime."

"I'm sure that can be arranged."

Misty climbed out of the vehicle and came around to my side, helping me out. Once again, she slipped her arm around my waist. "Where to?"

I pointed to the steep stairs. "That way."

"You sure you can make it up those?" she asked warily.

"I'm good."

Together we stumbled toward them and I noticed she clung heavily to the rail with her free hand and she helped me up. When we reached the door she lifted my keys, looking at them. "Which one opens your door?"

"That one," I replied, pointing it out. She quickly unlocked it and guided me inside.

"Let's get you tucked into bed, shall we?"

"No! Not the bedroom. I can't sleep in the bedroom."

"Okay," she said, slightly drawing the word out after my neurotic outburst. "Where do you want to go, then?"

"To the couch, please. I've been sleeping on the couch lately."

"It looks like a very comfortable couch." She guided me in that direction and I plopped down on it.

"Are you going to be all right?" she asked. "Is there anything else I can do for you before I call a cab?"

Staring at her, I couldn't get over how beautiful she was. "Stay with me," I said, not caring if I sounded like a fool.

"Excuse   me?"   she   asked,   fidgeting

nervously.

"I won't do anything. I just don't want to be alone right now. Stay with me for a while." I extended my hand to her, my arm feeling so heavy that it took an extreme amount of effort.

She studied me for a moment. "I'm not sure that's a good idea."

"Just for a little while," I said, seeing the struggle in her eyes. She wanted to stay. I was sure of it.

Hesitantly, she slipped her hand into mine and I pulled her down onto my lap. A soft gasp of surprise escaped her and I stared at her lips that were now very close to mine. I kind of wanted to kiss her, but I knew that wouldn't be fair.

"I'm tired," I said, leaning to the side and taking her with me as I stretched out on the couch. She was stiff for a moment and I pulled her closer. "I just need to hold someone— someone who isn't her," I whispered into her ear and she relaxed against me.

The scent of her perfume, or maybe it was her shampoo, filled my senses. She smelled different then Evie, but still so good. They were about as opposite as two women could get as far as coloring went, but they were both beautiful and sweet. And right now, at this moment, Misty felt so good in my arms.

"I wonder what my life would be like right now if I'd met you first?" I whispered, my eyes drifting closed heavily.

If she replied, I never knew it.

SMOLDER

CHAPTER TWENTY
Evie

I was doing it again . . . staring off aimlessly into space, that is. Thank goodness my last appointment of the day had come and gone. My mind was all over the place, except for my job. I felt pretty much useless these days.

A soft knock sounded at my door and Misty stepped inside. "Dr. McKnight? Can I talk to you for a minute?"

"My door is always open to you, Misty. You know that. Have a seat." Gesturing toward one of the leather chairs, I moved around my desk coming to join her.

She sat down, nervously playing with a button on the bottom of her pink blouse. I couldn't recall a time I'd ever seen Misty out of sorts. Something was clearly bothering her.

"What's on your mind?" I asked, suddenly hoping she wasn't giving me notice. Misty was the best secretary I'd ever had and I really liked her.

"Well, as you know, I occasionally go out for drinks with some of the other secretaries in the building."

"Yes," I replied, wondering where she was going with this.

"I went out last night and ran into Russ at the bar."

Just hearing his name on her lips made my heart clench as my pulse picked up speed. "Oh?" I said, hoping I sounded casual. "How is he?"

Sighing heavily, her shoulders slumped. "Honestly? He's miserable. He was drunk off his rocker and I had to drive him home so he wouldn't kill himself or someone else."

Wow. I didn't know what I'd been expecting her to say, but it certainly wasn't that.

"Once I got him home, he asked me to stay with him."

Again, she was fumbling with the button on her blouse. "Did you sleep with him?" I didn't want to ask that question, but I couldn't seem to hold the words in my mouth.

"Oh no! Nothing like that!" She looked horrified. "He just asked me to stay with him. He said he was lonely and he . . . ." Glancing at me hesitantly, she shook her head. "He said he needed to hold someone who wasn't you."

Ouch. That stung me hardcore.

"He pulled me down on the couch next to him and wrapped his arms around me. Then he passed out. I stayed with him for another thirty minutes, just to make sure he was really asleep, and then I hid his keys behind his television and typed my number into his phone and told him to call me so I could tell him where they were. After that, I called a cab and went back to the bar to get my car."

"Did he call you?" I was like a person staring at a horrific train wreck. I didn't want to see or know the gory details, but I couldn't manage to look away.

She nodded. "Yes. He called me this morning, apologizing profusely for how he'd behaved. I'm pretty sure he was quite mortified."

"I'm sure he was," I replied, my mind not quite able to get the image of Russ holding Misty out of my head. "Is there a reason you're telling me all this?" I wanted to get this awkward conversation over with.

"Well, he's hurting really badly, but he's trying to honor your wishes and move on. I felt bad for him and invited him to go out with a bunch of friends and me."

"Like on a date?" I couldn't help the way my eyes widened, feeling like I'd just been punched in the stomach.

"No!" she almost shouted in her rush to explain. "No, it's just a group of friends, no pairing off or dates. They're just a bunch of friends I hang out with occasionally—both guys and girls. I thought it might do him some good to get out and meet some new people. You know, to help take his mind off things."

I loved Misty. She was so sweet and caring. I also wanted to strangle her. I wasn't sure why. Obviously I didn't expect Russ to pine for me for the rest of his life, but I thought maybe he'd wallow a little longer than this. My heart hurt.

"Is that okay with you?" Misty continued. "I know it's awkward, since we work together. And I certainly didn't plan to run into him, but I did. I couldn't just leave him suffering that way. It was so sad."

The knife in my chest turned painfully, again, at her unspoken implication. He was hurting because of me; and because she knew me, she felt responsible to see to his wellbeing. It made total sense to my head, but my heart was having none of it. It wanted to shout at her and tell her to back off, that he belonged to me.

"I think you're very kind to introduce him to other people. I'm sure it would be very helpful for him to get out and socialize with others." I was totally lying—well, not totally. It would be good for him to get out. I just wished it could be with me. Then I thought of Kory and felt even worse. I made a commitment to him. I was his fiancée, and I owed him my loyalty.

"Have you told Kory about him, yet?" she asked.

I shook my head. "No, but I plan to this weekend. He's been through so much since he got home—hearing about Paul's death, trying to readjust to life, getting his appointments set up for his therapist, and trying to find a new job. It's all been thrown at him at once." I stared seriously at her. "He's struggling, too. His nightmares are horrendous. He won't even sleep in the same bed as me for fear he'll hurt me somehow." I wasn't sure why I was telling her all of this, but I couldn't seem to stop. The words were bubbling out of me before I could even consider them. "We haven't even slept together. I'm not sure why. I think he wants to, but he seems scared."

"It's been six years since he's been with you. Neither of you are the same people you were when he left for his tour."

"I know. So much has happened. But that's all the more reason for me to stick by him. He's been through hell for all those years. He almost gave his life for my brother and his unit members. Now he's lost my brother, his best friend, along with all those years of his life. For me to leave him now would be the most horrible, awful thing anyone could do to him."

"Are you trying to convince me, or yourself?" Misty asked, and my breath caught.

"I'm not trying to convince anyone," I replied indignantly. "I've made my choice."

"That's all I needed to know," she replied, rising. "Please know I'm so sorry you've been placed in the middle of this. I can't even imagine what it must be like to be in your shoes right now. I just wanted to make sure it wouldn't harm our relationship if I invite Russ to do things with my friends and me."

"You have my blessing." It was all I could do to force the words out. "I want him to be happy, too." That, at least, was the truth.

"Me, too. He's such a nice guy."

That was the understatement of the century. "I agree. He's wonderful." I caught myself staring at the door long after she'd exited the room and gone home for the night. My phone buzzed, interrupting my musings and I glanced down at it.

Finished for the night? The text from Kory made me smile. I'd just helped him get a new phone, but texting was a fairly new concept for him, seeing that he wasn't doing much chatting with anyone while he was a prisoner.

On my way now, I typed back. Can't wait 2 C U.

Same here, he replied. Hurry. I miss you.

***

"Hey, you," I said, entering the condo and tossing my keys and briefcase onto the stand near the door. "What are these delicious smells I'm smelling? Are you cooking for me?"

Kory laughed lightly, not looking away from the pot he was stirring, and it made my heart soar. He rarely laughed these days. "I would hardly call macaroni and cheese out of a box cooking, but I wanted to do something nice for you. I know things have been rough, and I've been pretty moody since I got back." Finally, he glanced up, making eye contact. "I just wanted you to know it doesn't have anything to do with you. I'm simply trying to sort things out in my head."

"I haven't thought that at all," I said, kicking off my heels and moving beside him. I placed a quick kiss against his cheek before going to the cupboard to get some dishes. Right now, in this moment, things between us almost felt normal, like the old days. This was definitely the most relaxed I'd seen him since he came home.

I hadn't pressed him too much after his initial arrival. Knowing that thinking about what he had been through was painful for him, I was trying to patiently wait for him to talk to me when he was ready. Mostly we'd discussed obvious things like Paul, and how much he'd missed me while he was gone. He spent most of the daylight hours at his parents' house, while I worked, and we'd had dinner a couple of times with my parents—but he hadn't breathed a word about what had been done to him. Not to any of us that I was aware of.

Hopefully the military was doing a good job of taking care of that. Apparently, he'd been through two weeks of therapy here in the states before he reappeared in my life.

"I was too messed up to come home right then." He'd told me when I asked him why the military hadn't notified his parents or me about him. "I needed some time before you found out, so I asked them to let me wait until after treatment. I figured it would be easier to keep you in the dark than have to wait, anxiously, until you could see me."

His words troubled me, but I left them alone, wanting him to continue to work through his issues in his own manner. He'd faithfully met with an Army psychiatrist every day, continuing his therapy. I did think it was helping, since he was starting to seem much more relaxed than when he first arrived. Whatever was going on with him couldn't be rushed. He'd lived through six years of who knew what? It could very well take him six years, or more, to work through everything. All I knew was I wanted him to find peace.

"How was your day?" he asked, pulling me back into the conversation.

"Long," I replied truthfully. "I'm glad it's over."

"I'm glad your home. I've been wanting to talk to you."

Attempting to mask my physical reaction to his words, I smiled, trying not to stiffen. His words both pleased and scared me. I wasn't sure if I was ready to hear the things he had to tell me.

"Well, I'm here. Feel free to talk away."

"After dinner," he said. "I want to enjoy a nice meal with you first."

That sounded foreboding. "Okay." I seriously felt like I spent my days walking on eggshells around him. I was terrified of doing something that might trigger an awful memory or make him uncomfortable somehow.

Carrying the pot to the table, he set it on a hot pad and began dishing food for both of us. I went to the wine rack and got a bottle, grabbing a couple of glasses, too.

Kory snorted. "Wine with Mac-n-Cheese?" he asked, smiling slightly.

"Only the best for my guy," I replied with a grin.

"You're too good to me," he said, sitting down and watching me as I poured our drinks. A wistful look passed over his face. "There were days I would've sold my soul to have a bottle of wine—or anything for that matter—drugs, alcohol, something to slit my own throat with."

Dropping to my seat, I stared at him, hoping abject horror wasn't written all over my face. I'd never heard him talk this way—ever. Kory was one of the most upbeat, positive people I knew. I didn't like hearing him sound so—broken. Yes, he had moments were the light really touched his eyes and he seemed happy he was home. However, most of the time he was quiet and sullen, following me with his stare as he sat lost in his own thoughts—thoughts I was terrified to ask him about, so I said nothing.

"I can't imagine what you must've gone through," I said, softly, not wanting to scare him away from talking.

"No, you can't imagine, and I don't ever want to tell you about it. I don't want to relive it and I don't want you to know." Capturing my gaze, he gave a wry smile. "I'd like you to keep the innocence that still shines in your eyes."

My heart clenched like it was in a vise. Just hearing these words from him led my mind to horrific places. If he was unwilling to share with me, then it was really bad. In the past, he'd shared everything with me.

"I simply want you to know that you are safe now—here in our home, and here with me. I love you. I never stopped loving you, and I will always be here for you. I give you my word. We'll get through this, both of us, together."

"Thank you." He made no move to eat, simply staring at me as if I were a mirage that might disappear. "That means a lot."

"I'd do anything for you."

"I know." He paused, still not eating. "Every day I wake up thinking I'll be back in that hole. Then I realize I'm here with you. I keep waiting to find out I'm hallucinating, that they've given me some drug that's made me go mad. If I really am crazy, and this is all some dream, then I hope I never wake up."

"What can I do to help you, Kory? Anything. Name it. I want to help you, but I don't know how."

"You're already doing it," he replied. "Just having you here with me is the best medicine I could ever receive. Don't give up on me. Not yet. I just need more time."

"I'd never give up on you," I replied, meaning every word.

CHAPTER TWENTY-ONE
Russ

Sadly, I was starting to believe in all that love-at-first-sight bullshit Cami and Dylan had been spouting off about for years. If I hadn't seen their love story in action, I would've never believed it. There was no denying the heat that radiated between the two of them from the moment Dylan laid eyes on her. He wanted her.

The same could be said for me. I'd seen Evie after I rescued her and something just clicked inside me. I wanted her and no one else, to the point of it constantly consuming my thoughts. However, unlike Cami and Dylan, I seemed to have made a royal botch job of my romantic scenario. Things were definitely not working out in my favor.

That mess had now led to me being included in a barbeque at the lake with Misty and all her friends. Misty was the only person I knew there; and while everyone was completely nice and welcoming, I noticed that I was following her around like a lost puppy, feeling a bit out of my element.

Grabbing a beer, I walked away from the barbeque pavilion and stood at the edge of the lake, watching the water ripple in soft gentle splashes against the shore. Slowly, my eyes drifted out to the place Evie had gone under— the place where both my life and hers had changed courses.

Well, at least my life had. Hers seemed to be trucking along just fine back on her original course. I didn't fault her. I would've made the exact same decision she did, if the situation were reversed. How could I walk away from someone I'd been crazy in love with all those years for someone I'd known for a few weeks? It didn't make any sense. She had totally done the right thing. Totally.

I intended to keep telling myself this until I believed it.

"Hey you." Misty's voice broke into my musings. "You doing okay?"

Glancing at her, I gave a half snort. "Just giving myself pep talks until I believe them. How about you?" My eyes never left her as I took a swallow of my beer. Damn she was pretty; and that bikini she was wearing, with the wrap around sarong, totally highlighted her rockin' body.

"I'm good." She smiled at me. "I'm really happy you came. Everyone seems to like you."

Briefly looking over at where the others were gathered around tables at the ramada, I grinned. "They all seem like pretty great people. You hang with a good crowd."

"I do," she agreed. "And I'd love it if you became one of those people, too."

"I'm here, aren't I?" I winked, sliding my arm around her shoulders and giving a light squeeze. "And while I appreciate the invite, I don't want you to think it's your job to cheer me up or babysit me. I'll work through all of this, I promise."

"You should know this wasn't a charity invite. I've liked you from the moment I met you. I invited you here because I thought you might enjoy the company. I mean, it seemed only fair, since I have slept with you already."

Laughter erupted from me and I squeezed her tighter. "I'm pretty sure I'm the only one who was doing any sleeping on that couch."

"True, I spent most of the time trying to figure out how to safely escape. You had me tucked up pretty tightly against you."

"Well, it worked," I replied. "It stopped the nightmares at least." Dammit. I'd said too much. It just slipped out.

"Nightmares?" she asked, looking at me curiously and I grimaced.

"Initially, when I first came to your office, it was for treatment of PTSD. Before I moved here with Cami and Dylan, we were all involved in a pretty gruesome hostage situation. I've still had some lingering effects from it that Evie, uh, Dr. McKnight, was trying to help me work through."

"So, are you doing any better now?" she asked, concerned.

"Not really. We didn't get too far into the therapy part before we decided to ditch it for a relationship thing."

"That, right there, is what surprises me," Misty said.

"What do you mean?"

"I mean, Dr. McKnight and men . . . once Mr. Presley died, or was rumored to be dead, Dr. McKnight never showed any interest in anyone again—ever. I haven't known her the whole time, but her secretary prior to me filled me in on a lot. All I know is that it doesn't matter how hard guys pursued her, it was like she didn't even notice there were other men on the planet—until you came along. So something about you caught her eye, big time."

Kory Presley. I couldn't remember if Evie had told me his last name or if I'd read it in the paper, but even his names sounded more deserving than mine. "Either that, or she was finally lonely enough to let someone else take advantage of her."

Misty snorted. "No one takes advantage of Dr. McKnight. She'd sooner kick a guy in the balls than let him screw her over. She's one tough cookie. Just the fact that she let you in tells me exactly how she felt about you. I'm positive she's hurting just as badly as you are."

"Except she has him." I couldn't let that go. Images of the two of them wrapped up together in her bed, doing things she'd recently done with me, constantly flooded my mind, filling me with jealousy.

"There is that," she agreed, not sugar

coating for my benefit. "But now you have me." She gave me a sidelong glance. "If you want me, that is."

I stared at her, slightly overcome with the desire to kiss her, but not wanting to make a mess of things either. That didn't stop me from leaning in closer though.

"I mean, no strings attached, right?" She continued to ramble on. "I know you're just coming out of a relationship, well, sort of a relationship and you need time to grieve and all. I'm not trying to push you into another one or anything. I just want you to know if you ever need a friend, or whatever, I'm here for you."

"Misty."

"Yes?" Her wide eyes looked up at me and she swallowed hard.

"Shut up," I said with a laugh. Leaning closer, I placed a light kiss on the top of her head. "I appreciate everything you're trying to do and I'm thrilled to have you as 'a friend, or whatever,' okay? Take a breath. It's all good." The "whatever" was not lost on me. I'd been around plenty of girls to know that the "whatever" had been the most important word of the conversation. She was telling me she liked me and was open to more of a relationship with me, if I was ready.

I wasn't sure if I'd ever really be ready for another relationship. But now that Evie had made her feelings clear, there was no reason for me not to jump back on the dating bandwagon. Yes, my heart was hurting, but maybe the best way to get over that would be for my heart to turn attention to another heart.

I liked Misty a lot; and aside from the fact she worked for Evie, she was exactly my type. The idea of dating her right away filled me with hesitation, though. I didn't want her to be a rebound relationship or a mercy date, or anything like that. If I dated her, I wanted it to be purely based on the fact that I wanted to date her, not because I was trying to get over Evie.

"Would you like to go for a little walk with me around the lake?" Misty asked.

"Sure," I replied, my arm still draped around her shoulder. She didn't make any attempt to remove it, so I left it there. It felt good.

Sounds of nature filled the air around us, birds tweeting, the soft breeze rustling through the leaves, the sound of the lake water lapping gently against the shore, our shoes crunching against the gravelly path. Everything about today felt good—better than I'd felt in the last few days anyway. That, right there, should be a big sign. I was having fun and I wasn't plastered drunk. I'd been drunk pretty much every minute of the week that I wasn't on call.

Halting, I dropped my hand from her shoulder, grabbing her hand instead, and lacing our fingers together. "Go out with me next weekend." It wasn't really a question. I wanted more of what I was feeling right now—more living—less sorrow.

"Are you sure?" She hesitated. And so I hadn't been able to read her eyes, I would've thought she was playing around, protesting in order to look good, so to speak. But she wasn't. There was genuine concern and worry there.

"Do you think it will hurt her if we date?" I asked, continuing to observe her reactions, and she sighed heavily.

"Maybe; but if it does, she wouldn't tell us. Evie is the kind of person who would cheer us on, hoping we could find happiness, too, even if it was awkward for her."

"It would be awkward for me, too."

"How awkward?" Her eyes never left me.

"Our relationship was very . . . physical."

"Oh. I see." She stood there for a few moments. "I'm surprised, really. I knew she'd sworn off men that way."

I chuckled. "Yeah, she had. What happened between us was kind of unplanned and very spur of the moment. It caught us both by surprise." My thoughts were instantly back in that kitchen, and then in my bedroom.

Shoving the images of Evie out of my mind, I knew I needed to move on instead of constantly reliving those memories. She'd made her choice. It didn't include me. End of story. Move on.

"So, about this weekend? Is that a yes or a no?"

Smiling, she shook her head. "What did you have in mind?"

"Something totally boring like dinner and a movie. You can even pick what you want to eat and which movie to see. I'm easy."

"Are you?" Laughing, her eyes twinkled, her smile shining bright and white against her tanned skin. "I'll have to see how easy."

"Please do," I continued, urging her on. "Life has been way too celibate around my place lately."

She made a sympathetic frowny face. "Aw, poor little guy hasn't got any for over a week and he thinks he's dying, huh?" She was totally teasing me.

"Hey," I replied with a nonchalant shrug. "Us guys, we have needs." I could totally play this game with her. Leaning in closer, I whispered into her ear. "And there's nothing little about this guy." The beer was making me brazen—maybe I shouldn't have anymore.

This was a strange conversation to be having with Misty, but for some reason it seemed to be helping me immensely. Life wasn't over merely because Evie dumped me. Really, who else could she choose? If Kory made her happy, then I was happy for her. And if her hot, sexy secretary wanted to date me, then by all that was holy, I was going to let her. It sure as hell beat being alone.

Besides, I liked this girl; and the more I was around her, the more I liked her. Maybe she was exactly what I needed to move on.

Her eyes sparkled with humor. "Really? Now I'm totally intrigued."

I grinned. "I thought you might be." Shit, all she needed to do was look down at my swim trunks to verify my statement. These shorts weren't supposed to come with a tent. Oddly enough, instead of feeling badly for having this reaction to her, I felt amazingly good instead.

Gathering her into my arms, I pulled her

against me. "Next weekend?" I asked again, trying to steer this runaway train back onto the right subject.

"Pick me up at the office at six on Friday."

My heart raced at her words. I was actually excited for this. "I'll be there at six PM sharp." This time I dropped my lips to hers.

Chapter Twenty-Two
Evie

"So, why did you want to come out here today?" Kory asked as we exited the vehicle. "Other than the fact that it's a beautiful Sunday."

"Well, I know you've struggled with being able to talk to me about some of the things that happened to you. I have, too. I thought bringing you here might help me talk about them with you."

"Do you still swim here like we used to?" Kory asked, smiling.

"I did," I replied, leaning against the hood of my car. "Up until a few weeks ago, I used to come out here pretty regularly, at least when the weather permitted it."

"Then why'd you stop?" he asked, casually leaning beside me, close enough to be close, but still not touching. He didn't touch me near as much as he used to. It was like he was afraid of me or something.

"I got a cramp in the middle of the lake, the last time I went out. I almost drowned. Thank goodness the local fire department was having their annual barbeque on the other side of the lake. One of the firemen happened to see me go under and he jumped in and swam out to help me." I didn't make eye contact with Kory, instead reliving the memories in my head—the sounds of the water, the pain in my side, the gasping for help. "I didn't know he was coming for me. I thought I was going to die."

"It was that bad?" Kory asked, sympathy and concern evident in his voice.

I nodded. "I remember the exact point I knew I was going to die because suddenly you were standing there, in front of me, with your arms outstretched. I thought you'd come to take me with you."

"Wow."

"Right before I could go to you, something grabbed my hair and began yanking me to the surface. The firefighter had managed to find me, even under the water, and he rescued me."

"Thank God for well-trained firefighters," Kory said, slipping his arm around my shoulder and hugging me to him. At first I stiffened in surprise, but then I melted into him, missing the contact we used to have like this.

"There's more," I said, knowing this would probably push him away a little. I didn't want to do that. He'd been too far away for too long.

"Go ahead," he encouraged.

"Well, shortly after I was rescued, I found

out the very same firefighter who'd rescued me had scheduled an appointment with me for PTSD. He tried canceling, due to conflict of interest, but I asked him to keep coming. I wanted to help him."

"Did he agree?"

"Yes, in the beginning, but he didn't want the friends that he lived with to know why I was seeing him." I glanced at Kory. "I can't break confidentiality, but he had good reasons for not wanting that information to get out to them. Anyway, his friends came to the mistaken conclusion that we were dating and we just let them think it."

I paused, trying to decide how to continue, but I was unsure. I didn't want to hurt him.

"The two of you became an item as a result, didn't you?" he asked, filling in the blanks for me.

I nodded, tears flooding my eyes. "I didn't set out to be unfaithful to you. I guess all those years without you finally caught up to me and Russ filled a void I'd really needed."

"Russ? Is that his name?"

"Russ Weston, yes. It's sad, too, because under normal circumstances, you both would probably really like each other. You know, if I wasn't standing in between the two of you."

"Evie, you can't be unfaithful to someone you thought was dead. There's no way I'm going to hold that against you. The real question is, am I the one you want?"

"I'm here, aren't I? I've been all yours since the moment you came back. Not that it means that much."

"Why do you say that?"

"Because look at us. You've been here for how long now, and you have yet to touch me. You're very careful around me. I know you've been through a lot, but I'm beginning to wonder if you really want to be with me anymore."
Might as well get all the cards out on the table.

"I'm not necessarily trying to avoid you, Evie, rather I'm trying to avoid things that will bring us both pain. I'm not the same man who left you. That person is inside me somewhere, along with all his great memories, but I don't know that he will ever be my 'normal' self, again."

I scooted closer to him, laying my head on his shoulder. "I know you're different now, but I'm here for you. Really. I want to help you however I can." I was beginning to wonder if we'd ever come back to some sense of normalcy in our lives, but I was determined to stand by him. I owed it to him after all he'd been through.

My eyes drifted around the edges of the lake, resting on a group of people who were barbecuing a short way from our location, the heavenly smells from their food floating into the air, making my mouth water. Two people further down the shore were wrapped in each other's arms and the guy seemed to be showering the girl with kisses. Suddenly the girl said something funny and the guy tipped his head back and laughed hard.

Instantly I froze, recognizing that laughter.

Peering closer, my heart sank when I realized it was Russ and Misty I was looking at. Tears threatened to spill from my eyes and I broke away from Kory.

"Uh, I don't feel like sitting out here any longer. I'm kind of hungry. Want to go get something to eat and head back to our place?"

Kory shook his head. "Let's just go home and finish this conversation. We can make something to eat there."

"Okay." I didn't wait for him to usher me into the car, I simply went to the driver's side and slipped in. I couldn't seem to break my gaze away from where Misty and Russ held each other, red-hot jealousy pouring through me.

Just some friends getting together, my eye, I thought. *She wants him as badly as I do.*

I was being totally selfish and needed to get over myself. There was no way I could choose one guy and hope the other spent the rest of his life yearning for me. Russ was young—of course he'd be looking for someone else. It wasn't like we had dated this huge long time or anything. It only seemed this difficult because I hadn't been with Kory again physically yet. Once we crossed that line, everything would be okay. I just knew it. Now I simply needed to convince Kory.

***

"Come here," Kory said as soon as we reached the condo, closing the door behind him.

"What's wrong?" I asked, noticing his concerned expression. Moving closer, I slipped my hand inside his.

"Nothing is wrong, at least not for me where

it concerns you." He slipped a hand into my hair, his thumb brushing against my cheek. "I'm sorry I showed up and put your life in such a tailspin. And I'm sure this Russ guy probably hates me for stealing you away from him; but damn, Evie, I sure am glad you picked me."

"Are you?" I was trembling under his touch and soft words.

"I need to show you something." Leading me through the living room and into the bedroom, he paused at the foot of the bed, smiling at me before taking a deep breath. He started to unbutton the top of his fatigues, the only thing I'd seen him dressed in since his return—except for a brief stint in his full dress uniform when he was presented his medal.

My nerves skyrocketed and I placed my hand over his, stilling him. "You don't need to rush into anything on my behalf."

"I'm not. I'm legitimately choosing to share this with you." He continued to unbutton, shrugging out of them and then pulling off his t-shirt underneath.

I gasped, one hand covering my mouth, my other reaching behind me for the bed and I sat down, shocked. "What did they do to you?" I managed to choke out as I stared at his once beautiful body, now heavily scarred and puckered.

"They tortured me. A lot."

He didn't shrink away as my fingers reached out, tracing the horrific lines that been left on him.

"Does this hurt?" I asked, not wanting to

cause him any pain.

"No. In fact, right now, I'd say I feel better than I have in a very long time."

Fingering a rough looking hole in his upper abdomen, I glanced up at him and he nodded. "The gunshot wound." Pointing to a few others, he continued. "These weren't from torture, I got them in the helicopter crash." Slowly he turned around and I wanted to faint at all the thick striped scars along his back.

"They whipped you," I said aghast, afraid to even touch him.

"They did many things to me."

"Tell me," I said, wanting to know.

"No, because then you will be their victim, too."

"I'm already their victim!" I shouted a little too loudly, and he flinched, turning to face me, again. "I became their victim the day they took you from me. I want to know what they did to you damn it! I want to make sure someone pays."

Kory grabbed my hands. "They did pay. All of them." That was obviously all he was going to offer.

"Well, good. They deserve it," I said weakly, almost as an afterthought. "And you deserve the best of everything life can give you."

Smiling, he pulled me to my feet. "I'm working on it."

"Why did you show me all this, now?"

"I didn't want to scare you away. Plus, I was worried you'd be repulsed and want nothing to do with me."

"Kory, I'm so grateful you're alive I don't see scars, I just see miracles. I'm so happy you're alive."

His mouth quickly descended, his full lips pressing against mine. I could sense the need inside him, yet he still seemed to hold back.

"What's wrong?" I asked, pulling away.

"I'm pretty scarred up on my legs, too."

"I thought we established I don't care about your scars." I tried to kiss him again, but he pulled away. "Would it help if we turned off all the lights? Would that ease some of your fears?" I asked.

"It would," he replied with a wry laugh. "But I've waited so long to see your body beneath mine again, that I'd really like to leave the light on."

"Then trust me, Kory. Trust me to love you as much as I always have."

Pausing only a moment longer, he nodded and carefully began removing my clothes. His fingers were shaking so badly at times that I had to help him. But soon he had me gathered in his arms and carried me from the foot to the head of the bed.

I made a special point to not openly gawk at any of the trauma to his body, wanting him to know that it didn't influence me in any manner. Instead, I succumbed to his heated kisses and touches, some familiar, others not so much, but all enjoyable as each of us reacquainted ourselves with the other.

Briefly I wondered if Russ and Misty would end up this way, in bed together. Russ had begged me not to sleep with Kory, but there was no way I could deny him. There was no way I'd ever be able to tell this man no after what he'd been through. And from the way Russ had looked with Misty today, I could tell he was trying to move on, and he looked to be doing a pretty good job of it.

I didn't know why it bothered me so much. I'd made my choice. But for some reason, I hated knowing that Misty was probably going to find out just how good Russ was in bed. He was incredible, and I missed being with him like that.

Jerking my attention away from Russ, I forced myself back to the present, allowing my body to respond to Kory and his affections. Before long, we were both panting, reaching the crest of completion together, amid gasps and shouted names.

Kory fell against me, kissing my face and smiling. "Thank you. That was even better than I remember it."

"It was really good," I replied, running my fingers up and down his back like I used to and then pausing because the scar tissue was so unfamiliar.

I really sucked. My first time with my returned-from-the-dead fiancé and I'd practically spent the whole time wondering if Russ was doing Misty. There were no bigger assholes on the planet than me, right now. How could I be so cruel?

Kory obviously didn't notice the self-hatred going on at the moment because he just kept smiling and kissing me in random places.

"If it's okay with you, I'd like to go again. It's been a while, you know?"

I laughed, both at his humor and my stupidity. "You may help yourself to me as often as you like Mr. Presley. I quite enjoy being with you."

"That's always good to know. This time I want to take my time."

Keeping me occupied all night long, he reminded me of many of the reasons I'd initially fallen in love with him. Now, if I could just stop comparing all those reasons to Russ, I'd finally be able to move on and give Kory the life he deserved.

CHAPTER TWENTY-THREE
Russ

I hadn't heard anything from Evie since the last time we talked together. On the other hand, Misty and I had been texting back and forth and calling each other every day. We'd developed quite the friendship between the two of us, and I enjoyed how down to earth she was about everything.

She had also been my inside spy to all things Evie, whom I was pretty sure had resumed her physical relationship with her fiancé at this point. Misty said he was constantly showering her with gifts and that the two of them acted like kids who had just fallen in love.

Evie hadn't said anything in particular about her relationship to Misty, but Misty was pretty sure there was some kinky stuff going on with Kory and Evie behind closed doors. Having been on that ride, and knowing how quiet Evie was not, I agreed with her assessment that the two of them were sleeping together again.

That decision pretty much put the final nail in my coffin. It was safe to say that I was completely out of the picture where Evie was concerned. While this didn't do much for my own self-esteem, I was really enjoying getting to know Misty better and the two of us had a lot in common.

Misty had even stopped by my work, one night, and brought cookies, enough for the entire crew. That instantly won them over.

"What's going on with you and these two girls?" Dylan asked me after she left.

"What do you mean?" Groaning over a chocolate chip cookie, I took another bite.

"I mean you've been practically pining over Evie, but now you're seeing this other girl all the time."

"I like Misty," I said defensively. "Besides, she was there for me when no one else was."

"Hey, I don't care which one you're banging. I just want you to be happy and not get caught up in some massive love triangle or something."

I snorted. "Trust me there is no triangle going on. I've had zero contact from Evie and, according to the rumor mill, she and Kory are going at it like rabbits. I think it's pretty safe to say she's over me."

"Are you over her, though? That's the real question."

I shrugged. "I'm working on it. So far, Misty's been a good distraction for me, not to mention that she usually has insider information."

Dylan appeared to ponder this for a second. "Hmmm. Just promise me one thing."

"What's that?"

"If you decide to take your relationship with Misty to the next level, make sure you're doing it because you have feelings for *her*, not because you're using her to erase another girl you have feelings for. She deserves better than that."

"I agree completely," I replied, having already thought that myself. "I don't want Misty getting hurt either. I really like her."

"Good, then promise me I'm not going to need to clean any surfaces in my kitchen in the near future."

I laughed. "That was totally an accident."

"You don't accidentally slip and fall into a woman's vagina, Russ. I'm pretty sure it was intentional sex."

Chuckling, I shook my head. "You know what I mean."

"Yeah, I do." Punching me lightly against the shoulder, he stood and pointed at me. "I'm serious, though. Any sexy stuff going on between you and whoever needs to be happening in your part of the house—with the door closed." Turning he walked into the other room. "Oh, and with a new bed, too," he hollered, his words carrying through the station.

"Already ordered," I called back to him. "It delivers this week."

"Good. I'm glad we won't have to put up with any more of those squeaking springs. What the hell took it so long?"

"I had it custom made—from the Amish—in Pennsylvania."

Dylan reappeared, gaping at me. "Seriously?" he asked and I nodded. "Well, they sure took their damn time. I'm happy to hear it's coming."

No happier than I was. I was tired of sleeping on the damn couch and I needed to get everything that reminded me of Evie out of my head. She'd clearly moved on, proving that she hadn't ever considered our relationship as deeply as I had. Now it was time for me to move on, too. Only this time, I was going slowly. There was no way I was jumping into bed any time soon with Misty. I wanted time for the relationship to build naturally, and reduce the risk of someone getting hurt. Maybe I should ask her if she had any missing boyfriends she was longing for, just to be safe.

Yes, this time was different. Slow was the key.

***

"Shit! Holy hell! Yesss!" I dragged the word out long and loud. "Dammit, Misty. You're killing me! Yes! Yes! Right there!" I closed my eyes, complete ecstasy flooding my body at the mere touch of her hands. "Holy cow, how you ended up as a secretary with hands like these, I'll never know. This is the best massage I've ever had. I swear I've had a knot right there for months!"

"Oh, you know this because you get massages a lot, do you?" she teased, working her fingers into the tightened muscles of my shoulders as I lay on her table.

"Not a lot, and definitely not this good. You're like a magician with those hands."

"Well, you better keep it down a little, or Cami and Dylan are going to think I'm up here giving you the happy finish. I swear, I'm blushing with all the hollering and groaning you've been doing during this."

Of course, me being a guy and all, her words immediately inflamed other parts of me. Rolling over, I stared at her, the sheet tucked around my waist hiding nothing. "Just so you know, I'd be okay with the happy finish in the future if you ever feel the need. I'm all for helping you stay up on any necessary skills." I raised an eyebrow in invitation.

Her eyes trailed a path over me, resting on the sheet and staring at it like there was a potential bomb underneath it that was ready to explode . . . which, really, there was.

Laughing, she shook her head at me. "What happened to wanting to take things slow?"

I sighed, throwing an arm over my eyes. "If we go any slower we will be at a standstill."

Giving a slight laugh, she nodded. "This is true."

"How many dates have we been on now?" I asked, trying to count up the last several weeks we'd been seeing each other.

"I've lost count, but they were all good."

"Yes, they were," I agreed. And truthfully, I'd wanted to sleep with her after each and every one; but I'd managed to keep waiting. Only now, I didn't know what we were waiting for.

It was obvious we were great friends, and it was obvious the attraction burned hot between us. It was also obvious that Evie wasn't going to be changing her mind. I'd seen her out and about with Kory a couple of times, and the two of them stuck to each other like glue. Thankfully, I'd seen them before they saw me, so I was able to ditch away. I didn't think anything would be changing on that front.

It was crazy how much all our lives had changed since Evie's near drowning. I often wondered if Misty was the one I was meant to have met through all this. There was never any guessing with her. She seemed totally, one hundred percent, into me. I didn't ever have to wonder about things with her or beg her to give me a chance while she mourned for someone else.

I liked all that. It said a lot. Somewhere in my head I realized that if Evie came right now and asked for me back, I'd have a hard time letting go of Misty. I was falling for her, and that had never been my intention to begin with. It had just sort of snuck up on us. At least I hoped there was an "us." Misty had never pressed me for anything more than friendship.

"Think this table will hold us both?" I asked, teasing her as I ripped the sheet away and dropped it to the floor. "It would give me a better, complete assessment of your massage skills."

She laughed, shaking her head, blushing heavily at my obvious lack of clothing. "I bet.

You know, if I was licensed still, I'd lose my certification for this."

"Good thing you aren't still licensed. Besides, we can just list this under the sensual massage category, can't we?" Grabbing her bottle of oil, I lubed up my hands. "Take your shirt off and get on the table. I need to massage some things on you."

She laughed harder. "I'm going to get into so much trouble with you, aren't I?"

"Most likely. But I swear it will all be fun trouble. How's that?"

"Sounds great to me."

I watched greedily as she removed her clothing and crawled onto the table face down. Yeah, her body was just as I thought, rockin' awesome. Not an ounce of fat, but curvy in all the right places.

I knew nothing about giving a massage, so I simply started running my hands over her, rubbing the oily concoction into her skin.

"Mmmmm. That feels so good."

"Keep moaning like that and you're going to get the happy finish before you get the rest of your massage."

She laughed. "Maybe we should just get that out of the way now, so we don't have to worry about it later."

She was teasing me, but I was all for the plan. I liked Misty, a lot. And while we were great friends, I was more than willing to see where a friends-with-benefits relationship would take us. Maybe it would work out, maybe it wouldn't; but the two of us could have fun while we tried to figure things out along the way.

"I'm in total agreement with this assessment."

Laughing again, she shook her head, rolling on her side and propping her head up as she stared at me. "I can't ever tell when you're just messing with me, Russ, or if you're serious."

Staring at her for a moment, I decided to take the open opportunity. I slid my oily hands to either side of her head and bent to kiss her—deeply. Sparks rushed through me when she slipped an arm loosely around my neck, a low moan escaping her. Pulling back slightly, my eyes briefly fell to her lips before moving back to her beautiful eyes. "Any questions?" I asked. "Or do you require more demonstrations?"

"I think I got the message." She smiled seductively. "Should I scoot over?"

"Nah. It just so happens I have this really great new bed. I think we might fit better on it."

"Wow, I actually get to touch the new bed? Look at how special I am."

"Hey, I let you help me get it all put together."

"And then you refused to let me lay on it," she reminded me.

"I wanted to lay on it first," I replied, laughing. "Besides, I was tired and seeing you laying on my bed would've required me to take things to the next level."

"Hmm. I have a hard time believing that," she replied with a smirk.

"It's part of the unspoken guy code. If you have a hot girl on your bed you have to do her."

I grinned, winking at her.

"And what is the guy code if your girl is on a massage table?"

I allowed my gaze to move over her from head to toe. "Then you definitely get the happy finish."

"Do me a favor?" she asked, laughing.

"Anything."

"Don't ever become a licensed massage therapist. You'd end up in jail quicker than you can imagine with this kind of talk."

"This kind of talk is only reserved for my 'special' clients."

"So I'm special?" There was laughter in her voice, but a hint of seriousness in her eyes.

"At the moment you are my only 'special' client." Reaching out, I began rubbing my oily hands over her exposed chest.

"Why is it I think this would be the most massaged area on my body if you were my masseuse?"

I shook my head. "Honestly, I have no clue, because I can think of something I'd much rather massage on you. It happens to be my 'specialty' for my 'special' customers."

"And what 'specialty' is that?" she asked, her eyelids growing heavier and her voice huskier.

"It's a special internal massage. It really gets the blood pumping through all parts of the body. It causes the body to tense from the friction and then literally explode with release. It's one of the best stress relievers out there. You really should try it."

Biting at her grin, Misty stared at me with

smoky eyes. "And are you licensed to practice? I want to know I'm getting the very best treatment."

"All I can give you is my 100% satisfaction guarantee. I've never had any complaints yet. Only rave reviews."

"Well, then it looks like I've come to the right guy."

I shook my head. "Not yet, but you will really soon, I promise." She laughed at my joke, shaking her head. Scooping her off her massage table, I carried her to my room and practically tossed her among the pillows. Her laughter echoed through the space and thankfully, the huge bed didn't even make the tiniest squeak.

Quickly, I climbed on next to her, staring down at her pretty features. "You sure about this?" I asked seriously. "We're about to cross a line right here. I want to make sure you're comfortable with it because I don't want things to get weird for us later."

"I'm completely comfortable," she replied, slipping her hands around my neck and pulling me closer. "If you want the truth, I've been wondering what was taking you so damn long."

I grinned. "Things have been a little harried. I promised Dylan I wouldn't rush into anything new."

"He's a good friend. I love that you have him and Cami in your life."

"And Piper. Don't forget her. I claim that kid as my own."

She giggled. "So I've noticed. I think you'll make a great dad someday."

"Not right now though," I interjected. "Right now, I need to keep practicing my baby making skills so I get it just right when it's time."

She totally snorted and grinned. "Is that what you're calling it?"

"I am. And since I hate to fail any kind of testing, I say we get onto the practicing right away."

"I'm ready. What's the hold up?" Leaning forward, she captured my lips, her soft hands running down my body eagerly.

Yep, I was definitely feeling very happy right now.

In fact, I intended to get my happy finish many times tonight.

CHAPTER TWENTY-FOUR
Evie

"Have a seat, here, and we'll go over your chart, together," Dr. Emily Daughtry said, gesturing to one of the chairs in front of her desk.

Sitting, I folded my hands primly in my lap, waiting for her to speak, though I was pretty sure what she was going to say.

"First, I want to offer you my congratulations. You're pregnant!"

I attempted to muster a smile, but had no way of knowing if I actually pulled it off.

"Judging from the date of your last period," she continued. "I'd say you're around eight weeks' gestation."

Eight weeks. Eight weeks. Eight Weeks? The words reverberated over and over in my head. This was Russ' baby, for sure. I didn't even know Kory was still alive eight weeks ago.

"The rest of your lab work looks good; so

unless you have any more questions for me, I say we get scheduled for your next appointment in a month. Does that sound good?"

"Huh?" I was still lost on the eight weeks and what this particular baby would mean to my life right now. I'd been so caught up with everything else, I hadn't been paying attention to my body.

"Shall I schedule you for a month from now?" she asked, again.

"Actually, could you give me some information on abortion?" My voice was shaking, but I couldn't make it stop. "I haven't decided if I'm going to keep this baby."

Settling back into her chair, the doctor stared at me. "I can definitely give you a referral to an abortion clinic, but I like to talk to my patients a little bit before I send them there. Abortion is a big decision—one that will affect you emotionally for the rest of your life; so you need to make sure you don't rush into anything you might regret, later. Also, if I may ask, is there a particular reason you're leaning this direction? Remember, everything you say here is confidential."

I gave a wry laugh. "My life is so screwed up right now, I don't even know how to process this latest development."

"I've seen a little about you in the news lately. I understand you were rescued from a near drowning and you had a previously presumed dead fiancé return from overseas. Is that correct?"

I nodded.

"And you don't feel he's ready for a baby

yet? I know life has probably been pretty traumatic for him."

"It's not that," I said quickly, seeing she was heading in the wrong direction. Sighing heavily, I looked her straight in the eye. "The baby isn't his."

Those words put such finality on my situation.

"Oh. I see. Yes, that does complicate things."

I hated that she thought I was some cheating tramp. "Even though I thought Kory was dead, I still waited for him—mourned him every day. That day—when I was rescued—well, the firefighter that rescued me, he and I kind of started a relationship. But when Kory came home, I chose him. He was still my fiancé as far as he was concerned and he lived with me. What else could I do? He needed me."

"So, you broke things off with the firefighter, not knowing you'd conceived a child with him?"

I nodded, dipping my head into my hand as a sob escaped me. "What am I going to do?"

"Well, if your relationship is over with the firefighter, and you're in a committed relationship with this other man, maybe abortion is the best option for you."

"I just . . . I can't . . . I don't know . . . ." I stared at her through my blurry water-filled eyes. "I'm still in love with him. I never stopped loving him—the firefighter, that is. I don't know if I can abort his baby. It's a piece of both of us." Several hysterical sobs escaped me. "I love Kory, too, though. How can I help him through everything and ask him to raise another man's child? He has so much on his plate right now."

"Sounds like you have a lot of things to consider," she said sympathetically. "Tell you what, I'm going to give you several brochures. I have some on abortion and adoption, as well on how to deal with a pregnancy that has occurred outside the bounds of a relationship. Maybe that will help you know what direction to go."

"Okay," I said, feeling like a steamroller had just hit me. I needed all the help I could get. While I didn't necessarily cheat on Kory—I mean he was dead after all—it still felt like I did.

And Russ. *How the hell do I tell Russ?* I'd broke off with him fairly harshly, thinking that stopping cold turkey would be the best way for us. Now I was pregnant with his child. I couldn't go back to him—he was with Misty now. Besides, if the two of us ever got together, I wanted it to be because we loved each other, not because we goofed and I got knocked up.

I really wasn't sure how Kory would take this news either. We'd both sort of taken for granted that we would move on with our future together . . . at least I did. We'd never actually sat down and really discussed it in depth. I'd assumed he returned to his old life because that's what he wanted. It's what I would do.

Everything was moving in a hazy dream-like status right now. I took the offered pamphlets Dr. Daughtry handed me, shoving them into my purse. I promised to call her if I needed to talk to her about anything, and she even gave me her after-hours number.

I didn't remember the walk to my car, but once I slipped inside, I leaned over the steering wheel and let the water works loose.

Russ and I were having a baby—maybe. I was terrified, heartsick, overwhelmed. I had no idea what this revelation would do to my future. And I didn't know if I had the guts to get an abortion. I couldn't just put the baby up for adoption either. Russ would have to sign away those rights, as well. I knew there were lots of families out there that wanted babies and couldn't have them.

Of course, that was my problem. I wanted this baby, too. But I didn't see any way I could keep it and keep Kory, unless he was willing to raise another man's child. If he broke up with me, there was no way in hell I was running back to Russ. I'd put him through enough already. I wasn't going to have him thinking he was merely my second choice. My feelings for him weren't like that.

I adored Russ. I was crazy about Russ. Walking away from him was the hardest thing I'd ever done in my life, but I'd made a previous commitment to Kory, and I always honored my commitments.

"Yeah, and now look were that got you," I said out loud, dropping my visor and looking in the mirror, attempting to wipe away the dark smudges beneath my eyes. Well, at least I had some time still before I started showing. Maybe I could come up with a good solution in the next couple of weeks.

Sliding my keys into the ignition, I couldn't

help resting my free hand lightly on my stomach. Regardless of the incredibly bad timing of this event, a tiny part of my heart was thrilled to know that a piece of Russ was growing inside me.

Our relationship might have been short, but it was definitely intense. Our feelings for each other had been real—and now that "real" had taken on a life of its own. Under any other circumstances, I would've been thrilled to receive this news. Unfortunately, this baby could possibly derail everything instead.

Carefully pulling out of the parking space, I turned my car toward home—and Kory.

***

"What's the matter?" Kory asked, his eyes full of concern the second I stepped into the apartment.

Sending him a half attempt at a smile, I shook my head. "It's just been a long day, with a few unexpected curveballs." I kicked my shoes off, not able to stand being in heels for another minute, and I tossed my keys and briefcase on the stand by the door.

"Let me grab you a glass of wine. That will help you unwind."

"No!" I practically shouted, holding a hand up in the air as I warned him to stop. "My stomach is a bit on the queasy side today. Alcohol will definitely not help."

"Are you still feeling sick? You've been through a lot lately. Maybe we need to get you in to the doctor and see what's going on. Of course, like I said before, you've been through a lot. It could just be stress."

"Kory, I'm pregnant." I just blurted it out there, seeing the immediate shock on his face, but at least it shut him up. Going over to the couch I plopped down with a sigh, happy to get off my feet.

"Are . . . are you sure?" he asked, not moving from the same place he'd been standing.

"I came straight from the doctor's office, so unless their blood work and urinalysis is wrong, then yep. I'm having a baby." Tears welled in my eyes as I continued to stare at him, knowing my next words were probably going to make him feel like he'd been shot all over again.

"Oh." He sank down into the chair opposite the couch. Quiet for several long moments, I gave him his space to absorb the news. "I don't understand. We've been really careful to use protection."

"Um, about that." Tears flooded over the rim of my eyes and a giant knot appeared in my throat. "If the timing is accurate, which I'm pretty certain it is, this baby isn't yours."

Silence. He simply stared at me, shock obviously getting the better of him. I couldn't even imagine what he must feel like.

"And it really sucks, too," I continued on, trying to fill the emptiness. "I mourned for you all those years. I swore I'd never move on. Then, the second I changed my mind, fate gave you back to me. And now this."

"Didn't you use protection?" he asked, his voice soft, but the pain extremely visible in his eyes.

"We did, mostly. But there was this one time—the first time—it was sort of spontaneous. Neither of us expected anything like that to happen. We weren't prepared for it."

"The jerk can't keep a damn condom in his wallet?" Kory spit out angrily.

"I don't know. If he does, we didn't think about using it."

"Come on, Evie. As long as I've known you you've been on the pill. You're telling me that didn't work either?"

Sighing heavily, I tried not to allow his angry words to affect me and drag me into an argument. "I'd lost the man of my dreams. I wasn't planning on ever being with anyone ever again. There was no reason to be on the pill."

"Obviously there was," he replied, gesturing toward my stomach.

I picked up one of the throw pillows on the couch, covering my belly. Suddenly I felt the need to shield the little life in there from the words being said out here.

"I'm really sorry about this, Kory. It certainly wasn't intentional."

"Are you going to keep it?" he asked, fidgeting restlessly in his seat.

"I haven't decided yet," I answered honestly.

"Wow. Just wow." Standing, he paced across the room. "I can't believe you'd disrespect me in this manner."

"Ouch. That stings. What in heaven's name have I done to disrespect you? This happened when I thought you were dead."

"I'm talking about now. You said you hadn't

decided whether or not to keep it."

"Yeah. So?"

"Do you really expect me to raise some other guy's kid?"

"Well, I figured we could tell Russ together, and see what role he would like to play in the child's life. But yeah, I thought you'd be a great father figure for him or her. Am I wrong to think that?"

"Yes!" he shouted, still sounding extremely frustrated. "I mean, look at me, Evie. I'm barely functioning from day to day. I spend my life going to therapy and hoping I won't explode from all the crap I'm carrying inside me. I have no idea how long it's going to take me to get back to some semblance of normal. I'm not a good fit to be around kids."

"But look how much you've improved just since you came home! It's going to keep getting better. Maybe having a family will help you through your therapy and give you a new place to redirect your attention. Love can conquer many things."

"Not this, Evie. Not this."

"What are you saying?" My lower lip trembled as I spoke, despite my trying to remain calm.

"I'm saying I don't want kids—ever. Not my own, and definitely not some other guy's."

"We always used to talk about how many kids we wanted to have. Don't you remember?"

"Things have changed, Evie!" He yelled and I started crying in earnest, my hands covering my face as I sobbed. "Maybe we're just trying too hard to put a past back together that wasn't meant to be."

"Please don't say that." I spoke in a hiccupping voice.

Finally, a morsel of sympathy appeared on his face. "We aren't the same two people. Can't you see that? We've changed. Yes, we were good before, but that was . . . it was before. We were still kids who believed life was all sunshine and roses. Now, everywhere I look, I just see death. Death of platoon members, death of my best friend, even our relationship reeks of death. You and I are struggling here, Evie. Struggling bad. I know we've been trying to work our way back to each other, but it's like we're just going through the motions.

"And now this. Don't try to deny it. I know you're still in love with him. I know you still want him."

"I chose you!" I shouted, jumping up from the couch and throwing the pillow at him. "I chose you! It was always you. Don't you try to put this failure off on me. I've been killing myself trying to help you acclimate to society."

"And that's exactly my point. It shouldn't be this hard. Should it?" Silence fell between us as we stared at each other. "Hell yes, I love you. And you'd better damn well believe it. Thinking of you every day was what got me out of that hellhole. You've already saved me, Evie. You don't need to keep trying."

"What are you saying?" I rubbed the back of my hands against my eyes, trying to brush the tears away. This couldn't be happening, not after everything we'd been through to be back with one another again.

"I'm saying that coming back here was a mistake. I'm unable to move on because too many things here remind me of the past and everything I've lost. I've been thinking about this for a while, but didn't know how to approach the subject with you." He looked so sad. "I need out, Evie. I need to move away, go somewhere else, a place where my life isn't all about how things were before or what happened to me while I was gone. I want to go somewhere far away from here and get a fresh start—a new perspective on things."

"Without me," I added, sinking back to the sofa. Placing my elbows on my knees I curled my arms around my head, feeling like my whole world was crashing in around me.

Suddenly Kory was there on the floor, kneeling in front of me. "Listen to me, babe. I swear, this is going to be better for both of us."

"How?" I asked incredulously, only able to feel the pain of my heart being torn from my chest.

"You're still in love with him. Now you're having his baby. Go to him. Tell him. This might be the life he wants, too."

I snorted; and it wasn't even a good snort, but a pathetic half attempt. "Russ is already dating someone else. I think they're getting pretty serious." I paused, taking in a deep breath. "Besides, I chose you over him. No guy wants to feel like they're the second choice."

"Was he ever really the second choice?" Kory

asked. "Or were you just being loyal, like you always are?"

"I never stopped loving you, Kory. Not for one minute. I was in agony thinking you were dead."

"I know that. I believe you. But still, you managed to move past it and give your heart to someone else. If I really was your 'be all end all' in this life, do you think that would've happened?"

There was no way for me to answer that and he knew it. It made me even angrier.

"What do you want, Kory?" I snapped—my heart, mind and soul on overload.

"I want you to give me your blessing to go out and search for a new life for myself. I want you to allow me a chance to look in the mirror every morning and not feel sorrow or regret. I want you to let me go."

Staring at him for several long moments, I could see the sad sincerity in his eyes. He really did want out. He really was through with me. I was shocked.

"I give you my blessing," I said very softly, my words accompanied by a fresh onslaught of tears. But immediately, my heart felt lighter.

It wasn't until that moment that I knew it was the right thing.

CHAPTER TWENTY-FIVE
Russ

"You're too cute, you know it?" I said, smiling at Misty as she helped me cook dinner on my new kitchen stove.

"How so?" she asked with a smile, not taking her eyes off her work.

"You do this cute thing with your tongue while you're chopping stuff." Now she looked at me. "Like this." I made the face for her.

"I do not!" Laughing, she elbowed me, her face flushing pink.

"You do! Don't be embarrassed, though. I like it."

"Sure you do," she replied, continuing to chop the vegetables for our stew.

"I do! It reminds me of that thing you do with your tongue when we are—,"

"Okay!" she said loudly, effectively cutting me off. "I get the picture."

Chuckling, I nudged her arm. "We haven't

christened the kitchen yet." I smacked a fist against the new granite counter top. "Look how sturdy this thing is. It's totally ripe for some action."

"Please, spare me," Misty said, rolling her eyes. "It wouldn't matter where we are or what we were doing, you'd still find a reason to have sex."

"Is that such a bad thing?" I replied with a grin, nuzzling my face into her hair and placing a light kiss there. "I thought you enjoyed all that."

"Oh, I do. Believe me."

"Then what's the problem?"

Stilling, she stared at the chopped veggies for a minute before looking up at me. "We need to talk."

Oh, that kind of sounded like the kiss of death to me—unless this was the famous "where is this relationship headed" conversation. That I could deal with. I'd been thinking about it a lot actually.

True, Misty and I never had the immediate fire I'd had with Evie, but things where comfortable with her all the time. She spoke her mind. She liked the same things I did. Plus, she was just flat out gorgeous, and a dream in the sack. She was everything I wanted in a girl—except for one thing.

She wasn't Evie.

Still, I'd grown to care very deeply for Misty in the couple of months we'd been together. I never asked her about Evie anymore, and she never volunteered any information. The two of us had grown close and become a couple. And while we were definitely having a great time together, I often wondered if there was a future in store for us or if we were just passing the time.

"Talk away," I said, encouraging her to get on with it. No sense playing the guessing game when she could just tell me what was going on.

"I was offered a job today," she said.

"Really?" I hadn't even been aware that she'd applied to other places. "I thought you liked working for Evie."

"Oh, I do. I love that girl. But this job is with a prestigious law firm in New York and there's room for me to work my way up the ladder."

I was completely dumbstruck, watching as she gathered the veggies and dumped them into the pan of boiling water.

"New York?" I managed to squeak out.

"Yep. I've already given Dr. McKnight my two weeks' notice today. So enjoy me now, because in two weeks I'm outta here."

There was this strange pang in my heart. I wasn't exactly sure why I was so upset. We'd never declared ourselves as being part of anything exclusive. We were more like best friends with extra benefits but, for some reason, I was really heartbroken about this news.

"So, you're saying I only have two weeks left to finish up all my fantasies with you and then you're disappearing from my life?" I attempted to make a joke out of it—you know, no biggie.

"That's right," she replied with a grin.

"Well, then forget dinner! We've got a

counter to break in right now. We're running out of time." I grabbed the hem of her shirt and she squealed and shoved me away.

"Don't you even try it, Russ. I swear I'll use this pan of boiling water as a weapon, if necessary."

I laughed, chasing her toward the living room. "No you won't. You love me too much." I captured her and the two of us fell to the couch together panting.

"I do love you, a lot," she said, breathlessly and smiling.

I grew serious. "I love you, too. You know that, right?" I brushed several strands of hair away from her face. "You've really helped me out through a rough time."

"And now my little birdie is ready to fly out of the nest on his own." Her eyes twinkled with humor. "My work here is done."

I started tickling her. "Your work isn't done until we consummate my new kitchen," I replied with a laugh.

"I'm not helping you consummate your kitchen!" Wriggling away from me, she ran across the room.

"Well, damn. I guess I'll have to find someone else to do it with me then."

"I guess so," she replied, not taking the bait.

"I can handle that you're leaving, since it's for something obviously important to you, but please don't tell me you're cutting off the friends-with-benefits package before you go. That would be a travesty."

"Oh, I see. You're okay with me leaving, as

long as you can sneak in a few more times before I do."

"Hey? Who said I was quitting? A flight to New York doesn't take that long. I'd happily come to visit and shag you there, too."

"I hope you'll be too busy to remember me."

I raised my eyebrows. "What the hell is that supposed to mean? I'm not so fickle that I'd ever forget you."

"I know you aren't. You're loyal—to a fault, almost. It totally reminds me of someone else I know. And that's the reason I'm hoping you will be too busy to think of me."

"You aren't making any sense." Rising, I stalked toward her. "How long do those veggies need to cook?"

"For a while," she replied, backing up as I moved closer.

"Good, because I've got a few other plans for you at the moment." She squealed as I swept her off her feet, flinging her over my shoulder and carrying her to the bedroom.

***

"Well, slave driver, I think that's the last of it." Smiling at Misty, Dylan and I jumped down out of the small moving truck. "You sure you don't need any help unloading this when you get to New York?"

Misty shook her head, grinning. "No. I have a few old friends from high school in that area. They promised to come help me once I get there."

"And by 'old friends' do you mean old boyfriends?" I asked, eyeing her suspiciously.

She'd been pretty adamant against me coming to see her in New York, even for a platonic visit. I'd gotten this whole big lecture, last night, from her about how it was time to stop moping around and move on with my life, that she'd merely been a distraction from reality for me while I needed it. And then she started kissing me and we made love one more time. It really was kind of weird, but there was no way I was passing up being with her again. I was going to miss her so much.

"One of them is an old boyfriend, yes," she replied with a smile.

"And the truth comes out!" I shouted facetiously. "She's getting rid of me so she can hook up with an ex. Admit it."

Laughing, she shook her head. "That's not what this is about. Not even a little." Turning to Dylan, she hugged him. "Thank you so much for helping me move. I enjoyed the short amount of time I got to spend with you and Cami."

"It's my pleasure," Dylan responded. "If you're ever back this way for a visit, be sure to drop by."

"I will." Misty turned to Cami, giving her a loose hug so she wouldn't smash baby Piper. "And thank you for the yummy looking banana bread. It's going to drive me crazy on the trip there."

"I cut it into slices for you, so you can eat on the way if you want. Or you can save it. I simply wanted to know you weren't starving when you got there."

"Well, you're sweet. I appreciate it."

Glancing at me, she smiled. "Take care of Russ for me too, okay? He's one in a million." Her eyes started to water as she approached me, sliding her arms around my neck. Lowering her voice for just my ears, she whispered. "I feel like Dorothy in the Wizard of Oz when she's telling all the people she loves goodbye. You're my Scarecrow. I think I'm going to miss you most of all."

Hooking my thumbs in her belt loops, I dragged her forward so she was flush against me. "Then why are you leaving? Or why aren't I coming with you?" I didn't understand. The two of us seemed to have an easy, relaxed relationship. Maybe it wasn't the epic love of all time, but I did love her. I didn't want her to go.

It was like she read my mind. "I love you, Russ, so much. But there's something better out there for you than me. And because I love you, I'm stepping aside so you can have it."

Okay, that made absolutely no sense to me, but what else could I do? "Thanks for being there for me when I needed you," I said. "You helped me get through a really difficult time."

"I know. And I hope your difficult times are behind you now." Hugging me tightly, she laid her head against me. "This is so much harder than I thought it would be."

Blinking away tears that were gathering in my own eyes, I agreed. I hadn't realized exactly how much I'd grown attached to having her presence in my life. "I love you. Be safe, and don't be a stranger."

"I love you, too," she whispered again, tears

falling as she stepped away from me. "Don't hate me, okay?"

I snorted. "I couldn't hate you if I tried."

"Yes, you could. Under the right circumstances."

Opening my mouth to ask her what she meant, I was interrupted by Dylan.

"I double checked everything on your tow bar. Your car is locked in there good for your trip."

"Thanks so much. I appreciate it!" She moved toward the U-Haul and climbed inside.

"Don't forget to take wide turns and give yourself plenty of time to move over in traffic," I called after her, suddenly nervous for her to be doing this by herself.

She laughed. "I will, Russ. Breathe. Everything is going to work out just fine."

I wasn't sure the erratic beating of my heart agreed, but I stood there as she closed the door, giving her one last wave. She started the truck and drove away without looking back, and I watched until she was out of sight.

"You doing okay?" Cami asked, stepping beside me.

"Strangely, I'm not. I didn't think it would be this difficult. She was good for me."

Cami nodded. "She was."

"I just don't know why it didn't work out for us. We got along great, you know?" I glanced at her briefly, before taking Piper from her and cuddling her against my chest. "Uncle Russ needs some baby loving," I cooed to the pretty little girl and she smiled. I kissed her cheek.

"You are growing up way too fast."

"I agree with that," Cami said, slipping her arm around my waist and the two of us walked over to where Dylan was waiting by our vehicles. He took Piper and buckled her into her car seat.

Sighing heavily, I cast my gaze back down the street, wondering if I might catch one more glimpse of Misty, even though I knew I wouldn't.

"Don't be sad," Cami said. "Yes, you guys got along great, but she wasn't the one for you. She did the right thing by letting you go, so you can have what you really want and need."

Turning around I gestured to the street. "Do you see the women lining up to catch me?"

Cami laughed. "Actually, I do."

I looked, again. "Then you better give me whatever you're smoking, because I'm telling you, no one is there."

"Give it time, Russ. You'll see." She walked around the passenger side of the Camaro and opened the door, sliding in beside Dylan. "See you at home."

I lifted my hand in a slight wave and watched them drive away. Long ago I'd given up on trying to decipher Cami's cryptic messages. When she wanted me to know what she meant, she'd tell me.

Hanging my head, I walked back to my truck, my life suddenly feeling empty once again.

CHAPTER TWENTY-SIX
Russ

Cracking open a beer, I sat in front of my television watching a baseball game. Okay, watching might have been stretching it a little. It was more like I was staring at the screen trying to figure out the mess that was my life and how I'd managed to let not one, but two, amazing women slip through my fingers.

Maybe I wasn't cut out for relationships. Maybe I was meant to spend eternity as the third wheel to Cami and Dylan. I could be like their really old adult child they adopted. Hell, in a few more years I'd end up in diapers—just like Piper—and I'd fit right in. No one would even notice. Of course, that would mean Cami and Dylan would probably be in diapers then, too. I shivered. That was gross.

Something had to give though. I wondered what Misty would think if I just happened to move to New York. Maybe if I were in the area, she wouldn't be opposed to continuing our casual relationship. Maybe then it would develop into more.

Oh, hell. Who was I kidding? She'd made it pretty clear that we were done. She'd been gone for a week and the only text I'd gotten from her was one saying she made it safely and would be busy settling in. There had been nothing else since then. We were done. She had moved on—literally.

And really, I was okay with it. Yes, it hurt. Yes, I missed her, but it had been nothing compared to what I'd felt after losing Evie. I was still feeling that one; and honestly, I was doing my best to not think of her at all, because it was just too damn painful.

I lifted my beer to my lips just as a series of tones went off from my hand held radio. Jumping up, I realized that they were the tones for my company—and we weren't even on shift. Immediately after that set, two more sets of tones went out, calling the other off-duty companies, too. Something bad was going down. Running to my bedroom I grabbed my shoes, keys and wallet.

"General page, general page, all companies, general page." The dispatcher's voice came through the radio right as I busted through my door, finding Dylan exiting the house from the kitchen door at the same time.

"Ride with me?" he asked breathlessly and I nodded, both of us racing toward the Camaro.

"All ambulance and fire units are needed for a massive structure fire at the Community

General Hospital. Repeat all ambulance and fire are needed at Community General Hospital for a massive structure fire. Please implement disaster scenarios at this time. This is not a drill. I repeat, this is not a drill. All off duty crews please report in with your gear. Be advised this is a large fire and patients are being evacuated from the structure."

"Holy shit!" I said, slipping on my boots as Dylan practically peeled out onto the street. "What the hell happened?"

"Copy, massive structure fire at Community General Hospital. Engine One is enroute." Sonny's voice came over the radio from the on-call crew at the station.

"Engine Two is enroute, also." The backup crew came on as they rolled out.

"Copy Engine One and Engine Two. Enroute time is nineteen hundred."

"Medic One and Medic Two are rolling, Code Three."

Goose bumps flooded over my skin as I listened to all the apparatus leaving the building. I knew we were in for a long haul with this one.

Dylan screeched up to the station, throwing the car in park and we ran inside, slipping into our turnouts as the rest of our crew pulled up and began dressing, too. Dylan was ready first, hopping on the truck and firing it up as we all climbed inside.

I jumped into the passenger seat, beside him.

"Let's roll!" he called out to the rest of the crew. "You can finish suiting up on the way." No one hesitated, immediately jumping on-board as he grabbed the radio. "Dispatch, this is Engine Three. We're enroute to Community General."

"Copy Engine Three. Enroute time nineteen hundred and six, please switch to secure channel four for more instructions."

"Copy Dispatch, switching channels."

"I got it," I said, wanting him to keep his eyes on the road. He handed the radio to me. "Engine Three tuning in for command instructions."

"Engine Three, this is command." The chief's voice crackled through the radio. "We need your crew to suit up for an interior strike. It's looking like a gas leak caused an explosion. The gas company has cut power, but the fire is roaring pretty hot on the right wing of the building."

"The right wing? Isn't that the emergency room?" I asked in horror, staring over at Dylan and he nodded grimly. Nerves shot through me. We knew people in there. Friends. Coworkers. "Roger. Gear for interior attack. Where do you want us to stage?"

"You'll be staging on the left side of the building. We will send a crew to run your truck. We need all of you inside evacuating patients as quickly as possible. An emergency tent is being set up in the parking lot of the medical offices, next door. Any emergent patients will be transported by helicopter and ambulance to other facilities. Your job is to get every last patient out and to that staging area. Copy?"

"Copy, evacuate all patients to staging area."

"Once you get everyone out, then we'll look

at moving you to interior attack, if needed."

"Copy."

"Wilcock, this is your show, son. Make me proud," Chief Daniel's added, and Dylan's jaw tightened as he nodded.

Briefly clicking back to the main channel, I radioed the dispatcher. "Engine Three is on scene."

"Copy Engine Three. Nineteen Ten."

I wrote the time down and immediately switched the radio back to the operations channel. Jumping out, I noticed Anderson, from the on-duty crew, running toward us.

"Give me your command board, Wilcock," he ordered as he approached. "Chief wants me to keep track and run your truck so you can go inside with your crew."

Dylan didn't question him at all, simply reaching behind the seat and grabbing the white board with the Velcro tabs on it. He quickly peeled off his smaller nametag and placed it under "Interior Search and Rescue." The rest of us did the same.

"I want everyone in full masks and gear. We have no idea what's happening with smoke in there. Once we get inside, we need to search and retrieve those who are in the most danger from the fire first. Dawson, grab the extra fire extinguishers, too." Turning to Anderson, Dylan continued. "Get someone to drop and prime the hose off this truck and run it to the building, just in case we need it."

"I'm on it," he said, quickly getting on his radio and asking for more help.

The adrenalin caused Dylan's voice to rasp. "Command, Engine Three crew is entering the building from the north doors. We have five men all together. Anderson is running the truck."

"Copy Engine Three. Be safe and work fast."

"Save the world," Dylan said to me, seriously.

"Save the world," I replied back.

The five of us rushed into the building, mass chaos greeting us. People were running everywhere, shouting orders, crying, and desperately trying to get patients out of the structure.

"Give me that," Dylan said to a police officer holding a megaphone, snatching it from his hand. "Listen to me!" he shouted into the amplifying device. Barely anyone looked at him. Ripping his mask off, he shouted again. "Listen to me! We're here to help you, but we need your cooperation, please! I just need a second!"

Finally, people started turning toward him.

"We need everyone to calm down and act in an organized manner. I know the hospital has disaster protocols you've all been trained for. Follow those protocols; do them quickly, but efficiently. We need to avoid any more injuries. We want to get these patients out in an orderly fashion. Who is in charge in here?"

"No one." One of the nurses spoke up, tears streaking down her face. "The doctor in charge was with a patient in the part of the building that exploded.

"Okay, listen up, everyone. From now on Nurse . . . ," he paused, looking   at her nametag. "Nurse Ritchey is in charge. If you have a question about what to do, ask her." He stared at Nurse Ritchey. "You up for this? It's show time."

She nodded and he handed her the megaphone.

"Tell me how to get to the patients who are in the most imminent danger from the fire."

"Go to the end of the hall and turn left. At the end of that hall is a set of double doors. That whole hallway is right behind where the fire is currently burning. A couple rooms from the west end have been evacuated already, but that's it."

"That's the ICU, isn't it?" I asked, as I listened to the directions she gave and she nodded. "They need to stay on all their machines, if at all possible."

Shit. This wasn't going to be easy. "How many patients are left on the floor?"

"It holds twenty, so eighteen if they're full."

"All right. We're on it. You start evacuations in this area."

Not wasting another second, the five of us ran down the hallway, following the directions she'd given us.

"Russ, you're with me," Dylan ordered. "You other three go left. Start at the rooms furthest away and work your way back to this point. Make sure you get medical personnel out with you, too."

I was surprised to find the nurses still at their stations, wearing masks to try and combat the smoke that was filling the area, terror in their eyes."

"You!" Dylan pointed to one nurse. "Go with them and tell them everything they need to bring. And you!" He pointed at the other nurse. "Come and do the same for us." She kept in step with us as we went to the right.

Glancing briefly at her nametag, I saw her name was Sarah Layton. She looked really scared, but she nodded.

Dylan lowered his mask back in place and we turned and ran down the hall to the farthest room. "As soon as you help us with this patient, I want you out of the building. We need to get you out of this smoke. Do you understand?"

Sarah nodded, not even trying to argue. We entered the room on the left side at the end of the hall, since that side was closest to the fire. An elderly man lay there, sleeping, seeming completely oblivious to what was going on around him. I saw he was on a ventilator. Quickly, the three of us packaged him up, getting him ready to move. As soon as he was ready, I unlocked the brakes of the bed and pushed it toward the door.

"Dammit," Dylan cursed. "I wish I could stay behind and package these others."

I knew it was against the rules for us to be alone—our training was set up on a strict buddy system. "So give this guy to the other three. Each of them can push a gurney out, together, and you and I can stay behind and package the rest so they're ready to go when they come back in."

"Great idea," he said, radioing to the other guys. As soon as we handed off the patients and nurse to them, the two of us turned toward the other rooms.

"Command, Captain Wilcock, reporting. Three patients are on their way out, along with two nurses, escorted by firefighters Camden, Tell, and Stromboli. Weston and I are staying interior to package more patients. Be advised we are retrieving from the ICU."

"Copy Captain Wilcock, three patients and two nurses coming out with Camden, Tell, and Stromboli. Weston and Wilcock remaining interior in the ICU."

Confident that his message had been appropriately received, we turned into the next room, this one containing a young woman who looked like she might have been in a car accident with all her cuts and bruises. She was also on a ventilator, but she wasn't asleep—her eyes wide and frantic as we entered.

"It's going to be okay," I said to her as we moved swiftly around her bed gathering things she needed. "There's a fire, but we are here to evacuate you to a different facility, okay?"

She nodded slightly.

"Don't be afraid when you go outside," Dylan added. "There are a lot of emergency crews here helping, so it's going to be loud and a bit chaotic; but we'll make sure you get taken care of."

As soon as she was ready to go, we pushed her out into the hallway until we reached the door to the next room. "You'll be able to see us from here, but we've got to step away and get all the patients unhooked and ready to go.

Another team of firefighters is on their way in to take you out," I said, leaning over and maintaining eye contact with her.

Following our previous routine, we packaged the young man in the next bed who, according to his chart, was here after an attempted overdose. He certainly didn't look like he wanted to die right at this moment, begging us to get him out. I noticed he had leather restraints, so I figured he was still on a suicide watch. Maybe today would help him change his mind.

Pushing him out into the hall, we moved both him and the woman down to the next door, going in and repeating the same procedure again. I glanced at the ceiling nervously. The smoke was definitely getting thicker in this area. With all the oxygen in here, this place was ripe for an explosion. We needed to hurry.

The third patient was out of the room just as our three crewmen reappeared. We handed the patients off to them and began our task again, working as fast as we could. Before long, six more patients had been delivered to safety.

"Dylan, I can feel the heat. I think the fire is in the ceiling above us." Glancing up, I watched as thick, dark smoke seeped in from between the ceiling tiles.

"I think so, too. Two more runs, Russ. Then we are done. We've got to get these people out of here."

Three more were safely delivered to our crew—only three more to go. The ceiling groaned heavily overhead and the smoke increased.

"Captain Wilcock to command," Dylan said into his radio.

"Command, go ahead Wilcock."

"We need an interior attack in here. No flames yet, but the smoke is getting very heavy. According to our information, we still have three patients to evacuate from this department. Fire is imminent, I repeat, fire is imminent."

"Copy. We will get a hose into you pronto."

Dylan and I quickly packaged the next two patients, this time taking them completely out into the exterior hallway to get them away from the worst of the smoke. As soon as we saw the crew returning for them, we turned to go back for the remaining patient.

"We've got the last one!" Dylan shouted. "Make sure they get some line in here fast."

Bursting through the double doors, we ran to the closest room. There was a loud creaking sound and I glanced up just as the ceiling gave way, fire shooting through the tiles as the debris fell directly on top of me, knocking me to the floor.

"Russ!" Dylan's terrified scream reached me at the same time the pain did and I hollered, my leg pinned beneath a beam. I knew right away it was broken from the angle it was at. "Russ!" Dylan screamed again, grabbing a fire extinguisher and spraying the burning tiles around me.

"Go!" I yelled at him, waving him off. "Get the patient! I'll be fine!"

Dylan glanced up through the gaping hole to the flames billowing overhead and then back at me, his eyes wide.

"Go!" I shouted again. "Save the patient!" I knew the odds of me getting out of here alive weren't very good, but I needed to get him out of here.

Dylan stood firm, bending to try and lift the heavy steel beam off my leg, but it wouldn't budge.

"Go!" I said again, staring into his tear filled eyes as he glanced down at me. "Just go!"

"I will not leave you behind," he said, slowly and clearly, as if he were trying to punch his words home. More debris fell from the ceiling, landing right behind Dylan. Suddenly, fire was everywhere.

Grabbing his hand, I stilled him. "Go! Cami and Piper need you. You have to go!"

"Shut up, Russ!" he shouted angrily at me. "I'm not leaving you behind. Do you hear me?"

"Then we're going to die in this place together! Is that what you want—for Cami to be a widow and Piper to not have a dad? Get your ass out of here. I mean it!" I was screaming at the top of my lungs.

Dylan shook his head, clapping his free hand on top of mine. "You go, we go," he said, quoting our favorite line from the firefighter movie *Backdraft*.

"Really? I'm about to die here, and all you've got is *Backdraft*?" I teased, trying to lighten the whole terrible situation.

More debris fell, this time blocking our exit.

"Dammit!" I yelled. "Now look what you've done. You're trapped here with me. This is so stupid. Stupid!" I punched my fist against some of the fallen debris. "Dammit, Dylan! Why?"

I could see the tears streaming down his cheeks through his mask. "You came for me once—put your life on the line for me and my family. I swore, in that moment, I'd do whatever it took to protect you. So, if I die today, I die trying to save you, Russ. You're my brother and I'm not leaving you behind."

I couldn't respond, my voice too choked up to acknowledge his words. After all those dumb nightmares about Dylan choosing Cami over me, all the trauma and stress I'd put myself through because of it, and now he was making the ultimate sacrifice on my behalf. He could've gotten away. He could've made it out.

But he didn't. He stayed so I wouldn't die alone.

I loved him so damn much.

CHAPTER TWENTY-SEVEN
Evie

Once again, I was glued to the television watching the horror unfold in front of me. I was the worst of Lookie Lou's or rubberneckers, or whatever they were called—people who tried to see what was happening during dire situations.

And this situation was definitely dire.

I knew Russ and Dylan would be at this fire. Everyone was at this fire. Shoot, mass crime could be being committed across the city right now and no one would notice because they were all tuned in to the devastation on television, just like me.

News crews had cameras everywhere, and I found myself flipping through channels as I tried to find the best coverage.

"We have new information coming in right now, " a female reporter was saying from the scene. I stopped on that channel, anxious for any news. "As we said earlier, it appears there has been the loss of several lives in the initial explosion near the Emergency Department here at Community General Hospital. The next wing that was immediately threatened was the ICU. An attack team was sent in to rescue those patients and we are happy to say that triage is stating that all patients from that wing are accounted for. Unfortunately, we are now hearing that two of the firefighters involved in the rescue of those patients are now, themselves, trapped. From what we've been able to garner on radio traffic, one of those firefighters is pinned beneath a beam of some sort and he and his coworker are unable to get out. We are trying to get confirmation of this now."

"Wow, Jeanine, that's just terrible." The news anchor's voice broke in. "We are definitely sending all our prayers to those brave firefighters who put their lives on the line every day. Do we have the names of the men who are trapped?" he asked, wanting to add even more sensationalism to the drama unfolding.

"They haven't released the names, needing to contact the families first. I can tell you that the crew members inside the building responded to the fire on Engine Three, and are part of Company Charlie under the command of Captain Dylan Wilcock."

I didn't hear anything else, a silent scream escaping my mouth as I sank to the floor. It was Russ in there. I knew it. I could feel it in my bones. My hand went to my belly and the life that grew inside there, a life Russ still didn't know about.

Hands shaking, I reached for my phone on the coffee table and scrolled for Cami's phone number.

"Hello?" she answered, her voice trembling.

"It's Evie," I said, my voice barely a whisper.

"Yes, it's Dylan and Russ." She answered before I could even ask. "I just got the call from the chief."

"Can I watch your baby or something, so you can go down there? I need to do something. I can't just sit here."

"I already have a sitter. I'll swing by and pick you up. I need someone with me right now who knows what I'm going through. Text me your address."

It was strange, really, knowing she'd never been to my house before. Of course, Russ had only been to my house once, and he was never actually inside. "Okay. I'm ready. I'll be waiting for you out on the sidewalk."

She hung up.

I turned toward the television, just in time to see them showing some more minor explosions and my heart wrenched painfully inside me. The man I loved was in that mess. I would probably never see him again. *Why? Why had I taken so long to go and talk to him?* Misty had encouraged me to go visit him before she left. She didn't know about the baby, though, and I didn't want him to feel trapped, like he had to marry me or something. I didn't want him to feel like he was my second choice. He wasn't.

"We're being told that while the gas has

been turned off in the building, there are still several explosives in the building, primarily oxygen tanks. These could possibly be what we are hearing with these smaller explosions." I couldn't stand to listen to the news any longer. I needed to be there.

Slipping my shoes on, I raced out the door and down to the sidewalk, even though I knew it would take Cami several minutes to reach me. Pacing back and forth, I couldn't seem to stop chewing my fingernails.

Finally, after what seemed like hours, Cami's car rounded the corner. She paused long enough for me to jump inside and took off again.

Staring at her, I gave a wry laugh. "You look as bad as I do," I said, wiping at a stray tear.

"I'm terrified," she answered honestly. Glancing at me, she patted me on the knee. "Thanks for coming with me. I know you and Russ aren't an item anymore, but I know he still has strong feelings for you. I think he would want you there."

"I'm pregnant." I burst out, unable to keep it from her. "It's Russ'. He has to live, Cami. He has to. I've handled things all wrong!" I couldn't help the sobs that escaped me, racking my frame as I buried my face in my hands.

Cami continued to pat my leg. "Well, then Russ has to live, doesn't he? He'd be pissed if he died without knowing he was having a baby."

"And Dylan, too. Russ would never make it without Dylan. He loves him so much."

"Dylan feels the same about him. Neither of them would ever leave the other behind. That gives me some comfort, at least. That neither of them is alone."

Still crying, I didn't reply. Instead, I looked out the window, noting the massive clouds of black smoke filling the air down the road.

Cami pulled into the lot, identifying us both as spouses of the men trapped inside, and we were immediately redirected to the Command Center. As soon as we parked, we were ushered straight to the chief.

"Ladies," he said, acknowledging each of us. "Why don't you have a seat over here?" He gestured to two folding chairs.

"Just tell us, please," I said, not able to take it for one more minute.

"They're trapped just inside the doors to the ICU. The ceiling collapsed and Russ was pinned under the falling debris."

A whimper escaped me at his words and I covered my mouth, trying to listen intently.

"We know for sure that Russ has a broken leg and he's pinned under a steel beam. Dylan hasn't been able to lift it off him, but he refuses to leave him or try to find a way out for himself. We have hose laid in the building and crews are concentrating on knocking down the fire in their area, but things aren't looking really great at the moment."

"Why were they even in the ICU if all the patients were out?" I asked, demanding answers. I didn't care if I sounded bitchy. I wanted Russ safe.

"Apparently there was a miscommunication between the fire department and the nurses about how many patients were still on the floor. They thought there was one more, but there wasn't."

"So they're alive still?"

His face was solemn and there were tears in his eyes. "We have a radio set up on a secure channel for you ladies to talk to them."

Cami's face went completely ashen. "You don't think you can get them out, do you?"

"We wanted you to get a chance to . . . talk to them."

Say goodbye. That's what he meant to say. They wanted us to be able to tell them goodbye.

Woodenly, I followed Cami and the chief to the truck, climbing inside as directed.

"Who goes first?" he asked.

"Evie," Cami said. "It's most important she speak with Russ."

I knew how hard this must be for her and I flashed her a grateful look as I accepted the radio. Pushing the button, I spoke timidly. "Hello?"

"Cami? Goody, baby, is that you?" Dylan's voice came back.

"It's Evie," I said, my voice shaking terribly. "I need to speak to Russ."

There was a moment of silence and I waited, holding my breath. "Evie? Is it really you?"

Oh my gosh, he sounded so good.

"I don't have a lot of time, Russ, because Cami needs to get to talk to Dylan, too; but I just wanted you to know that I love you. I've always loved you. I never stopped." I didn't care who could hear me professing my love for him. I wanted the whole world to know.

"I love you, too, Evie. So much. I have no words to explain how much. I'm so sorry—for everything."

"Russ." I hated the finality he had in his voice, as if he'd accepted this was the end. "Russ, you can't die. I need you. I need you here with me—and our baby."

Silence.

"Come again?"

"I'm pregnant with your baby. I can't do this alone." More tears. "I don't want to do it alone. Not without you."

"What about Kory?" he asked.

"Kory is gone. His choice. And if you'll get your ass out of that damn burning building, I'd be happy to fill you in on all the details. But you have to come out!"

"Evie?"

"Yes?"

"Will you marry me?"

A half-laugh, half-sob escaped me. "Are you serious? Or did you get hit in the head?"

"I'm serious. I want an answer right now."

Could someone get dehydrated from crying too much? "If you will come out of that building I will marry you anywhere, any day, any time you want. Just say the word."

"Someone please get that in writing," his voice came back and everyone laughed.

"I need to go now," I said. "Cami needs her turn."

"I know. I love you, Evie. I love you! No matter what happens, don't you ever forget that, okay?"

More sobbing. "Okay. Don't you forget either. Now let Dylan talk."

Handing the radio to Cami, I absently listened to her and Dylan exchanging their love for each other. That was as far as they got. Suddenly there was a horrible sound coming from both, the radio, and outside. I looked up, just as part of the building collapsed.

The radio went dead.

"Dylan?" Cami screamed into the device. "Dylan?" she screamed again, louder. "Dylan!"

It was the last sound I heard. Everything started to spin and I passed out.

***

"Excuse me?" A voice penetrated the haze around me. "Could you move her gurney closer? I think she's finally waking up."

A slight feeling of dizziness passed through me and I felt myself moving. "What's going on? Where am I?" I asked, trying to focus on the nurse leaning over me.

"You're in our makeshift triage center," the nurse answered. "You passed out."

Immediately I remember the horror that cause me to faint. "Russ," I said in a panicked voice. "What happened to Russ and Dylan?"

A rough hand slipped into mine, squeezing tightly. My gaze drifted down, following the arm from my hand to the gurney next to me. "We made it out," Russ said. "The collapse caused the beam to shift and Dylan was able to pull me to a window."

Unimaginable relief poured through me. "Oh,

thank God! Thank God! He really does answer prayers!" Sitting up, I got off the gurney and stepped toward him.

"Ma'am, you need to lay back down," the nurse scolded, but I ignored her.

"Where are you hurt?" I asked, looking over his filthy body.

"I have a broken leg."

That was all I needed to know as I threw myself at his chest, wrapping my arms tightly around him as I sobbed. "I've never been so scared in my life." Lifting my head, I kissed him lightly on the lips, and he grabbed the back of my neck grimacing as he pulled me back.

"Kiss me like you mean it," he said; and I did, allowing his tongue to part my lips and tangle with mine.

After a few seconds, I pulled away. "Is Dylan okay?" I asked and he nodded.

"He's over getting oxygen on one of the trucks. He's with Cami."

"Good," I replied, kissing him again, not caring who was watching our public display of affection. If I could've, I would have crawled inside him. I needed to be closer, so much closer.

This time he pulled away, searching my eyes. "Now about that proposal. I intend to hold you to your word."

Smiling, I stroked his ash-laden hair. "You'd have a hard time getting out of it, Mister. I don't plan on ever letting you out of my sight again."

"Sounds good to me," he replied, his white grin flashing brightly against the grime. "You know, I bet there's a chaplain around here somewhere."

"No way," Cami's voice interrupted. "I know she said she would let you choose the when and where Russ, but I refuse to let you two get married in the middle of a triage zone. You can't even take her on a proper honeymoon until you get that leg fixed."

"There is that," he agreed with a sigh, not breaking eye contact with me. "I guess we have to wait. Sorry."

"As long as I get to be with you, I'll wait as long as needed." My heart literally felt like it might burst with joy. Why, oh why, had I ever been so confused over this man? No one had ever made me feel the way he did.

"I'd do it all again, you know?" he said, smiling.

"What?" I asked, not following.

"Run into a burning building, break my leg and almost die. I'd do it all again, just to hear you say you'd marry me." His hand drifted to my stomach. "And this little surprise. Well, I can't wait to be a dad."

Smiling, I kissed him again, and again, and again.

EPILOGUE
Russ

"Stop fidgeting," Dylan whispered in my ear.

"I can't help it. I'm excited," I replied back quietly. "What's taking so long?"

Dylan laughed. "Everything is running on time. Look, there's Cami, just inside the doorway to the house. That means they're getting ready to come out."

Music filled the air and I straightened, catching my mom's eye from where she sat in the front row of the garden with my dad. She blew a little kiss toward me. I smiled back at her, happy that they'd been able to come.

Cami slowly marched down the aisle and Dylan stirred beside me. "Isn't she beautiful? I swear I'll never get my fill of her."

"Pipe down, stud muffin. The two of you belong to me at least until the service is over. Then you have my permission to go knock her up with your next kid."

Dylan laughed, nudging me slightly. "There's Evie."

Like I could miss her. Damn, she looked hot. I couldn't take my eyes off her. Even with her giant pregnant belly, she still pulled off the stylish white wedding gown. It was gorgeous on her. I couldn't wait to take it off.

This day had taken forever to get here. Evie and Cami insisted my leg be healed before we got married. Unfortunately, that had taken a bit longer than planned. Two surgeries and several months later, I was finally given a clean bill of health and allowed to return to work.

Thankfully, Evie had been with me the entire time. She sold her condo and moved in with me to help with my recovery. Even after all I'd been through with the fire, I never had any nightmares like I'd had from the trauma I'd experienced before. Dylan's staying with me had apparently taken care of the old nightmares and whatever deep seeded fear I'd hidden within me. And having Evie back in my life—well, that made everything perfect.

And now the day had finally arrived, the day we would make it legal, the day she would become mine completely. We were pushing this wedding pretty close to her due date, but extenuating circumstances had dictated our timetable. At least we'd be married before the baby was born.

Reaching where I stood, she and her dad paused.

"Who gives this woman in Holy Matrimony?" the minister asked.

"I do," her dad answered, passing her hand to mine.

"You're looking hot, Doc," I whispered in her ear as she stepped up beside me. "I can't wait to get you out of this dress." She blushed and elbowed me in the ribs.

Facing the minister, we both listened as he welcomed everyone and started the ceremony. I couldn't help constantly sneaking peeks at Evie, nor could I seem to wipe this damn grin off my face.

"Do you, Evelyn Sonya McKnight, take Russ Weston to be your lawful wedded husband, from this time forward, in sickness and in health, and cleave only unto him?"

Evie turned to me, a strained look passing across her face and she shook her head. "No," she whispered. "I can't. Not right now."

The guests in attendance gasped, and I stared at her in shock. "Wha . . . what?" I asked, flabbergasted.

Evie glanced between the minister and me, the grip of her hand growing ever tighter.

"Evie?" I said, totally confused and she gave a half-laugh, but it sounded pained.

"Uh, I think my water just broke," she said hastily, shifting a foot and revealing a puddle at her feet.

Eyes widening, I turned to Dylan. "Her water just broke," I said.

"Are you asking me for use of my kitchen?" Dylan asked with a grin, nodding toward the house.

"Hell, no. I'm asking you to go get the damn

car." Turning back to the minister, I looked him straight in the eye. "As of now, we are going to the bare bones of this ceremony. Do whatever you need to do to have us married before she gets in the car."

Looking shocked for a moment, he straightened himself. "Do you take Russ?" he asked.

"Yes, yes," Evie answered, signaling for him to hurry.

"Do you, Russ, take Evelyn?"

"I do," I replied, and Evie held her stomach as she groaned. I quickly swept her off her feet into my arms and began carrying her toward the gate where Dylan would be bringing the car.

"I now pronounce you man and wife," the minister shouted, running behind us. "You may now kiss the bride."

Without pausing, Evie and I shared a brief kiss and she groaned again.

"Not exactly the way I imagined it," she said through slightly clenched teeth.

"Me, neither, but it's legit—and that's all I care about."

Dylan pulled up outside the gate with the car. Jumping out, he opened the back door for us.

"One more thing," the minister shouted from behind us.

"What?" I asked, ready to get moving to the hospital.

"You both need to sign this. Here, and here." Slapping the wedding license on the top of the car, he passed me a pen. I quickly signed my name and gave the pen to Evie. I noticed her signature wasn't as neat as normal, but under the circumstances, I figured that could slide.

"Thanks for coming everyone!" I shouted to the guests. "Help yourselves to the refreshments. We're having a baby!"

Everyone burst into applause and cheers and Evie and I both smiled as I helped her into the car.

"I love you, Mrs. Weston," I whispered, kissing her once Dylan closed the door behind us.

"I love you, too, Mr. Weston," she added, smiling even though she was uncomfortable. "Let's go have this baby."

"Let's do it," I said, kissing her again.

***

The next morning, I simply watched my two sleeping girls, feeling very content with my life at the moment. Never, in a million years, would I have believed that things would've all ended up this way. Yes, we certainly took the long route to each other, but at least we made it.

"Excuse me, sir." A young woman stuck her head in the door, speaking quietly so she wouldn't wake Evie and the baby. "Would you like one of the morning papers to read while you're here?"

"Sure," I replied, and she brought one to me.

"Congratulations! She's beautiful," she said, peering into the bassinet. Lifting the card on it, she smiled. "Zoey Lyn. What a great name! Well, get some rest while you can."

I watched as she left the room and then opened my paper, groaning at the headline that greeted me.

Hero Firefighter Ties the Knot With Doctor He Rescued and Gets a Baby, All in Same Day!

Rolling my eyes, I glanced down at the article.

Russ Weston, known to many for his daring firefighting heroics and the lives he's saved, tied the knot yesterday, with local, renowned psychiatrist, Evelyn McKnight. The couple, whom the general public has affectionately started referring to as "Revie," also welcomed a baby daughter, shortly after the ceremony.

Revie, I thought, shaking my head. *Oh for heaven's sake, who comes up with this crap? I'm screwed as soon as the guys at the department get a look at this.*

Closing the paper, I folded my arms, choosing to stare at my pretty girls instead. *Revie,* I thought again. Yes, I would be catching a lot of flak over that one; but somehow, having these two beauties in my life made me feel like I could take on the entire world.

In that moment, I realized I finally had everything in my life that I envied about Cami and Dylan's. I'd never been so happy—so content. Everything was perfect.

Well, okay, maybe not exactly perfect. I did miss my honeymoon, after all. But, as soon as Evie was able, I'd spend the rest of my life making it up to her, over and over again.

Yep, the future was looking pretty damn good.

About the Author:

Lacey Weatherford is the bestselling author of the popular young adult paranormal romance series, Of Witches and Warlocks, and contemporary series, Chasing Nikki, Crush, and Tell Me Why. She has always had a love of books and wanted to become a writer ever since reading her first Nancy Drew novel at the age of eight.

Lacey resides in the beautiful White Mountains of Arizona. She lives with her wonderful husband and children along with their dog, Talley, and cat, Minx. When she's not out supporting one of her kids at their sporting/music events, she spends her time reading, writing, blogging, and visiting with her readers on her social media accounts.

Visit Lacey's Official Website:
http://www.laceyweatherfordbooks.com
Follow on Twitter:
LMWeatherford
Or Facebook:
Lacey Weatherford